PRAISE FOR ADAM MITZNER

A Matter of Will

"Business, blood, and deception help make this an exciting and fast-moving yarn. Fine fare for thriller fans."

—*Kirkus Reviews*

"[An] engrossing thriller from Mitzner (*Dead Certain*). The action never flags in this exciting cautionary tale."

—*Publishers Weekly*

"Mitzner is a master at making the complex understandable for the average reader while not letting the intricate details of the subject matter that supports his story weigh it down . . . *A Matter of Will* [is] a perfect vacation read."

—*Bookreporter*

"Mitzner really knows how to craft a page-turning mystery. A cover-to-cover read."

—*Press & Guide*

Dead Certain

An Amazon Charts Most Sold and Most Read Book

Authors on the Air Finalist for Book of the Year

"*Dead Certain* is dead-on terrific . . . It's an entertaining and riveting work that will more than hold your interest."

—*Bookreporter*

A Case of Redemption

An American Bar Association Silver Gavel Nominee
for Fiction

"Head and shoulders above most . . ."

—*Publishers Weekly*

Losing Faith

"Tightly plotted, fast-paced . . . Startling . . . A worthy courtroom yarn
that fans of Grisham and Turow will enjoy."

—*Kirkus Reviews*

The Girl from Home

"An engrossing little gem."

—*Kirkus Reviews*

THE
BEST
FRIEND

OTHER TITLES BY ADAM MITZNER

THE BEST FRIEND

A LEGAL THRILLER

ADAM MITZNER

THOMAS & MERCER

Published by Thomas & Mercer, Seattle

www.apub.com

Amazon, the Amazon logo, and Thomas & Mercer are trademarks of Amazon.com, Inc., or its affiliates.

ISBN-13: 9781542005753
ISBN-10: 1542005752

Cover design by Rex Bonomelli

Printed in the United States of America

To the real F. Clinton Broden,
2018 Texas Criminal Defense Lawyer of the Year,
and my friend since high school.

My guiding principle is this: guilt is never to be doubted.

—*Franz Kafka*

PART ONE

CLINT BRODEN

January–June 1986

1.

Twenty-seven-year-old women are not supposed to drown in the bathtub.

And yet that was what Nicky told me happened. At least that's what I thought he was saying. His words came haltingly, interrupted by sobs, so it was difficult to be sure. But not many things sound like "Carolyn drowned in the bathtub."

I had come to the office early that morning, although God only knew why. I had no clients requiring my legal services. Prior to Nicky's call, I was doing little beyond trying to will the phone to ring.

I think he asked me to come to his house, but after all this time, I can't be certain. It would have been a natural reflex for me to rush to my best friend in his moment of need.

After hanging up with Nicky, I considered calling my wife to share the news before heading up to Mount Vernon, but I thought better of it. Anne was likely still asleep, having been out late the previous evening filling the midnight slot at an open mic night somewhere in the Village, where she sang a few songs in the hope that an agent, record executive, or casting director would be in the audience. The death of my closest friend's wife justified waking her, but I decided instead to allow Anne to live a few more hours in ignorance so that I could break the news to her in person.

When I arrived at Grand Central, the big board told me that the next train heading to Mount Vernon had already begun boarding. I ran toward the track without even buying a ticket. It didn't occur to me until the train had left the station that I didn't know Nicky's address. He'd moved out of Manhattan only a month before, and the one time Anne and I had visited, Nicky picked us up at the train station. But I remembered it being walking distance from the Mount Vernon stop— one of the house's selling points, Nicky had said.

The train was nearly empty, which wasn't surprising considering I was doing the reverse commute slightly after the morning rush hour. It wasn't until we emerged from the Manhattan tunnels and bright sunlight streamed through the window that the magnitude of what had happened began to take hold. Nicky's new bride was dead.

———

Nearly an hour later, the train stopped at Mount Vernon. That was about twenty minutes longer than how Nicky had represented the trip when I teased him about being a suburbanite.

At the pay phone outside the station, the 411 operator gave me Nicky's street address: 116 Cahill Road. I recalled that their street was off the main drag, but to make sure, I asked the woman behind the ticket counter for directions.

"Straight along Main Street and about three blocks up it'll intersect with Cahill," she said.

It was actually five blocks away, but the streets were short. After I made the turn down Cahill, I didn't need to check the numbers to ascertain which house among the nearly identical white split-levels was Nicky's. It was the one with the police vehicles in front and an ambulance in the driveway.

A few neighbors had gathered on the sidewalk to gawk. I walked past them with purpose. A young police officer in uniform greeted me at the front door. He must have recognized me from court, because he asked, "Are you a lawyer?"

"Yes," I said with a smile that was inconsistent with the reason for my presence; back in those days, it wasn't often I was recognized as a lawyer. "Where is Mr. Zamora?"

The cop pointed into the house. As soon as I stepped into the foyer, I spotted Nicky. He was in the corner of the living room, his back to me. His attention was taken by two plainclothes police officers: big, burly men with thick heads of hair in sports jackets and slacks.

I made my way straight to my friend. Before I could intervene, one of the cops intercepted me with his body. "I'm Detective Lynch," he said. "And your name is?"

"Clint Broden."

"Mr. Broden, we're going to have to ask you to wait in the other room while we take Mr. McDermott's statement."

Nicky's surname is Zamora, not McDermott, which was Carolyn's family name. She had retained it for professional reasons. Nicky didn't react to the misidentification. He also hadn't acknowledged my presence. When I caught his eye, all I got back was a blank stare.

"Nicky," I said, hoping to break him out of his trance.

He blinked a few times, as if he'd just awakened. "Clinton," he said, almost like a question. It was then I noticed that his shirt was still damp. He must have found Carolyn in the bathtub and pulled her out.

Nicky and I weren't huggers. Even at our weddings, where we'd each stood up for the other as best man, neither of us engaged in any greater expression of intimacy than a pat on the back.

The one exception to our mutual disdain of physical affection occurred when we were twenty and both juniors in college. My parents had been killed by a drunk driver the night before, but word had reached me only that morning. I had returned home in a daze, unable to fathom the sea change in my life that had come without warning and left me alone in the world. That reality came painfully to the fore when I reached my house and realized that there was no reason to enter. Instead, I went to the Zamoras' home, which was across the street.

Nicky and I were both only children, and we'd moved in and out of each other's homes in our childhood with such regularity that we were more like brothers than most actual brothers I knew. I was sitting in their living room when Nicky entered. He must have hightailed it down from Vermont the moment his parents told him the news.

He ran right up to me and pulled me in, holding on tight. I think he even kissed my cheek. I know he said, "I love you, Clinton. We're your family now."

That memory was front and center when I saw Nicky on the day Carolyn died. As he had with me, I embraced him and held on tight.

"I'm sorry, Nicky," I said. "You know I love you."

The police allowed us a moment but not much more than that. "Excuse me," one of the detectives said. "I'm afraid you're going to have to leave."

Nicky and I separated. "I'd like to have a minute to talk with Nicky, alone, please," I said.

Detective Lynch didn't give my request a moment's thought. "No," he said flatly. "We'll be done very soon, and then you can talk with Mr. McDermott. But until then, I'm going to need for you to step into the other room."

To emphasize that my presence was no longer welcome, Detective Lynch's partner put his hand on my elbow. Their dismissal made my blood run hot. I yanked my arm away from him.

"His name is Zamora," I said sharply.

"What?" the detective said.

"Carolyn—his wife—her last name is McDermott. His name is Nicky . . . Nicholas Zamora."

Detective Lynch tried to put things back on track. He turned to Nicky and said, "Our apologies, Mr. Zamora."

Nicky made eye contact but didn't seem present. He gave no verbal response, and his expression remained unchanged.

Detective Lynch stared at me until I met his gaze. "You're still going to have to leave, sir."

I took another look at Nicky, who was obviously in shock. I played the only card I had.

"I'm Mr. Zamora's lawyer. So I'm going to have to ask the two of you to give my client and me a few moments to confer. After we talk, then he can continue with you."

This was checkmate. The only thing that trumps the police is the constitutional right to counsel.

The other detective looked like he wanted to take a swing at me, but Lynch seemed to understand that the power dynamic had shifted.

"We'll be right outside," he said.

I led Nicky into the guest bedroom. When Anne and I first got the tour of the house, Carolyn had made no pretense about this space being earmarked to become a nursery. The moment we entered the room, Nicky crumpled onto the bed. His hands immediately came up to his face, almost as if he were trying to hide. Then he began to cry, his body convulsing with each sob.

In short order, a knock came on the door. I was opening it when a push came from the other side.

"I'm sorry to interrupt," Detective Lynch said, "but Detective Mercado and I need to finish taking Mr. Zamora's statement."

"Okay," Nicky said, wiping his eyes.

I moved slightly to the side, allowing the detectives to face Nicky. At least now they weren't going to ask me to leave.

Had I truly been wearing my lawyer hat, I would have shut down the interrogation. But despite what I'd told the detectives, I was there as Nicky's best friend, not his lawyer. That Carolyn's death might lead to a criminal charge was the furthest thing from my mind.

Detective Lynch resumed the questioning. "Mr. Zamora, did you call 911 as soon as you woke up, or did some time elapse between when you got up and saw your wife was not in bed with you and when you made the call?"

Carolyn's workday typically started early, especially after they'd moved to the suburbs and she'd tacked an hour on to her commute. Nicky's job, on the other hand, had a starting time of five o'clock, when he began tending bar at a dive in Murray Hill. I had no idea what time he began working what he'd always referred to as his "real" job, writing during the day, but I doubted very much it was as early as Carolyn's workday began. All of which meant that Nicky being asleep after Carolyn had already left their bed was hardly surprising and certainly no reason for him to call 911.

Still, Nicky seemed baffled by the question. "When I woke up, Carolyn wasn't in bed. I don't know what time it was, but I remember thinking that she was probably already at work. I got out of bed and went into the bathroom to . . . you know, brush my teeth. And . . ."

He resumed the position he'd been in before—hands cupping his face—and he let out a wail.

It was a sound I previously couldn't have imagined coming out of Nicky, and I flinched visibly at it. But the detectives didn't budge. Instead, Detective Lynch continued his line of inquiry.

"Were you home last night?"

Nicky needed a moment to answer that too. "Yes. I don't work on Sundays."

"And after you saw your wife in the bathtub, what did you do next?"

"I . . . I pulled her out and started doing CPR," Nicky said.

The mental image made me wince again: Nicky vainly trying to blow air into Carolyn's lungs.

"Did you think your wife might have taken her bath in the morning?" Detective Mercado asked.

"I don't know."

"So you don't recall if she took a bath last night?"

The question implied the answer. Carolyn must have drowned the night before, which meant that she had been dead for hours when Nicky pulled her from the tub and administered CPR.

Nicky didn't respond. It seemed as though the question hadn't registered.

Detective Mercado asked it again. "Did your wife tell you she was taking a bath the night before?"

"Tell me what?"

"Do you remember your wife telling you last night that she was taking a bath?" Detective Mercado asked slowly, leaving a beat between every word, as if talking to someone with a mental defect.

"She did take baths at night. That way she could sleep later in the morning."

Detective Lynch: "Did she take a bath last night?"

"Yes . . ."

Detective Mercado: "So she went in the bath last night, and you discovered her this morning, and yet you still thought that she might be alive?"

"Is she alive?"

Nicky sounded hopeful, as if everything he had experienced up until that moment might have been wrong. I shuddered at the thought that the detectives would now be forced to tell him again that his wife was dead. It would be like him hearing it for the first time.

Better that it come from me.

"Nicky," I said softly, "Carolyn's dead. She drowned in the bathtub. The detectives are asking you how she looked when you first saw her this morning."

I turned to Detective Lynch to gauge whether my paraphrase of his question was what he was trying to ascertain. He didn't give me any reaction. His focus remained solely on Nicky.

Nicky shook his head slightly, as if pushing away something negative—the horror of what he'd seen, perhaps. Then his face dropped back into his cupped hands.

2.

I first met Carolyn at a bar in midtown Manhattan. It was in late September 1985. The last vestiges of Hurricane Gloria were leaving the tristate area. The storm's impact had been less severe than predicted, but the rain was still coming down hard enough that I was drenched by the time I stepped inside.

Despite the understated surroundings, I suspected that every patron had a six-figure income. The dress code for men seemed to require bold-colored braces and power ties, and a sizable percentage wore blue shirts with contrasting white collars.

We were all coming from work, but our uniforms were as varied as our professions. I was wearing a suit and tie, all of it purchased from a discount men's store. Carolyn also wore a lawyer costume, but hers was more expensive than mine: padded shoulders and pinstripes, befitting an era when *Dynasty* set the tone for woman's fashion. Nicky was in his standard starving-artist getup—faded blue jeans and a black turtleneck sweater.

When Nicky set up the meeting, I assumed Carolyn was just another one of his sexual conquests. Someone who would burn bright for a few weeks and then go the way of the dodo bird. Many who came before her had followed exactly that trajectory, and I assumed there were many more to come.

"You'll like her. She's a lawyer like you," Nicky had told me.

In point of fact, Carolyn McDermott was a lawyer nothing like me.

She was a third-year associate at Martin Quinn, one of the biggest law firms in the country. An associateship there was the brass ring of the legal profession—at least until you came up for partner in the next decade. Even in the mid-1980s, they paid law school graduates $65,000, which was more than twice what I earned, and I'd already been practicing for four years. You didn't get hired there without a perfect résumé. Nicky'd boasted that Carolyn had an Ivy League education and a clerkship with a well-respected federal judge before joining Martin Quinn.

My own pedigree had afforded me a path through the relative underbelly of the legal profession. Undergraduate and law school at St. John's, which was second-rate in every way but its basketball team. Despite the fact that I'd gotten pretty good grades, no law firm would have me upon graduation, so I'd joined the Office of the Federal Defenders of New York—the FD, for short. For the next four years, I represented the vilest form of scum imaginable—drug dealers, wife beaters, rapists. When I left the office, my win-loss record at trial was 7–28. Although those were hardly Hall of Fame stats, nobody else among the office's sixty-seven lawyers had even won twice.

I might have spent my career as a public defender had it not been for the fact that in some years my wife took home more than I did in her hodgepodge of jobs—waitress, babysitter, vocal tutor, actress. When I first mentioned that I was thinking of leaving the FD to go out on my own, she asked, "Can we afford it?" My answer—"Can we afford it if I stay?"—was only partly meant to be clever.

Unspoken between us was that when Anne turned thirty, I started becoming aware of her biological clock, even if she preferred to ignore it. Part of me thought that if I led by example, taking a job I didn't necessarily love because that's what grown-ups thinking about the future did, Anne would follow suit.

It had not worked out that way, at least not so far. To the contrary, whenever I mentioned that she might want to transition into a more stable lifestyle, she always used Nicky as a shield. "Are you also telling your best friend that he should have a regular job and give up his dream of becoming a novelist?"

The opening of my eponymous law firm taught me that being your own boss means you can actually lose money working. If it were not for court-appointed work, I would have gone under, but the thirty-five dollars an hour I was paid for those cases was scarcely enough for me to be able to pay my office rent.

My hours at the FD had been long, but at least when I left for the day, I was on my own time. Private practice worked the opposite way. If I had no billable work from nine to five—which was often the case—I had to work twice as hard after hours to drum up business. That meant attending bar association meetings that began at eight o'clock or taking out prospective clients or those I hoped would someday be business-referrers for drinks or dinner. Whatever the cause, I rarely arrived home before ten. By that time, Anne was usually out, participating in various open mic sessions. Our schedules made it akin to a harmonic convergence when we were together and awake at the same time.

Which was why I had hoped that Anne would join me to meet Carolyn. At the last minute, though, she had canceled. One of the Upper East Side families that paid her roughly my hourly rate to tutor their off-key daughter on vocal techniques had asked for an "emergency appointment" to prepare for an upcoming middle school audition.

"I'll catch Nick's next conquest," she told me. "Probably be next week, anyway."

I chuckled at the dig. In the movie version of Nicky's life, his past girlfriends would appear as a montage of beautiful women differentiated by hairstyles and clothing but always well endowed. Here's the kicker, though—they were always smart. Not a bimbo in the bunch. Not even the rebounds or the one-night stands. Each new girlfriend was, as Nicky put it, a woman of substance.

From her résumé, I already knew that Carolyn fit that last criterion, but upon catching sight of her, I realized she also would have been heartily welcomed into the club of prior Nicky paramours based on her physical attributes alone. She was six years younger than Nicky, which was about as young as he could have gone at the time and not been a thirtysomething dating a grad student. Her figure strained against the buttons of her blouse, and the McDermott surname fit his penchant for Irish women, although Carolyn was black Irish, with dark, almost black hair and an alabaster complexion. Combined with sapphire-blue eyes, she had a certain Snow White vibe.

"Carolyn, this is Clinton," Nicky said.

"Clint," I corrected. "Unless you call him Nicky, in which case you can also call me what Nicky calls me."

She laughed. "Nicky?" Apparently, she had not been briefed on that point.

"Call him Clint," Nicky said with an eye-roll for my benefit. "It's the third iteration of his name since we've met. His given name is Francis. Then he was Clinton through high school, and somewhere along the line he became Clint. I think it makes him feel like Dirty Harry."

"To be fair, no one ever called me Francis. Not even my mother."

"Clint it is," Carolyn said with a smile. "Now, Nicky, can you get me a beer?"

Nicky laughed. To me he said, "I told you, right?"

Nicky got up and made his way to the bar. As soon as he left, Carolyn slid down the bench until she was against the wall, sitting directly opposite of me. The bartender was busy, which meant that I'd be alone with her for the next few minutes.

"So you're the one and only Clinton—I mean Clint—Broden?"

"Guilty as charged."

"I've been excited to meet you because . . . well, the way Nick talks about you, I didn't think you could actually exist. He seemed to be describing . . . I don't know, a superhero, maybe."

"You sure he was talking about me?"

She made a face like she might have been mistaken, but I knew it was a put-on. Living with Anne had alerted me to the difference between good and bad acting.

"Let me see," she said, in mock thought. "Are you the smartest guy he's ever met? And have the most beautiful wife?"

It's hard not to like someone after an introduction like that. But even if she had been less kind, I couldn't have helped but like Carolyn. She was exactly as Nicky had described, and I thought that, despite my best friend's seemingly impossibly high standards for women, he might have finally found the woman of his dreams.

———

The next day, Nicky wanted to see me again at the same bar. I assumed that he wanted to get my views about Carolyn, or to brag about how his evening had ended with her. But when we sat, he handed me a shopping bag that contained his completed manuscript.

"Hot off the presses," he said. "I want you to be the first to read it."

This was only the second time I'd been given the honor of reading his work, and to my knowledge, it was only the second time he'd completed a manuscript. His first effort had been an outgrowth of his senior-year college project. That book was about two childhood friends from a middle-class, outer-borough neighborhood. Although he took pains at the time to emphasize that it was a work of fiction, it wasn't too difficult to decipher that I was Clay, best friend to the story's protagonist, Nate. The plot revolved around a can't-miss business deal. At first, Nate tried to entice Clay into joining the venture, but Clay saw the danger and cautioned Nate to back out. Four hundred pages later, all Clay's concerns were proven true, but Nate prevailed on the last page, outwitting his business partners and escaping to a Caribbean island with a suitcase full of cash.

The book was good enough to capture the attention of a well-respected New York City literary agent, but they couldn't sell it to one of the big publishing houses, although at least two publishers said that they wanted to read Nicky's next novel. The agent told Nicky not to lower his standards and accept a deal with a smaller press; instead, he should write something new.

I thought it a tremendous success that Nicky's first effort had piqued an agent's interest and resulted in favorable reactions from the major publishers, but Nicky was devastated. The rejection might have been the first he'd ever suffered, at least of any consequence.

I'm not sure he wrote another word for the rest of our twenties. At least he didn't mention anything that got further than the "idea stage," and he never asked me to read anything. Then, around the time that Anne and I got engaged, he mentioned that he was back at it, working on something he was very excited about.

Apparently, it had taken him three years to finish, but there it was, what looked to be at least a ream of paper in a shopping bag. I glanced at the title: *Precipice.*

"Is it about two best friends from Astoria?"

He laughed. "I'm tempted to tell you that you'll find out when you read it, but no. It's a love story, actually."

That surprised me a bit. I hadn't thought Nicky knew enough about love to write a love story. A young buck who has sex with hundreds of women? *That* he could write. But love? It seemed outside his scope of experience.

"I can't wait to read it," I said. "Fair warning, though, it may take me a while. I have this appellate brief due in two weeks. Unfortunately, all my reading's going to have to be case law until that's submitted."

He seemed disappointed that he'd have to wait before getting feedback.

"Why don't you ask Carolyn to be your first read?" I suggested.

"I don't think so. To be honest, I don't think there's a real future there."

"Why? She seemed great."

"I know. I was just thinking . . . I don't know, just . . ."

"No, you're right, Nicky. That sounds like a perfectly good reason to break up with a beautiful, intelligent woman."

"You got lucky. Anne was practically the first woman you were serious about. That's why you can't understand what it's like to be with someone who you think is great, smart, beautiful, and you have amazing sex, but you still have that nagging feeling like they're not the one for you."

"That's the most pathetic thing I've ever heard," I said with a laugh. "You almost make me glad that beautiful women aren't constantly throwing themselves at my feet. If you want my advice, and I know you don't, but that doesn't mean you shouldn't take it, give Carolyn some more time. I think there's something real there."

"I'll take it under advisement," he said.

It turned out that he did more than that. Not two months later, they were engaged, and their marriage came a month after that. Then, as soon as they returned from their honeymoon, they moved to the suburbs.

And now, a month after that, Carolyn was dead.

3.

Nicky said he was fine to stay in his house, but I suspected he had no idea how he'd feel once he was alone, so I told him that he didn't have a choice in the matter, at least not tonight. After a brief back-and-forth, he agreed to take the train back to the city and stay with Anne and me for the night.

On the ride back into the city, Nicky told me that he had taken "something" to calm himself, so if he got a little loopy, I shouldn't be concerned. He didn't get loopy so much as sleepy. When we got back to my apartment, I delivered him into the bedroom and told him to rest.

Nicky was still asleep when Anne came home. It was about three in the afternoon. Anne was wearing her gym clothing and still sweating. When she saw me in the living room, she looked like she'd seen a ghost. By the fear in her eyes I first thought she had already heard the news about Carolyn, but then I realized that her concern stemmed from my being home in the middle of the workday. As if only some type of tragedy could explain it.

"I have some very bad news," I said. "Carolyn died this morning. An accident. She drowned in the bathtub."

Anne reacted with silence. It reminded me of what I'd gone through earlier that morning when Nicky called to impart the same news: a delayed response because the statement made zero sense.

Twenty-seven-year-old women are not supposed to drown in the bathtub.

"Nicky's here," I said. "He's resting in our bed. He called me right after he discovered her body, and I went straight to their house. The police were already there. I stayed with him until they left. He's . . . well, you can imagine. Devastated. He took something to calm himself, and then he felt tired. I didn't want him to be alone."

Anne took in the information, nodding as I spoke. Then she said something I would hear many times over the next six months: "How can you even drown in your own bathtub?"

"She must have hit her head or something. Maybe getting out and she slid back in."

Anne brought her hands to her mouth, clearly shaken as she absorbed our new reality.

———

Nicky and I met shortly after my family moved to Queens, when I was eight. My mother had excitedly told me that our new neighborhood was named after John Jacob Astor, who was the richest man in the country at the beginning of the twentieth century. I later learned that the town elders had hoped that by calling their village Astoria, the town's namesake would invest in the neighborhood, but Astor gifted the village only $500, and he actually never set foot in the place that bears his name.

Even without his largesse, however, Astoria flourished. The 1960s brought an influx of Greeks into the neighborhood, as was evident by the Greek restaurants, Greek bakeries, and Greek Orthodox churches. One such place was the Apollo Market, owned by Nicky's family.

I met my future best friend on a muggy August day, about a week before we began fourth grade. Our apartment was stifling hot, and I had no friends to play with outside. In what was a first, my mother gave me a nickel to buy a pack of baseball cards, simply so I'd leave the apartment and stop sulking.

Even though Nicky was only eight, he was working the market's cash register. He urged me to open my pack in front of him. I cracked the gum in two, giving him the bigger piece, and he looked over my shoulder as I shuffled through the cards.

"Mickey Mantle and Whitey Ford in the same pack!" he exclaimed. "I've never seen that before. You must be the luckiest kid in the world."

I've often wondered if Nicky and I would have been friends had our bond not formed so early. Not because I wouldn't have wanted to be his friend—everyone wanted to be around Nicky. He had that sense of ease that you hoped would rub off on you; simply being close to him bathed you in the warmth of the sun that seemed to perpetually shine on Nicholas Zamora. I brought little of that to the table. Although I was a decent athlete, puberty was not kind to me. I topped out at five foot six on my toes and could no longer compete athletically with boys like Nicky, who were half a foot taller. But through our school years, he kept me close, never dropping me for his jock buddies or the girls who flocked around him.

After my parents died, I lived with Nicky's family during college vacations until graduation, which his parents attended in my parents' stead. Then Nicky and I shared a walk-up apartment in Hell's Kitchen. I worked as a paralegal for a big law firm while going to St. John's Law at night. Nicky tended bar at night while he claimed to be writing the great American novel during the day, but to me it seemed as if he spent most of his free time drinking and bedding beautiful women.

We were still sharing that same place when I met Anne. Back then she joked that she wanted to get married just so she'd have only one husband, not the two she currently felt wedded to because Nicky and I sometimes seemed joined at the hip. The joke was on her, of course. Even after Anne and I were married, the three of us remained inseparable.

Losing my parents had already conditioned me to accept that the unthinkable sometimes happens, and always without warning. Yet

Carolyn's death still shocked me. I couldn't believe she was actually dead.

Anne, on the other hand, had never suffered a loss of this magnitude, and therefore had the belief that the world made sense and was safe. For her, Carolyn's death was unfathomable, a breach of the world order upon which she relied. Whereas I imagined myself in Nicky's place, wondering how I would go on if Anne had died in such a freak accident, my wife undoubtedly saw her own mortality in the randomness of Carolyn's death.

Whatever Nicky took to calm himself, it knocked him out good. He was still fast asleep at ten, when Anne would have otherwise headed out to do her open mic set. Tonight, however, she stayed in, and we spent the evening—our first weeknight together in weeks—watching television.

"How is Nick going to go on after this?" she asked.

"What choice will he have?"

"I don't think I could . . . if something happened to you, I mean."

I smiled at her. "Nothing is going to happen to me. But I know what you mean. I can't imagine my life without you either. I know it's not the most romantic notion, but something I learned when my parents died is that you don't decide to go on after a tragedy, you just *do* because . . . well, it's the only path available. You're never the same after, and I'm certain that will be true of Nicky too."

"Promise me that you'll never die, Clint."

"I promise," I said with a smile. "Never. But only if you promise too."

"Yep. Never."

At midnight, we moved Nicky to our sofa. Once we were back in our bed, Anne quickly drifted off, but I knew sleep would be elusive for me. At the forefront of my restlessness on the night of Carolyn's death was something that Anne had told me a few months earlier. At my urging, Nicky had allowed Anne to be the first reader of his manuscript.

She appeared to be engrossed from the first page, and she read late into the night to finish the novel. When I heard her put the manuscript back in its paper bag, I asked for her review.

"It's great," she said.

"Nicky swore to me it wasn't about him and me. Was he lying?"

"No. Well, not entirely. It's still about him, but you're not in it, at least as far as I could tell. The main character is this guy who's just like Nick, or his view of himself, at least: a wildly talented artist destined for greatness. Hence the title—*Precipice*—because he's on the verge. But then he falls in love with a woman who threatens to ruin his life."

"What happens in the end?" I asked.

"She dies," Anne said. "So it all works out for our hero in the end, after all."

4.

The St. Ignatius Church was spectacular in every way, from the enormous bronze doors providing the gateway from Park Avenue to the Palladian arched windows that captured the eye immediately upon entry. The main sanctuary was the epitome of Baroque architecture, with polished pink marble pillars supporting a seventy-foot arched ceiling, and a central aisle more than twice that long.

It was the same church where Nicky and Carolyn had been married only five weeks earlier. Approximately a hundred guests had filled the chapel for their wedding, but five times as many came to pay their final respects to Carolyn. Martin Quinn lawyers were out in full force, as were the Zamoras' neighbors from Astoria, many of whom I hadn't seen since childhood. As I took in the mourners dressed in black, I couldn't help but recall the contrast to Carolyn in her magnificent white wedding dress, and how the bridesmaids had looked like bursts of flame in red gowns.

It had been four days since Carolyn's death. Or three, depending on whether the count began on Sunday night or Monday morning, when Nicky discovered her body. It had snowed every day during that stretch, something the weatherman claimed hadn't happened in more than fifty years.

Two days earlier, on Tuesday, the *Challenger* shuttle had exploded on live television, killing all seven astronauts, including Christa McAuliffe, the elementary school teacher on board. Nicky and I had been watching from my living room. I'd thought that the diversion might be good for him. To be part of something uplifting, rather than continue wallowing in his grief. As the rocket disintegrated in front of us, leaving only twin smoke trails, Nicky looked at the screen without saying a word. It was almost as if he had expected the disaster, because in his new mind-set, everything ended with senseless death.

Anne had tried to engage Nicky about the arrangements for Carolyn's funeral, but he was unable to handle even the most routine tasks. As a result, Carolyn's parents had planned the funeral as a full-on ecclesiastical affair, despite the fact that Carolyn had used the term "lapsed" whenever describing her Catholicism, and Nicky hadn't set foot inside a Greek Orthodox Church in more than twenty years.

The McDermotts were a large clan. They occupied the entire first row on the left side of the sanctuary. I immediately recognized Carolyn's parents from the wedding. Carolyn's father had reminded me of the butler in the movie *Trading Places*, and her mother must have commented at least three times about the beauty of the flowers. Like everyone else who had come to mourn after having attended the wedding, the McDermotts looked like pale imitations of the vibrant, joyous people they had been only last month.

Carolyn's siblings—her two brothers and one sister—sat beside their parents. Their significant others, along with aunts, uncles, and cousins, sat in the rows behind the immediate family.

Nicky sat in a pew across the aisle from the McDermotts. Beside him were his parents. The seating required that only immediate family occupy the first row, which was why Anne and I sat directly behind the Zamoras.

I had last seen the Zamoras at Nicky and Carolyn's wedding. They'd been as happy as I could ever remember them being. They danced the Kalamatiano, the traditional Greek wedding dance, with gusto, and then Nicky's father did the Hasapiko (which I always thought of as the Zorba the Greek dance) like a man half his age. But in the five weeks since then, they seemed to have aged a lifetime. For the first time, they appeared old and fragile.

Carolyn's older brother, John, gave the eulogy for the McDermott family. He spoke for about ten minutes, telling the mourners that his sister had sung in the church choir as a young girl, been a standout soccer midfielder in high school, been a member of the debate team in college, and graded on to the law review. He talked about her time at Martin Quinn, and how their entire family believed that only greater things lay ahead for their Carolyn.

What John didn't say, however, was word-one about Carolyn's marriage to Nicky. Perhaps the omission was because he was yielding that part of Carolyn's life to her husband, but it seemed more likely that the family held Nicky responsible for Carolyn's death. It wasn't hard to see it that way through the McDermotts' eyes. During the twenty-seven years that they had been charged with safeguarding Carolyn's well-being, she had thrived, racking up one accomplishment after another. Nicky had assumed that role for only a few months, and yet Carolyn had drowned in the bathtub on his watch.

Nicky had always been a natural at public speaking, but he was in no condition to address anyone regarding his wife. The few times Anne and I had tried to engage him to discuss what he was feeling, he'd had difficulty putting together a coherent thought. I told him that it would be understandable if he declined to speak at the funeral, but he said he couldn't live with himself if he didn't.

When it came time for him to speak, he looked like the same old Nicky: handsome, confident, totally in control. I could barely align the person delivering the eulogy with the shell of a man who had been living with Anne and me for the past four days. He spoke for nearly twenty minutes, without notes, and without faltering. It was a speech that struck all the right notes of melancholy and charm, joy and tragedy.

After the mass, as the mourners made their way to the cemetery, Anne and I sidled up to Nicky. The snow had stopped falling, at least for now.

"How are you holding up?" I asked.

"It's harder than I thought it would be, and I thought it was going to be fucking impossible."

At the gravesite, we stood beside Nicky like pillars keeping him upright, each of us holding one of his hands. After the priest had recited the appropriate psalms, two men in overalls lowered the casket into the grave. I honestly thought that Nicky was going to collapse, but instead he leaned more heavily on us until the service finally concluded.

Nicky, Anne, and I walked back to his car together. As we approached the parking lot, I saw two familiar faces. At first, I thought I knew them because they were partners at Martin Quinn; then I assumed I recognized them from court. Instead, they were the two police detectives from Nicky's house on the day Carolyn died.

Detective Lynch nodded when we made eye contact, and then a thin smile came to his lips. I turned away, not acknowledging our brief connection. It was not the circumstances that kept my expression in check, but my sudden awareness that the police didn't believe Carolyn's death had been an accident.

5.

Nicky wanted to return to his own house that evening.

"I've imposed on you and Anne enough," he said.

I told him it was too soon, but Anne pulled me aside and said that Nicky was right. Not that he'd imposed on us, of course, but that he had to get back to living his life at some point, and there would never be a *right* time. At least if he did it tonight, she reasoned, I could go with him and help him settle in.

"Make sure he's got food in the refrigerator and throw out anything that smells. That type of thing. And, of course, make sure there are no reminders of Carolyn's death. After he's settled, you can take the train back into the city."

As soon as we arrived at Nicky's place, he made a beeline to the kitchen. He returned with two tumblers and took them over to the credenza in the living room that he kept stocked with alcohol. He pulled out a bottle of Johnnie Walker.

"Pour one for me and I'll join you in a minute," I said, trying not to make my agenda obvious.

The master bedroom was on the first floor, at the back of the house. The bathroom was not en suite but located a few feet down the hall. It had been four days since Carolyn's death, and in that period, scores of law enforcement personnel had traipsed through. If I'd hazarded a guess at what I would find, it would have included some blood, if Carolyn had indeed struck her head. Perhaps water that had collected on the floor but not yet evaporated. At a minimum, I assumed that towels would be strewn about. To my surprise, though, the room was pristine. Not so much as a Q-tip out of place.

Carolyn's presence was everywhere, however. Her toothbrush, contact lens case, glasses, hairbrush, makeup bag, and magnifying mirror were on the bathroom sink, and her towel and robe were on a hook beside Nicky's. I was tempted to hide it all but feared that Nicky would find the absence of Carolyn's things even more unsettling, so I left everything exactly as I'd found it.

When I joined Nicky again in the living room, he was on the sofa, his glass now half-empty. A second glass, untouched, awaited my return. When I took my drink, I contemplated toasting Carolyn's memory but thought better of it. Perhaps, I thought, Nicky wanted some time to reflect in silence. So I sat beside him, and we drank without saying a word.

Finally Nicky said, "I know it's what everyone says, but I really can't believe she's gone. She should be here with us right now. Not . . . six feet underground in a box."

"It's a terrible, terrible tragedy," was all I could think to say.

"We were talking about having a baby," he said. "In fact, the last discussion we had was about that. How wonderful it would be to have a child. I asked her if it was the right time for her, career-wise, and you know what she said?"

I shook my head.

"She said that any time is the right time to have a baby." He shut his eyes and winced. "What day is it, anyway?"

It took me a moment to recall. "Thursday."

"I don't remember if I ever called the bar to tell them that I wouldn't be coming in."

"You asked me to do it," I said. "Remember, nearly the entire staff were at the funeral?"

The reference to the funeral apparently required him to finish the rest of his drink. Then he walked back over to the credenza, grabbed the bottle, and brought it back to the sofa.

"Slow down there, cowboy," I said.

As if I hadn't spoken a word, Nicky poured himself another double, then topped off my glass. "If you can't get stinking drunk with your best friend on the day of your wife's funeral, alcohol should never have been invented in the first place."

Within the hour, the whisky began working its magic. Like everything else in Nicky's life, he had mastered alcohol. It took much more than he'd imbibed to get him drunk, but it was enough for him to smile from time to time and allow his mind to range to matters other than his wife's death. Of course, it was not nearly enough for us to move the subject away from Carolyn entirely.

"I know that everyone thought we were crazy. That we'd gone from meeting each other, to getting engaged, to getting married, and then moving to the suburbs in . . . what, four months? And there were times when I heard this voice inside my head saying, *Slow down. What's the hurry?* But I told it to shut the hell up. Wanna know why?"

I nodded.

"I thought, here's finally a possibility for me to have what Clinton has. For once, maybe, do it like he does, just a little bit. And I didn't want to let that chance slip through my fingers."

I'd spent most of my life wishing I were more like Nicky. In the competition of our boyhood, I'd never been the winner. Nicky was more handsome, a better athlete, and even a more promising student, his writing noteworthy among the English faculty as something to be encouraged, whereas my teachers always saw me as more of a grinder. When the movie *Amadeus* came out, my first reaction was that if Nicky and I had lived in late-eighteenth-century Vienna, we might have been Mozart and Salieri.

"It's something they never tell you when you're in school," he said, almost as if talking to himself. "Everyone—parents, teachers, coaches—they always say that the key to success is to follow your passion. But the real key is to find someone you love who loves you back. After that, nothing else really matters. I learned that from seeing you and Anne together, Clinton. I wanted that too."

———

Anne was waiting up for me. I don't think she had expected for me to stay so long at Nicky's, and the fact that I was still smelling of booze after the train ride back must have surprised her too. But Anne wasn't the type to scold, especially when I was on a mission of mercy. She told me to take a shower and then come to bed.

"How'd he seem when you left?" she asked when I returned to the bedroom, my hair still damp.

"I'm not sure, to be honest."

"That's not very comforting."

"I assumed you wanted me to tell you the truth," I said with a smile. "For public consumption, I'd say that he's devastated but very strong, and in time he'll be okay."

"How long do you think it takes before you're *okay* with your new bride drowning ten feet away from you?"

"Which is why that's what I'm saying for public consumption. Between us, he'll obviously never be okay," I said. "He told me that Carolyn wasn't pregnant. He said that they were still talking about it."

The disclosure seemed to surprise Anne. She had more than once said that pregnancy was the only thing that would have made sense about the whirlwind nature of their romance, and now she was left without even that explanation.

"He said something else too," I offered, not sure whether sharing this bit of intelligence with Anne was wise. "He said that he moved so quickly to marry Carolyn because he wanted what you and I have."

She responded with a quiet laugh. "Do you think he was hoping that in a few years that he and Carolyn would hardly ever see each other?"

The comment stung. Anne must have seen my displeasure, because her smile quickly vanished.

"I'm sorry, Clint. No, what Nicky said was sweet. We're lucky to have what we have. Call me greedy, but I just want more of it, that's all. Do you know how many times in the past week I've heard someone tell me that this is proof you need to live every day like it's your last? And the thing is, I'm not sure there's any bigger lie. Can you imagine if people really lived every day like they were going to die tomorrow? Who would go to work? Who would exercise? Who would pay their bills? And don't get me started on the fact that most people would immediately binge on drugs and hookers if they thought they'd be dead in twenty-four hours."

"Not me," I said, looking into her eyes. "I'd spend it with you."

Her smile reappeared, but it didn't reflect that she believed me. It was the look you give a child who's telling you what Santa's going to bring.

"Maybe if you knew it was your last," she said. "But since we're not afforded that luxury, tomorrow life will go on as if we have all the time in the world, and whatever cautionary tale could be gleaned from Carolyn's death will be forgotten. You'll go to work and be there past ten. I won't be home when you roll in, because I'll be out chasing my dream. It'll be the same as it's always been."

"Maybe we should think about changing that, then."

"Maybe. But what would that even look like? You want to go back to the FD? Should I give up on singing? Is that going to make either of us happier?"

"Are you not happy now?"

She exhaled deeply, which answered my question. I knew that this was not the best period of our relationship, but until that moment I hadn't thought Anne was unhappy. Perhaps no one ever does until it's too late.

"No, it's not that, Clint. I'm happy. I'm just not enamored by our circumstances at the moment. I'm sorry, I don't know what I'm really trying to say. I'm just a little freaked out about all of this. I can't get out of my head that no one dies in the bathtub unless . . ."

"Unless what?"

"Unless they want to."

It was further testament to my failure to see the obvious at times, but I was so fixated on my immediate conclusion that Carolyn's death had been a tragic accident that I hadn't given any thought to the idea that she might have committed suicide. That would make much more sense than an accidental drowning, of course. She might have taken a handful of pills and then slipped away peacefully in the warm water. But despite the logic, I didn't want to believe it.

"Why would Carolyn kill herself? She was a newlywed, good career, new house. The world was her oyster."

"Yeah, I know," was all Anne said in response.

"You think she wasn't happy with her life? Suicidally unhappy?"

"How can you ever know?"

"She didn't leave a suicide note," I said, even though I knew from my FD days that many suicides don't leave notes. For some people, the act itself is the only communication necessary.

Anne let my comment be the last word, but the thought that Carolyn had taken her own life had taken root. I had always imagined that Carolyn had been the one who put the whirlwind nature of Nicky's transformation in motion, with him trying to apply the brakes but failing. But perhaps I had it all wrong. Maybe that transformation was exactly what Nicky craved, and in his rush to get there, he pushed Carolyn into a life she didn't want, until she thought death was her only escape.

6.

I hadn't been back at the office since I got Nicky's call that Carolyn was dead. But when I returned the next Monday, it was as I'd left it. If any clients—or, more importantly, prospective clients—had called while I was away, they hadn't left a message.

Even without any new messages or clients, I had a full slate of after-hours events scheduled. Two bar committee meetings, a memorial service for a recently departed judge I'd never heard of, and drinks with a law school classmate who'd been promoted to deputy counsel at a small brokerage firm, making him ripe for future business. As Anne had predicted, I was back to living my life as if Carolyn had never died.

My one paying client at the moment was Ruth Lewis, a woman who had been indicted for writing checks made out to cash and forging her boss's name. She had come to me in the circuitous way that I got most of my clients in the early part of my career—by referral from another lawyer. In her case, a lawyer who handled the divorce of the friend of a friend of Mrs. Lewis and gave her my name because he owed me a favor on account of my helping his nephew with a DUI.

A less likely looking felon than Ruth Lewis would have been hard to imagine. A flea of a woman, with an old-fashioned bouffant hairstyle and even more dated eyeglasses, she was sixty-eight years old and unwed, although she had been married briefly in her early twenties. She had adamantly refused to discuss the circumstances that led to her being not married, and given how many years had passed, I didn't think it would be relevant. I did ask her to confirm that her husband hadn't died under mysterious circumstances, which she did with an "Oh my, no."

This was our second meeting. Our first was at her arraignment, two weeks earlier, where I got her released on her own recognizance.

"I graduated from high school in 1939," Mrs. Lewis had told me in the courthouse hallway. "My senior year, I won a statewide competition for typing. Ninety-seven words per minute without a mistake. And that was on an old manual machine. Some of the girls were a bit faster, but if you made a mistake, they deducted it from your score. After graduation, I started to work for these three men. Mr. Goldenstein was the man who actually hired me. He was an older man, although I assume now that he probably wasn't much older than fifty. There was another man who was older still, a Mr. . . . I don't remember his name right now, but it'll come to me. And Mr. Harris. He was the youngest of the three by far, but still older than me, of course. The three of them weren't partners, but I worked for all three. On Fridays, I'd go to them one at a time, and each would give me four dollars. They didn't even just hand me an envelope with the twelve dollars. I actually had to go into their offices separately. Each one would reach into his pocket to pay me for the week. Sometimes, one of them didn't have the cash. When that happened, I'd have to go back to his office on Monday and ask again.

"Anyway, Mr. Harris left that office a few years later and asked me to come with him. After another move or two, we ended up at BBDO, which back then was the biggest advertising agency in the world. Mr. Harris had a corner office high above Madison Avenue. He used to say to me, 'Remember when we were in that dump on Seventh Avenue with those old codgers?' A few years after that, he left BBDO to go out on his own, and I followed him again."

She had the wistful sound of someone recounting her first love. Of course, if she was in love with him, it was unrequited, as Mr. Harris had filed a criminal complaint accusing her of embezzlement.

"I'm telling you this," she continued, "so you'll understand that Mr. Harris was family to me. I would never steal from him. Not in a million years. I swear on my life."

I told her that I believed her. Then I sent the copies of the allegedly forged checks to an expert for a handwriting analysis. He confirmed the checks were definitely not signed by Mr. Harris. He also told me that the forgeries were good—very good, in fact. "Someone took a lot of time practicing," was the way he put it.

My modus operandi, then and now, was to lay out the facts for the client. Then I'd say that it was my job to explain how the prosecutor would view those facts and, if it came to that, the conclusion a jury would reach if asked to render a verdict. That way, I could stay in the client's good graces by claiming that I believed in their innocence, but my advice was based on the likelihood that others might not. I maintained that position right up until the moment they confessed their guilt.

It was my hope that Mrs. Lewis would reach that point in the next five minutes.

She sat in my office, her hands knitted together, resting atop the purse that sat on her lap. She declined my offer of water, coffee, or tea. From the look on her face, she seemed to be expecting me to share good news.

"I have some hard facts we need to discuss," I said. "As you know, the prosecution has a handwriting expert who will testify that Mr. Harris did not write the checks made out to cash. To rebut that, I needed to get an expert who would testify that he did. Unfortunately, my expert also told me that there's no way Mr. Harris wrote those checks. That's just science. Which means we have to accept as a fact that someone was forging his name."

If Mrs. Lewis sensed that the walls were closing in on her, she didn't show it. In fact, she displayed no expression whatsoever.

"Our expert also told me that whoever forged Mr. Harris's signature had seen it enough times to be able to make a pretty convincing copy. On top of which, it had to be someone who had ready access to his checkbook. In light of the fact that Mr. Harris is unmarried and without family, and you had the responsibility of paying his bills, we can expect the prosecution to claim that only you had that type of access."

I paused to see if this was enough to elicit a response. Perhaps she'd tell me about others with equal access. But Mrs. Lewis remained still, staring at me as if waiting for me to get to the point.

"The police already know that your fingerprints are on each of those checks. As we discussed, that's not incriminating in and of itself because you handled Mr. Harris's finances. However, they must have already reviewed your bank records, and that means that any deposits there that match up against the check amounts will be powerful evidence against you. I suspect that they're also checking surveillance footage at the banks, to match it against the timestamp for the deposit of the checks. Even if the person who made the deposits was careful enough to avoid the cameras, the tellers might be able to make a positive ID based on a photo array."

I thought the circumstantial case I'd presented would be enough to convince Mrs. Lewis that this was her last opportunity to take responsibility before the evidence made her guilt a foregone conclusion. But she didn't budge. Instead, she looked at me through her cat's-eye glasses with a challenge in her gaze.

"I can probably get the DA to consider a suspended sentence," I continued. "Your age, and the fact that I'm certain Mr. Harris doesn't want this incident to become public, would push them in that direction. They're only going to go for it, though, if you also pay full restitution. And the window on that type of deal will close quickly. When it does, they're going to insist on jail time."

Some clients confess at this point, realizing their lie has been revealed. Others double down. They swear that the evidence must have been planted or that there's proof still to be uncovered that will exonerate them.

Mrs. Lewis was quiet for a good minute. Then she said, "I have two questions, Mr. Broden. The first question I have is how much would the restitution be?"

The indictment claimed that Mrs. Lewis had written $38,000 in forged checks, a fact of which she was well aware. Her question told me that she likely had stolen far more. Rarely do the police figure out the full extent of anyone's crime, which puts the lie to the idea that crime doesn't pay. My guess was that she had been forging Mr. Harris's name on checks for years—maybe since 1939—making the grand total of her ill-gotten gains possibly in the mid–six figures, if not more.

"A little under forty thousand," I said. "We can try to negotiate the number based on your financial circumstances."

She nodded and continued to show me a world-class poker face. "Second, if I plead guilty, will you refund some of the retainer I paid you? I only gave you the five thousand dollars because I assumed I'd be going to trial. If I knew I was going to plead guilty after meeting you only twice, I wouldn't have paid you that much."

She said this with a straight face too. As if the fact that she had lied to me about her guilt should be held against me and not her. I was about to tell her that the retainer was nonrefundable, and that it was fine by me if she wanted to go to trial and risk a prison sentence so that she could get her $5,000 worth in legal fees, when my phone rang.

Normally I wouldn't answer during a client meeting. However, it was now obvious that Mrs. Lewis would be a former client soon.

The caller was Nicky.

From the way he said my name, I knew he was in distress. My mind flashed to his call of a week ago, when he'd sounded much the same before telling me that his wife was dead.

"I've been arrested," he said. "They think I killed Carolyn."

7.

My legal practice was exclusively New York City–based. I handled both federal and state matters, but I never ventured outside the five boroughs to do it. I hadn't even considered that the police and forensic people who occupied Nicky's home after Carolyn's death were Westchester County employees, not NYPD. It was a stupid thing not to register, as I'm certain their identity was emblazoned on every windbreaker, bag, and patrol car I saw that day.

But when Nicky said he'd been arrested, he told me he was being held in the Westchester County jail. It was in Valhalla, northern Westchester, nearly two hours outside Manhattan.

There was no mistaking the building for anything other than a jail, but it was still a step up from the MCC—the Manhattan Correctional Center—where those awaiting trial in Manhattan were held. For one thing, it didn't stink. This facility was also clean and extremely well lit. The visitors' room reminded me of a high school cafeteria, with rows of Formica tables filling the room.

I explained to the guard that I was an attorney, here for a legal visit. He escorted me to a private room without windows that was the size of a broom closet.

It took another hour for Nicky to arrive. I feared the worst—that he had been involved in an altercation with a hardened criminal and been hurt. But when my friend appeared at the door, he didn't look any worse for wear. In fact, considering that my recent interactions with him had been in equally dire circumstances, I might have said that he looked good. He was clean-shaven and smiled when our eyes met. I instinctively extended my hand to greet him. It was only when Nicky didn't reciprocate that I realized his hands were cuffed behind his back.

"Are the handcuffs really necessary, officer?" I asked.

"Protocol," the guard said, not the least bit sympathetic to Nicky's plight.

Nicky wriggled into the seat, his arms dangling over the back of the wooden chair uncomfortably.

"I'm going to need him to use his hands to communicate certain things with me," I said to the guard. "How about if we meet in the middle? Cuff one hand—his left, preferably—to the chair. That way I don't have to report to the judge that I was unable to deliver effective counsel to my client before his arraignment because of *protocol*."

Without further discussion, the guard did as I requested, securing Nicky's left wrist to the chair, then leaving without another word.

"How are you holding up?" I asked Nicky.

"I've been better. Not going to lie about that. How could they think I killed Carolyn?"

Because twenty-seven-year-old women are not supposed to drown in the bathtub.

"I don't know anything about their evidence," I said instead. "But right now, that's of secondary importance to getting you out of here. The arraignment is at four. I don't want to sugarcoat things. This is a murder charge. The bail demand is going to be high."

"How high?"

"Could be a million dollars. And bail may not be on the table at all."

"Jesus."

"Assuming the judge sets a bail amount that you don't have in cash, you can post a bond that's backed by something of that value. So the immediate question is what kind of assets you can pull together."

"I've got nothing, Clinton. We used all our savings to buy the house."

"How much did you put down?"

"Ten percent. Something like twenty thousand."

That obviously wasn't going to do it.

"What about your parents? Do they own their home without a mortgage?"

Nicky's parents still lived in the same brick-front home where he'd grown up. When my parents died, I sold our home for about $150,000. Even with the red-hot real estate market since then, I couldn't imagine the Zamoras' house was worth more than $250,000.

"I think so."

"And your dad's store? Does he own the building it's in?"

Nicky nodded.

"Anything else? Stocks, bonds, retirement funds? For either you or your parents?"

This time a headshake.

I made a quick estimate and concluded that his total assets might enable him to pledge $500,000 or more. Hopefully that would be enough to satisfy the judge that he wasn't a flight risk.

"Okay. After we're done in here, I'm going to call your father. I'll ask him to meet us at the courthouse and to bring the paperwork showing ownership of the house and the store."

I was asking Nicky for permission, but he didn't seem to understand. Rather than offer his assent, he said, "I don't understand why this is happening."

This time I said it aloud. "Twenty-seven-year-old women are not supposed to drown in their bathtub, Nicky. The prosecution is looking for a reason that Carolyn died. Clearly, they have some evidence that suggests that you—or somebody—killed her."

He didn't utter a word of protest. Instead he asked, "What's going to happen next?"

"I'm not going to see you again until you're brought into the courtroom to be arraigned. Until then, you don't say anything to anyone. If anyone approaches you, tell them that you invoke your right to counsel. When I see you in court, I'll waive reading of the indictment, and then the judge will ask you to enter a plea. That's when you say, 'Not guilty, Your Honor.' And that's all you say. Say it strongly, but don't shout. Then the judge will ask the prosecutor for his position on bail, and we'll argue it out. You were born in Queens, right?"

"Yeah."

"Aunts and uncles live there too?"

"Yeah. My mother's two sisters. My father's sister too."

"Good. That'll help. It gives you ties to the community."

Nicky adjusted his position, and the handcuff clanked against the metal chair leg.

"Anything you need to discuss with me before I reach out to your dad?"

He didn't hesitate. "I didn't kill Carolyn."

I smiled. "Nicky, that was the last thing you needed to tell me. I know you didn't."

———

The courthouse was in Mount Pleasant, a location chosen apparently without irony. It was housed in a two-story cement structure with a dome and two oversize windows that looked out on the street like giant eyes. In addition to housing the courtroom where Nicky would be arraigned, all town business took place in this building, from getting a marriage license to recording real estate deeds.

The courtroom looked nothing like the baronial chambers in which Manhattan judges presided. The room was carpeted, a dingy, gray, industrial weave. The courtrooms in the city had stationary wooden benches for the spectators, but here I sat in an actual chair that was not bolted to the floor.

All but a few of the twenty or so chairs were occupied, but none by anyone who appeared to have business before the court. That meant they were reporters, which prompted my first realization that Nicky's arrest was going to make the news. It should have occurred to me before. Everything about the crime was tailor-made for the tabloids: successful, well-educated, young, Caucasian couple who had it all until the husband murdered his wife.

Nicky's parents sat beside me in the gallery's third row. The fragility I had observed at Carolyn's funeral now seemed to consume them. They were proud people, and the specter of their son being under arrest for murder seemed more than they could handle.

"He's innocent, Andres," I said. "There's nothing anyone can do about being wrongly accused."

Nicky's father couldn't even meet my eyes to answer. Instead, his mother said, "Thank you, Clinton. Thank you for being his friend."

At twenty minutes after two, the judge entered the courtroom. Despite the modest surroundings, the judge's arrival came with the same pomp of every courtroom I'd ever been in: the clerk banging on the door, ordering all to rise, and announcing His Honor.

Judge Raymond T. Carson was in his midfifties. His dark hair was slicked straight back, and he wore black plastic eyeglasses that gave him a bit of a Clark Kent quality, at least based on the George Reeves version that had played on WPIX 11 when I was in elementary school. After taking his seat, Judge Carson smiled, apparently pleased to be working to a full house.

"Welcome, everyone," Judge Carson said. "Please, be seated."

He nodded at the court officer, who must have doubled as a local cop, because he was wearing a policeman's uniform. "The People of the State of New York versus Nicholas J. Zamora. Case Number 86 CR

113101. Top count of the indictment is section 125.25 of the New York Criminal Penal Law, murder in the second degree."

The charge was not a surprise, but hearing it still caught me off-balance. Nicky had now been formally charged with murdering his wife.

In New York State, murder in the first degree is limited to killing a police officer and a few other special classes of people, mainly those involved in the justice system. Killing your wife in a premeditated fashion was charged as second degree. New York didn't impose the death penalty for second-degree murder, but Nicky was still staring down the possibility of life in prison if convicted.

As I got up to enter the well of the court, I turned to look behind me, back to the one and only entrance into the space. Nicky was making his way in, his hands again cuffed behind his back. Another local police officer was guiding him down the corridor. I joined him when he passed the first row, and we walked together to the small table in front of the judge. The prosecutor was already in place. He looked to be my age, clean-cut the way prosecutors usually are.

"Waive reading of the indictment," I said.

This was a given in criminal practice. As a vestige of a bygone era, the law required that the defendant be read the charges aloud in open court. Not only was it a gigantic waste of time, but it was painful for the defendant to hear the awful things he'd been accused of doing.

"That's not the way we do things here," Judge Carson said. "First, I need your appearance."

In Manhattan, you give your appearance to the court clerk before the judge takes the bench. That way, the proceeding can begin as soon as the judge arrives. In Mount Pleasant, apparently, no one was in a hurry.

"Assistant District Attorney Barry Mendelson, of the Westchester County District Attorney's Office," the prosecutor said.

"F. Clinton Broden, New York City. Counsel for the defendant."

"Now, Mr. Broden, is it?" Judge Carson asked.

"Yes, Your Honor."

"Would you like Mr. Mendelson to read the indictment, or do you waive reading?"

He said it with a mocking smile. It was his way of telling me that I wasn't in Kansas anymore. I'd heard about other New York City lawyers getting hometowned outside the five boroughs, but this was my first time being on the receiving end.

"The defense waives reading," I said.

"On the only charge in the indictment, murder in the second degree, how does the defendant plead?"

I nodded for Nicky to say his line. "Not guilty," he choked out barely loud enough for me to hear, much less the judge.

Still, it was enough to make the record, because Judge Carson quickly asked, "Mr. Mendelson, what is the People's position on bail?"

"Thank you, Your Honor. Mr. Zamora is charged with murdering his wife of only a month by drowning her in the bathtub. The savage nature of the crime makes Mr. Zamora a danger to the community. In addition, he has no ties to Westchester County. No children. The defendant is therefore a definite flight risk. The People therefore request that Mr. Zamora be held without bail."

Prosecutors are no different from defense lawyers—we both set out extreme positions, pushing the bounds of truth to the breaking point.

"Mr. Broden?"

"Your Honor, I will spare the court the usual recitation of how flimsy the People's evidence is because I recognize that the seriousness of the charge alone warrants meaningful bail. But it should be set at the lowest level that will ensure Mr. Zamora's appearance at trial. Contrary to the ADA's claim, Mr. Zamora has extremely significant ties to the community. He grew up less than thirty minutes from here, in Queens. His parents still live there, and they are in the courtroom today."

I turned and motioned for Nicky's parents to stand. Mr. Zamora managed a crooked smile, but his wife buried her face in her handkerchief.

"Mr. Zamora's parents are willing to post the home they have lived in for nearly forty years and the business that has been in their family even longer than that, a grocery store in Queens. They will also pledge the building it occupies, which they also own. The value of this package is going to top out at five hundred thousand dollars," I said, deliberately lowballing it. "That is a significant amount, especially to people of the Zamoras' means. I therefore respectfully request that you select a bail figure that they can achieve."

The judge's gaze went past me and focused on Nicky's parents in the gallery. Then he turned back to Nicky.

"Sir, do you love your parents?" Judge Carson asked.

The question must have confused Nicky, because he didn't immediately answer. Then he said, "Yes. Very much."

"Do you promise me that if I free you on bail, you're going to come back here to face trial?"

"I promise."

Judge Carson looked down at the indictment, no doubt to recall Nicky's name. "Believe me, Mr. Zamora, I will not hesitate to take your parents' home and their business from them if you do not. Do you understand that?"

"I do. I swear."

Judge Carson gave a single nod. "Bail is set at five hundred thousand dollars."

8.

More than five hours after the arraignment, Nicky still hadn't been released. I canceled my after-work appointments and settled in for what I expected might be a long night. My main concern was that, despite the judge granting Nicky bail, if everything wasn't finalized soon, Nicky would still end up spending the night in confinement. As each hour passed, the ranks of the reporters dwindled, undoubtedly because they too expected there'd be no photo op today.

A little before seven, Nicky passed through the gate. By that time there were only two or three news outfits still in attendance. They took their pictures and asked for a comment, to which I responded, "Mr. Zamora is innocent of these charges and will prove that at trial."

We drove back to Mount Vernon in silence. I had been prepared for Nicky to pepper me with questions during the car ride—about the evidence, the likely jail time if he were convicted, the odds that he'd win at trial, or simply what would happen next. But he didn't say a word. He stared out the window, as if the answers were to be found on the highway.

I periodically looked in the rearview mirror to see if we were being followed, but a picture and a quote were apparently all the reporters wanted. When Nicky and I pulled into the Skyline diner, we were alone.

"How's the food in the joint?" I asked Nicky when we sat, my effort to inject a little levity.

He smiled for a moment, then looked at me with meaning. "Seriously, Clinton, thank you. For everything, man. I—"

"No need. I'm here for you. Just like I know that if someday my freedom depended on you writing a really good book, you'd be there for me."

He laughed. "You know I would."

"One thing, though. You know the old expression about the lawyer who represents himself in court . . ."

"Fool for a client, yeah."

"Well, I'm not sure having your best friend as your lawyer makes you much smarter than that. Which is my way of saying that, starting right now, you have to think only of yourself."

Instead of turning somber, Nicky smiled, as if to acknowledge that had never been much of a problem for him.

"What I mean to say is that you can't feel any obligation toward me, Nicky. There's a reason that doctors don't operate on family members, right? It's not because of shaky hands; it's because the emotional bond can cloud your judgment. This is your life we're talking about. Win or lose, I go home when the trial's over. So if you want a lawyer who you can curse out, or even if you're thinking about suing for malpractice when it's all over, if it came to that, I can get you names of people I think are terrific, and I'd be fine with that. I could help out in some other way, or provide no legal services at all and just be your friend."

"You may have a fool for a client, Clinton, but I have the best criminal defense lawyer in New York City." He smiled. "Besides, who else is going to do it for free?"

"I do come cheap, that's true. But all kidding aside, just remember this, and we don't have to discuss it again, but you should fire me the second you think that I'm not the right guy for this."

"Deal," he said, still smiling. "Maybe the one thing that won't suck about being wrongly accused of murdering the woman I loved will be firing your ass."

Needless to say, I wasn't worried about being fired. My concern was that my best friend was going to end up serving life in prison because of me.

———

After we ordered, while we were waiting for the food to arrive, I told Nicky what I'd learned about the case against him.

"The indictment doesn't say much, which is pretty standard. It just repeats the elements of the crime and alleges that you did them. I asked the ADA to put some meat on those bones, but he said it wasn't his case and he was just there for the arraignment. Apparently some guy named Brandon Sherman is the ADA in charge. I'll reach out to him tomorrow."

"Why do they even think Carolyn was murdered?" Nicky asked. "It was obviously an accident."

"Without seeing their discovery, particularly the autopsy, it's impossible to know for sure. But with the lawyerly caveat that this is pure guesswork, and everything I tell you could be proven wrong, the fact that they made the arrest a week after Carolyn died tells me that the autopsy didn't support an accidental death. I had a few theories as to how Carolyn might have died. I'm sure you did too. A brain aneurysm or a seizure, or maybe she had a reaction to some medication she'd started and it caused her to pass out. But the autopsy must have disproved those possibilities. It likely shows that she was in perfect health and didn't have any drugs or alcohol in her system."

"But why would that make them think that I murdered her?"

His naivete on this point surprised me.

"Nicky, if the autopsy didn't show a medical reason for her to pass out, then there was probably a contusion on her head or something. Maybe she slipped getting out, but the DA could have concluded that someone hit her. And you were the only other person in the house. They weren't thinking about other suspects."

Nicky winced at the suggestion. "Jesus."

"I know. But here's what worries me: I don't believe that just a bang on the head would be enough for them to indict. They must have more than that."

"Like what?"

"A reason why you wanted her dead. In a spousal situation, one that isn't going to involve child custody, it usually comes down to money or infidelity. Sometimes it's both."

He was shaking his head to deny either possibility, but I asked the question anyway.

"Did Carolyn have any family money? Like a trust or something like that?"

"No. The McDermotts are reasonably well off, but nothing like that."

"Life insurance?"

"No. I'm screwed financially now. Without Carolyn's paycheck, I won't be able to pay the property tax on the house, much less the mortgage."

"Okay. So there's no financial motive. What about infidelity? Yours or hers?"

"We're still newlyweds. I don't know what it was like with you and Anne, but Carolyn and I were still having sex every night and twice a day on the weekends. There's no one else, I swear. For either of us."

The financial part I accepted at face value. If Carolyn's parents were millionaires, I would have known about it, and lying about insurance money made no sense because Nicky must have known it would be easy to prove. The infidelity, however, was another matter. I didn't know Carolyn well enough to pass judgment on whether she would cheat on her new husband, but I'd known Nicky to step out on prior girlfriends.

But, like he said, Carolyn and he were newlyweds, and there was no reason for him to marry her if he had someone else on the side.

"So that's the good news, then," I said. "There is no motive."

———

"Do you think it's possible?"

Attorney-client privilege does not have an exception for wives. Although Anne could not be compelled to reveal anything I said to her under the doctrine of spousal privilege, repeating what a client told me, even to Anne, was still an ethical breach. But Anne and I had always talked about my cases, and usually that included my revealing things that I would never tell someone outside of the attorney-client privilege. Something about Nicky's case could come up that I'd shield from Anne in the future, but I was not going to draw the line at general questions like the one she was asking now.

"Absolutely not," I said.

In response to my full-throated denial, she nodded, but in a way that suggested she did not believe as strongly as I did in Nicky's innocence. I didn't begrudge her this doubt. She didn't know him like I did.

"Why do they think he killed her?"

During the early days of our marriage, Anne would listen to the fact patterns of my cases as if I were recounting the plot of a particularly good novel. After a few years, she came to assume the dispassionate air of a juror, rendering judgment after I'd laid out the evidence. By this point in our marriage, however, Anne's interest in my work had waned. On those occasions when I'd come home to share some new evidence I'd unearthed, more often than not she'd say that my cases all blurred together in her mind.

It was only natural, however, that Nicky's defense reawakened her interest in my work. And being married to a defense lawyer means that you acquire some of the tricks of the trade. In Anne's case, she was a natural cross-examiner. Her question about my opinion of Nicky's guilt had revealed only that I loved him; now she was attacking the issue from another angle.

"The indictment didn't specify a motive. That's not unusual, though. Motive isn't an element of the prosecution's burden, and they usually like to play it close to the vest. Besides, in a spousal situation, the motive could be virtually anything. The usual things, of course, are money or infidelity, but Nicky's emphatic that neither of those things were issues between him and Carolyn."

"There's got to be a reason why they think he killed her," Anne said.

The prosecution would argue otherwise. They'd say that it doesn't matter why. That people fly into murderous rages over nothing all the time. Nicky could have been triggered by a sudden request to do the dishes.

But I believed the answer to Anne's question was much simpler.

"There is a reason," I said. "It's that they're wrong."

Again, I wasn't sure she believed that. And like before, she deflected my certainty to address a logistical issue.

"So what's next?"

"Preparing for trial."

"Are you up for that?"

There were a multitude of meanings packed in that one question. *Am I capable of representing someone in a murder case?* I'd done two murder cases, but both were gang killings between drug dealers with long criminal records. In neither did my clients put on a defense, and both were convicted. Or maybe Anne wasn't questioning my bona fides, but instead asking if I was ready to represent a friend. And not just any friend, of course. Nicky was my oldest and dearest friend. My wife was well aware that in the few previous instances someone I knew socially had asked me to represent them, I'd declined for the reasons I'd already shared with Nicky. It was also possible that Anne wasn't concerned about Nicky, but about our finances. The trial would occupy at least the next six months of my life and require my full-time attention. She knew from experience that, a month or two after the case ended, I'd lack regular work because I hadn't been able to accept new clients during the trial. She also knew that I would never in a million years charge Nicky a dime. From a financial perspective, this meant that representing Nicky would be the rough equivalent of taking a half-year, unpaid sabbatical. Our bank account didn't reflect that I had that luxury.

"Yes," was all I said.

9.

A criminal defense begins by demanding the prosecution share its evidence. More often than not, that demand is met by stonewalling. Then, shortly before the trial date, the prosecution produces what in the jargon of criminal defense is referred to as *Brady* materials, the constitutionally required minimum of information, which amounts only to exculpatory or impeachment evidence. Other than that, the prosecution has limited discovery obligations pretrial, and they typically hold even that back until the last possible moment.

It was therefore something of a surprise when, less than two weeks after I made my demands in Nicky's case, I received the forensic evidence. This was not necessarily good news. Prosecutors respond early only to demonstrate they have the defendant dead to rights, in order to set the stage for a guilty plea. The criminal-law equivalent of shock and awe.

The evidence consisted of thirty pages of medical reports and half as many autopsy photographs. The pictures were graphic—Carolyn's dead eyes staring at me—but it was the medical analysis that mattered, and to decipher that I needed an expert's assistance, which was why George Graham was now sitting in my office.

I met George when I was at the FD, and he worked for the New York City Medical Examiner. It didn't take me long to realize that George was the ME you wanted on your case. Not only because he was smart and thorough, but because he gave it to you straight, whereas many of his colleagues thought of themselves as part of the prosecutorial team, which made defense lawyers the enemy.

George left the ME two years ago after being railroaded by his boss. He never told me what happened, but I'd heard from others that when Ben Kornitzer stepped down as the city's chief medical examiner, the Mayor's office spoke to the rank and file to get the lowdown on Paul Zimmerman, who at the time was the First Assistant and the odds-on favorite to be offered the top spot. Reading the writing on the wall, the members of the staff sang Zimmerman's praises, which is another way of saying that they lied. Except George. He wasn't built that way. He told the truth—that Zimmerman was a second-rate pathologist who likely had a drinking problem and definitely had anger issues. Of course, the story ended the way anyone could have predicted: Zimmerman got the job anyway, someone told him about George's comments, and George was sent packing.

On the bright side for George, a former ME who goes into the expert-witness business is in high demand. As soon as George put out his shingle, he became the first call for every defense lawyer, and price was never an object. Unfortunately, the same Boy Scout impulse that lost George his job made him a difficult expert. Put another way, George wrongly thought he was being paid for his expertise; the truth is, defense lawyers retain experts to provide helpful testimony.

The one and only time we discussed it, I told George that he'd more than double his client list if he were a bit more flexible in his opinions. "I'm not saying that you should lie," I said, "but sometimes you could tell me that there are other possible scenarios, and that's all I need."

"Let's be honest," he said. "Defense lawyers don't want a black doctor as their expert. And the last thing I'm going to be is a black doctor willing to say whatever it takes to get paid."

I'd retained George to consult on at least ten cases but had put him on the stand only twice. In the others, I couldn't get the opinion I needed and ultimately had to retain an expert who was willing to testify in line with my defense. However, the only two cases I won were the ones in which George had been my expert.

"So what have you got for me?" I asked.

"First thing. Cause of death was drowning."

"No real surprise there. She was found in the bathtub."

"I know. But it's not like a blow to the head or a heart attack or aneurysm is present. So I think that probably goes in the bad news category. Because you have to explain that she somehow drowned in her bathtub without a clear precipitating medical cause. The ME has time of death as the night before, between midnight and four a.m."

I was focused solely on the precipitating cause, hoping that George's claim that there wasn't a "clear" precipitating event meant that there was at least an unclear one for me to work with.

"Were there any drugs or alcohol in her system?"

"She was on this new drug called Tofranil. It's used to combat anxiety and depression. It's still too new to have real data on it, but drowsiness is a side effect all by itself, and mixing it with alcohol, which she did, accelerates that process. She had a blood alcohol level of .04."

"How much is that in servings?"

"One. Give or take."

"And the drug . . . it's called Tofranil?"

He nodded.

"What was that dosage?"

"A hundred milligrams. Within the guidelines."

"So no possibility of suicide, then?"

"No. She took one pill and had, at most, a glass of wine. I'm not sure that even downing a handful of the stuff and following it up with an entire bottle of wine would have killed her, but she wasn't intentionally trying to cause herself to pass out in the tub, if that's what you're asking."

Even with suicide off the table, George had given me a drug that causes drowsiness, plus alcohol, all mixed in with a hot bath. I could definitely push that as a viable reason for Carolyn to pass out. But I knew there'd be more.

"So what's bad for us?"

"I'm not even done with the good news yet."

"Don't let me stop you."

"She was pregnant."

It shouldn't have jolted me. Anne had been speculating about it for months, saying that the only thing that explained the whirlwind nature of their romance was if a baby was on the way. But it was still a shock, especially because Nicky didn't know.

"How far along was she?"

"Not very. Five weeks."

I did the math in my head. They probably had conceived on their wedding night or during the honeymoon.

"Would she have known?"

"That depends on how regularly she got her period. If you subpoena her OB or even her physician, you'll find out whether she told either of them about the pregnancy—or if they told her. But she could have just as easily found out through a home pregnancy test."

"Does the alcohol level or the fact she was taking the depression meds suggest she didn't know yet? Would a doctor have told her to stop?"

"Not necessarily. Some OBs are okay with a little wine now and then. And I'm not sure that there's enough research about Tofranil and pregnancy for a doctor to take her off it. Again, I think it depends on the doctor and how strongly she felt she needed the meds."

"Does pregnancy increase the likelihood of her passing out in the tub?"

"Bingo," he said with a big smile. "I won't bore you with the medical reason, but pregnant women often feel dizzy and faint."

This was why George put the pregnancy in the good news category for the defense. I didn't see it that way, however. Whatever ground was gained by it being a possible contributing factor to her passing out would be lost tenfold when Carolyn's pregnancy was considered as part of motive evidence. An unwanted baby was powerful ammunition for the prosecution to argue that divorce—which now came with eighteen years of child support payments—was less appealing to Nicky than murdering Carolyn.

"Are you ready for the bad news?"

I wasn't, of course. I didn't want there to be any.

"Give me your worst," I said.

"She had some bruising."

He traced his finger along the autopsy photo of Carolyn. The picture was cropped to omit her nipples, but the top of her cleavage was visible. George pointed below her clavicle. Both sides. I knew instantly what he was going to say—that the placement was exactly where you'd put your hands on the body of a person you were trying to drown in a bathtub.

There had been other times in our working history that George had brought me scientific evidence that conflicted with my defense. Sometimes I pushed back, making him counter the various arguments that I expected to make when I heard the same points articulated by the other side's expert in court. But in none of those instances did I ever think George had made a mistake.

But this time he had to be wrong. There was simply no way the evidence suggested that Nicky had pushed on Carolyn's chest to keep her under the water until she drowned.

When I'd initially looked at the photo, I had assumed that the bruises were caused when Nicky tried to revive her. George immediately disabused me of the notion.

"Your guy says he did the CPR the following morning. By that time, she was already dead for something like eight hours. Without blood flow for that long, you wouldn't get bruising like this. I'm sorry to say it looks to me much more likely that this type of injury would have been incurred during a struggle in which she fought her attacker. The scratches on your guy's arm and the skin under her fingernail also fit that scenario."

Included in the photos was one of Nicky's forearms. They had some scratches on them, but nothing deep enough to break the skin.

"There's got to be another explanation. There's no way Nicky drowned her, George."

He shrugged, indicating that he was now going to give me ammunition that he didn't think would fire. "You could try the age-old defense that it was the result of rough sex. The problem there is that you're going to need a jury comprised of twelve virgins. Otherwise, they're going to know that it's a little odd that the man would bruise his lover by bracing all his weight on her torso, which is what would have to have happened for him to leave these kinds of bruises."

It was certainly a vivid picture. Nicky on top of Carolyn, his hands pressing on her upper chest, right above her breasts but below her collarbone, with her fingernails scratching at his arm. It seemed awkward. Not to mention unpleasant for Carolyn.

"And, on top of that, there's no evidence of sexual intercourse in the last forty-eight hours," George added.

"What if they used a condom?"

"Yeah, that's one way to go. But they wouldn't use a condom if she was pregnant. So that theory will only work if you can also prove that she didn't know she was with child. The prosecution's rebuttal will be that the most prominent bruising is lower than the rest."

He stopped as if his statement were self-explanatory. It wasn't. At least not to me.

"And?"

"Well, think about it. Most of the pressure applied from hands is from the thumbs." I nodded, but not because I agreed. I had no idea if that was right or not. I wanted George to get to the point.

"So that means in the typical way you'd think about someone's hands"—he put his own hands up, palms facing me—"the thumbs are facing up, which means when pressure is applied, the most prominent bruising will be either to the side or above, but not below."

I laid my palms flat on my desk, conducting my own experiment. The most natural position was what George had said, with my thumbs at a little more than a forty-five-degree angle above my wrists. Then I began to slightly rotate my hands, until my thumbs were pointing straight down.

"Not the most natural position," George said.

"But not impossible."

He rolled his eyes. His business was not about disproving impossibilities.

"There's another possibility I like better than the theory that your friend is a contortionist when he has intercourse," George said.

"Tell me."

George got up from my guest chair and stood directly over me. "If he was standing and she was on her knees," he said and placed his hands below my clavicle to illustrate his point. His thumbs were now in the right position, pointing downward.

"Wouldn't his hands be on her shoulders?" I asked.

"You would think. But maybe his fingertips were on her shoulders. Then it could line up. Does your friend have smallish hands?"

"I never measured them, but he's a big guy, six-two, so I doubt it."

"It doesn't necessarily correlate to height. Take a look at his hands next time you see him. If they're much bigger than yours, then if his hands were on her shoulders, his thumbs wouldn't line up with the bruising."

I considered how to word the next question. "Anything consistent with that theory in the forensics?"

"You mean is his semen in her throat? No. But if he ejaculated elsewhere, or she spit it out . . ."

I ran through my mind how this would sound to the jury. Midway through my thought process, I tried it out, hoping to get George's opinion.

"Ladies and gentlemen of the jury, you heard the prosecution place heavy emphasis on the bruises located on Carolyn McDermott's upper torso. It's practically their entire case, the only evidence that they have to suggest murder. There are many other interpretations regarding how Carolyn McDermott incurred that bruising that are completely innocent, however. Dr. Graham testified that the exact same bruising is consistent with sexual intercourse."

"*Might* have been caused by sexual intercourse is the best I can do, Clint," he interrupted. "And I'd also add that only if his hands were in the awkward position we discussed."

"But you'd at least wait for them to ask you that, right? You don't have to offer that opinion up on direct examination, do you?"

He smiled. "Does it matter when I say it if I end up saying it?"

"Hold that thought and let me get back to my summation." His nod told me the floor remained mine. "I know that this is a little graphic, but it's important that we not shy away from the truth because it is embarrassing. Dr. Graham was quite clear that the bruising lines up almost exactly with the possibility of Mr. Zamora standing, while his wife kneeled before him. A position that they very well might have taken part in while engaging in a sexual act."

George laughed. "That's the thing I love about you, Clint. You can turn a blow job into a defense for murder."

10.

On television, plea discussions are always held with the client present. I suppose writers do that to get the defendant's reaction to the offer without having to repeat the scene. But no defense attorney with a brain puts his client anywhere near a prosecutor. No matter how many off-the-record disclaimers are made before the meeting begins, letting a prosecutor even look at your client before trial is a mistake.

Which was why, when the Assistant District Attorney handling Nicky's case told me that he wanted to discuss "a pretrial resolution," I went alone.

The Westchester County District Attorney's Office was newer and cleaner than its counterpart in Manhattan, but that didn't mean it was anything more than a utilitarian government space. Assistant District Attorney Brandon Sherman's office was on the third floor, and my first impression upon meeting him was that he could be fairly described in the same way as his surroundings—newer and cleaner than his Manhattan counterparts.

His office was littered with boxes piled on top of one another and spread out against the walls. Each was labeled with a case name on the side: People of the State of New York v. a variety of surnames accused of criminal activity. The *v. Nicholas J. Zamora* box stood on the corner of his desk.

"Thank you for coming, Mr. Broden," he said as he extended his hand. He nodded at a clean-cut colleague also waiting in his office. "This is ADA Patrick Ferris. Please, have a seat."

Nicky had agreed I could take this meeting only if I made clear from the outset that he had absolutely no interest in taking a plea deal. Even without such instructions, I would have suggested as much to the other side, regardless of whether it was true. For me, the meeting was a one-way street: I'd get Sherman to tell me the evidence he had, and I wouldn't give him ice in winter.

Which was why, as soon as I took my seat, I said, "I'm here as a courtesy, but we're not interested in discussing a plea."

If my hardline approach surprised Sherman, he didn't show it. I suspected that many a defense attorney had said exactly the same thing to him at the beginning of a plea meeting, only to leave his office with a deal.

"Look, I know you don't know me, and I don't know you," Sherman said, "but if you did know me, then you'd know that I'm a straight shooter. I have no interest in making Mr. Zamora another notch in my belt, but I have every interest in punishing murderers."

The speech was over-the-top, even by prosecutorial standards.

"I appreciate hearing anything you have to tell me," I said. "Just don't expect it to change my mind. I know Nicky Zamora. I've known him since we were kids. And I knew his wife. Nicky loved her, and he didn't kill her."

"You've seen our *Brady* material and discovery. So you know what our forensic proof shows—the bruising on her body, the scratches on his arm that line up with the skin under her fingernails, and the fact that she was pregnant, which makes divorce a very costly endeavor for your client."

He stopped there, probably hoping that I would provide our rebuttal to this evidence. When I didn't, he continued with his prepared remarks.

"And I know that you're going to get some expert who, for the right price, will do his best to poke holes in all of it. But what's not in the discovery materials is our evidence of motive. Did your friend tell you that he was having an affair?"

I remained blank-faced even as the allegation shook me. Had Nicky lied to me about that?

"I take your silence to mean that this is new information," Sherman said with a slight smile. "His wife told several people about it."

"Who?"

"You should ask Mr. Zamora."

"I thought you were a straight shooter."

He chuckled. "Straight shooter, yes. An idiot, no. That means you should believe me when I tell you we have evidence of the affair, and if your client is claiming otherwise, well . . . that should tell you he's lying to you. And if he's lying to you about that, then I suspect he's lying to you about the ultimate issue too. Allow me to share something else with you."

He reached into his desk drawer and pulled out a file folder. Inside was an insurance policy. I saw Carolyn's name on the top, and then my eyes dropped to the amount: $200,000. I assumed the beneficiary would be Nicky, so what I looked for next was the date.

"He purchased it a month before her murder," Sherman said, a step ahead of me.

Her *murder*. Not her death. Her murder.

"There was also a second policy for fifty grand that Martin Quinn took out on her, and your client is the beneficiary of that too. So her death is a two-hundred-fifty-thousand-dollar payday for him. Not too shabby for a guy who makes most of his money from tips."

I scanned the pages. It was as Sherman represented, all there in black and white. Two insurance policies. One by Chubb, in the amount of $200,000. It was signed by both Carolyn and Nicky and dated January 9, 1986. The other was underwritten by Northwestern and appeared to have been provided as part of Carolyn's benefits through work. It had been taken out three years earlier. Carolyn's parents were originally listed as fifty-fifty beneficiaries, but on the same day she and Nicky purchased the Chubb policy, Carolyn executed a change-of-beneficiary form, making Nicky the sole recipient of the proceeds from her work policy.

I suspected Sherman was waiting for me to proffer some innocuous explanation for the policies, or maybe even for me to admit that he had me on this one. But I kept my mouth shut. He'd hear my view on the insurance policies at trial, and not a second before.

"Is that all you've got for me?" I said.

He smiled the cocky grin that prosecutors seem to be issued on their first day of work. "If we let this go to a jury, I'm relatively confident that I'll get a conviction. Twenty-seven-year-old women just don't drown in the bathtub, after all. But I also know that lots of things can happen in a trial, and so there's some chance, maybe ten percent, if I'm being generous, that the jury acquits. That means that a man who murdered his wife goes unpunished, and that's not good. So my boss is telling me that I can offer your client first-degree manslaughter. Between you and me, it's a gift."

Man-1 is still an intentional crime, but it doesn't include premeditation among its elements. It's the charge for a heat-of-passion murder. The penalty range is five to twenty-five years. While that's no walk in the park, it's far better than the life sentence Nicky would serve if convicted of murder in the second degree.

If we'd been negotiating, I would have countered that manslaughter in the *second* degree might be worth discussing with my client. The mens rea for that charge was recklessness, which would allow Nicky to claim that he didn't intend to kill Carolyn, and her death was the result of an accidental but reckless act. That version wouldn't match up with the evidence, but plea deals often suffer from that defect.

Man-2 was a Class C Felony, which reduced the potential jail to fifteen years on the high end, and to as little as one year, given a lenient judge. But my client's instructions were crystal clear on this point: I was not to indicate any willingness to consider a plea.

"I appreciate the consideration, but we're not interested in a plea. He's innocent."

"I've heard that before, Clinton . . . Can I call you Clinton?"

"Clint," I said, a correction I normally didn't make, but I didn't want the man prosecuting Nicky to call me by the same name my friend did.

"He's not innocent, Clint. I know you want him to be, which is understandable given your personal connection to the case. But let's be clear about one thing. No posturing. No bullshit. I'm telling you straightaway that Nicholas Zamora murdered his wife. And if I'm being honest with you, your client would be much better served if he had a lawyer who could get his head around that fact."

———

Later that day, I met with Nicky to discuss the prosecution's plea offer.

"There are a bunch of things Sherman said that we need to go over, but to get to the headline first, he put manslaughter in the first degree on the table—"

"No. I don't want to talk about a plea," Nicky said sharply. "I only said you could meet with him because you said we'd get some free discovery. Tell me about that."

I wasn't surprised by Nicky's initial reaction. Still, I'd be doing him a disservice to allow him to dismiss the possibility of a plea so cavalierly. I decided to table that part of the discussion. At least for now.

"Remember when we talked about possible motives, and I told you it was usually about love or money?"

"Yeah."

"They think they have both. On the money, they told me that you took out a two-hundred-thousand-dollar life insurance policy on Carolyn a month ago. And she also had another fifty-grand policy through work. You're the sole beneficiary of both."

He scrunched up his face. "I swear, I don't remember anything like that."

"The ADA also said that he has evidence you were unfaithful."

"What evidence?" he shot back.

It was the second-best response. That said, it was a natural reflex. I would have said the same if the accusation were made about me.

Still, I pressed him. "That's not a denial."

"Abso-fucking-lutely no," Nicky said with anger in his voice. "Is that a good enough denial for you?"

I smiled, my way of suggesting that I'd never doubted him for a second. "I'm just preparing you for testimony. And to answer your first question, they wouldn't tell me their evidence about the affair. They said to ask you about it."

"So they're bluffing."

"I don't think so. That's not to say, of course, that I don't believe you. I do. But it does mean that they *think* they have something to suggest an affair. He said Carolyn told others that she thought you were having an affair. Any idea who she might have said that to?"

"I can't imagine her saying it to anyone because it wasn't true. But she was closest with her sister, Allison. Maybe . . . I have no idea because I wasn't cheating and I don't for a second think that Carolyn thought I was . . . but if she had a suspicion or something, that would at least explain why the McDermotts saw me as public enemy number one even before the police did." He shook his head, as if to reject that thought out of hand. "No. I know what's going on. The police must have told her that they didn't have enough evidence to make an arrest, but I was the only guy who could have done it, and so Allison made the whole thing up."

That Carolyn's sister might have lied to the police to push them to arrest Nicky wasn't far-fetched. Family members will lie, cheat, and steal if they think it'll win justice for a murdered loved one.

I thought about probing further, telling him that I would make no judgment, even if he had been cheating on Carolyn. That's what I would have said to any other client, and therefore it should have been what I said to Nicky. Instead, I nodded and returned to the plea discussions.

"Like I said, they offered Man-1, which has a twenty-five-year top sentence. And I told them to pound sand. End of discussion. Just between us, I think they'll go down to Man-2."

"No," he said as defiantly as before.

"Nicky, Man-2 has a one- to fifteen-year range."

"I said no. How many times do I have to tell you that?"

Nicky was not the first client to declare that he would never, not in a million years, take a plea because he was innocent. In fact, most clients said that. And even with such a declaration, the vast majority of them still ended up pleading guilty in exchange for reduced or no jail time. The few who held firm were almost always convicted and ended up serving the maximum sentence.

"Forgive me for what I'm about to say, but it's important. Accepting a guilty plea doesn't mean that you are guilty. Think about it as if a doctor were telling you that you needed to have your leg amputated to save your life. No one wants to do it, but sometimes the risk of not doing it is so great that you choose something that's unthinkable because it's the better option. Or it's the only option to save your life. Look, if you got fifteen years on a Man-2 plea, I know that seems like forever, but it's not. You'll get out earlier on parole, and then you'll have your entire life ahead of you. Time to get married again, have children. Write. Do whatever you want to do. But if we go to trial and you lose, your life is over. You'll never have any existence outside of prison."

"I did not kill Carolyn," he said slowly, as if I were a child and he needed to enunciate each word.

"You're missing my point. I'm saying that your innocence—which I totally, one hundred percent believe—is also totally, one hundred percent beside the point. I'm only talking about the risk of you spending your life in jail—and the possibility of eliminating that risk."

"I understand exactly what you're saying. But the fact that I'm innocent isn't as irrelevant to the calculus as you're suggesting." He sighed, as if frustrated that I couldn't understand. "Clinton, it's *because* I'm innocent that I have faith I'll be found not guilty."

11.

That night, Anne and I both arrived home late and tired from a hard day at the office. Anne was complaining about her feet and back after the dance portion of an audition for a part she was certain she wouldn't get.

"I'm not sure how many more of these I have in me," she said.

Anne got this way every so often, but it usually passed.

"Like you always say, sweetheart, one audition at a time. The moment you land something, everything will look different."

In the past, she would have smiled and agreed when I offered this pep talk. Her protestations lately seemed more acute, though, and her willingness to risk rejection no longer so strong.

"If . . . *if* I land something." Anne's tone indicated no further interest in discussing her career prospects. "How'd your meeting with the ADA go?"

"Their case in a nutshell is that Nicky was in love with someone else and found out his wife was pregnant, which meant that he couldn't just walk away from her, so he killed her to collect two hundred fifty thousand dollars in life insurance proceeds."

"He took out insurance on Carolyn's life?"

I raised my eyebrows. "I would have thought you'd be more interested in the claim that Nicky was seeing someone else."

"I'm interested in both," she said. "Him screwing around doesn't shock me, but I can't see him killing Carolyn for money."

I was sure Anne didn't mean it that way; she sounded as if she could imagine him murdering his wife for other reasons.

"Fifty grand of the insurance was a work benefit. Nicky says he didn't know about it. He claims he didn't know about the other two hundred K either, but he must have known about it at some point because he signed the document. It's the affair part that bothers me. The ADA wouldn't tell me what they have, but he says Carolyn told people about it."

"What did Nick say?"

"He said it was absolutely, positively not true."

Anne gave me a look that suggested Nicky's denial settled the issue. I wished that it did, but the thought nagged at me. The evidence against Nicky was beginning to pile up.

When we were kids, Nicky and I used to say that if one of us ever killed somebody, the other would show up with a shovel ten minutes later, no questions asked. For me, it wasn't a joke. I was quite sure that was what I would have done.

Was that what I was doing now?

———

That night, I couldn't sleep. My mind was a never-ending loop of Carolyn in the bathtub. First, I imagined it as I hoped it had occurred. The way I'd tell the jury it had happened. Carolyn was alone. Relaxing. A glass of wine beside her. The steam rising from the water. Her reward for a difficult day of client and partner demands. Then she slipped away peacefully, unaware that her pregnancy, mixed with the wine, the Tofranil, and the heat of the bathwater, would cause her to pass out.

Next I saw Nicky waking in the morning to the other side of an empty bed. He groggily made his way to the bathroom, assuming today would be just another in his life. I imagine him with a smile on his face right up until the moment he saw Carolyn.

The scene the prosecution would be presenting to the jury would start like my version—Carolyn seeking solitude in a soothing, warm bath. But then something happened. Perhaps Carolyn confronted Nicky about his affair and they argued. Or maybe there was no trigger, and Nicky simply decided that was the night to put an end to the suffocating life he'd so quickly gotten himself into—marriage, house in the suburbs, baby on the way. However it happened, the prosecution would tell the jury that Nicky put his hands on his wife and pushed her down with such great fury that he bruised her while Carolyn fought back, scratching him as she struggled for her last breaths.

As if that weren't grisly enough, the prosecution's theory further postulated that after Nicky murdered his wife, he waited until morning to call the police, going to sleep while the dead body of the person he'd sworn to love forever cooled in the bathtub. Then, in the morning, with cold calculation, he staged the bathroom to reflect a frantic husband performing CPR on his dead wife.

George Graham had told me what a dead body looks like after nine hours in the water. Carolyn's complexion would have been blue. Not like a Smurf, but a hue that would have alerted Nicky, unless he was in a severe state of panic, that she was dead. And that owed to the fact that she had died faceup. Otherwise the blood would have pooled in her face, turning it a dark purple. Rigor had also already begun to set in, as the warm temperature of the water would have sped up that process. Which meant that when Nicky reached into the tub, Carolyn must have been ice-cold to the touch, and her arms and legs wouldn't have bent. Nonetheless, he had pulled her out and then pressed his mouth against her lifeless lips.

Nicky told me that he had no idea how much time elapsed as he tried to bring his wife back to life. But I could not imagine the scene for much more than thirty seconds without it becoming impossible to fathom. Nicky's alarm clock had been set for 8:15 a.m., and the call to the police came in at 8:55 a.m. Nicky's version of events meant he could have been performing CPR for as long as forty minutes.

Forty minutes. Assuming he took a breath every other second, that meant more than a thousand breaths he blew into his wife's cold, rigid, lifeless body.

It's a tried-and-true lawyer trick to make the jury experience the period of time in question. To ask them to look at the clock and watch the seconds tick by without offering any narrative. I wondered if Sherman would do it. *Forty minutes.* How could anyone perform CPR on a corpse for that long?

12.

There's an old joke that all of Russian history can be summarized in five words—*And then it got worse.* Criminal defense is the same way. It keeps getting worse right up until the day you hear *not guilty.* Of course, if you don't hear the word *not,* then things worsen from there.

Six months had passed since Nicky's indictment, and everything continued to get worse. His literary agent had put pitching *Precipice* to publishers on hold until he knew if he was representing a murderer. The house in Mount Vernon was on the market, but the broker had told Nicky not to expect a sale soon, as houses that had once been murder scenes tended to scare off potential buyers.

Worst of all, my efforts to delay the trial for as long as possible had been rejected by the trial judge, the Honorable Ross Asbill. When I played Little League baseball, common wisdom said that a walk was as good as a hit. The defense-lawyer version is that delay is as good as acquittal. In neither case is it entirely accurate, but in the same way a walk put a runner on base, a delay kept your client out of jail.

Unfortunately, Judge Asbill's judicial life had an expiration date of his seventy-seventh birthday, which was in early December. Under New York law, judges had a mandatory retirement age of seventy, which could be extended by three two-year terms. Each extension required Judge Asbill to go through a mental-competency screening, which he had always passed with flying colors. But December was his sell-by date, and there was no way he was going to retire before presiding over a front-page murder trial. He gave us the earliest available trial date on his calendar.

The first day of trial was only the third time I had appeared before Judge Asbill. During the initial pretrial conference, the merits of the case weren't discussed at all. The sole purpose of that gathering was to set the schedule through the final pretrial conference. The final pretrial conference had been held a month ago, my second appearance before Judge Asbill, at which His Honor had set the trial date.

The largest courtroom in Westchester County was only slightly smaller than the ceremonial courtroom in Manhattan. At the pretrial conferences, it had seemed even larger, due to the empty seats, but for the opening of the trial, the gallery was at capacity. Mainly press, of course, but the Zamoras and McDermotts were there too, on opposite sides, as they had been at the wedding—and at Carolyn's funeral, for that matter.

I had asked Anne to come, but she declined. It had been a running joke in our marriage that we never saw each other *perform*. Anne had always said my presence made her nervous. *I need to be someone else when I sing*, was how she explained it. *I just can't be that person when you're there.* I, on the other hand, liked when Anne came to watch me in action. The problem for her was boredom. In real life, trials are nothing like they're portrayed in fiction. Examinations can last days, delving into minutiae without ever leading to a last-second confession on the stand.

"I just can't," was her only explanation, but I knew what she meant. Boredom wasn't the issue this time; she didn't want to come for the opposite reason. It was hard enough for me to watch Nicky's life hang in the balance, but at least I was too busy defending him to contemplate the implications of a guilty verdict. That would have been all Anne could think about if she were in the gallery during the trial.

As we awaited the prosecution's opening statement in the courtroom, it seemed Nicky was the calmer of us two. As if his faith in the jury getting it right fueled his hope.

I had difficulty clinging to that fantasy.

Usually by the time the prosecutor delivers his opening statement, I have a pretty good idea of what I'm up against. That was not true this time. Although I knew the forensic evidence, I was still in the dark regarding the evidence they'd proffer to prove the affair—and Nicky's motive—if they had anything at all.

I was about to find out. Brandon Sherman had stepped to the podium to deliver his opening statement.

"Ladies and gentlemen of the jury, twenty-seven-year-old women simply do not drown in the bathtub without some type of outside interference," Sherman began. "And fortunately for us, this is not a murder mystery like you might find in an Agatha Christie novel, with a half dozen suspects, each with motive. There was only one person— only one—who could have murdered Carolyn McDermott. The only person in the house when she drowned in her bathtub. Her husband, the defendant, Nicholas Zamora."

Sherman had a smooth way about him. He spoke without notes, and he made strong eye contact with the jurors. The first half of his opening was devoted to demonstrating that Carolyn had, in fact, been murdered, rebutting any defense suggestion that her death had been a tragic accident. The bruising, the skin under her fingernails, and the scratches on Nicky's arm were the stars of this part, and in Sherman's telling, these things left no doubt that Carolyn had been murdered.

"Why?" Sherman asked, the obvious pivot to motive. Predictably, he told the jury that he was under no burden to tell them why. "If you believe beyond a reasonable doubt that Mr. Zamora murdered his wife, then the law is that you must convict. That obligation is no less mandatory if you don't know exactly why he did it. Even if you have no idea at all, for that matter. In other words, ladies and gentlemen, *why* isn't a relevant question. *Who* is all that matters. And the evidence will convince you beyond a reasonable doubt that the *who* is Nicholas Zamora."

He was right on the law, but I always found that a weak gambit. Juries want to know why. It is probably the most important part of the story for them. So much so that I've always thought that the prosecution did better when it had a compelling *why* and flimsier *who* case.

"But we know why too," Sherman said. "And it's as old a story as there is. Mr. Zamora was involved with another woman. We have ample proof of that. Expensive gifts—jewelry and lingerie—that were purchased by Mr. Zamora but not found in the Zamora-McDermott home because they were given by Mr. Zamora to his mistress. And you will hear testimony that Mr. Zamora checked in to hotels in New York City and paid cash. That's the behavior of a cheating husband."

———

Judge Asbill gave everyone a ten-minute break after Sherman's opening. As soon as the jury was excused, but before he dismissed the rest of us, the judge asked me if I was going to deliver my opening statement now or reserve it until the start of the defense case.

If ever there were a trial in which the defense would want to reserve its opening statement until after the prosecution had put on its full case, this would have fit the bill. I was still uncertain about the prosecution's theory, and I had a strong alternate theory of the facts that I could keep hidden from the prosecution's witnesses if I didn't open until after they had testified. But I had never declined to open immediately after the prosecutor. My belief was that any delay in addressing the jury allowed the prosecution's theory to solidify. The longer the jury listened to only one side of the story, the more difficult it would be for them to discount that story later, even if the defense demonstrated facts to rebut it.

"The defense will open after the recess," I told Judge Asbill.

"Very well, then," he said. "That'll be in exactly ten minutes. Don't be late, or we'll start without you." He grinned and banged the gavel.

Out of my peripheral vision, I saw Sherman receiving congratulatory handshakes from his seconds as they left the courtroom. I didn't have the luxury of stretching my legs, however. I needed the next few minutes to revise my opening so that it would rebut Sherman's allegations about the affair.

The problem was that I wasn't completely sure Sherman hadn't been telling the truth.

———

One of the unspoken dynamics in a murder trial is that the jury cannot restore the life lost. It is only empowered to take the freedom of the accused. Sometimes the best defense is to make them feel as if they don't want that responsibility.

"To hear Mr. Sherman tell it, this case is as straightforward as any scientific principle," I said at the beginning of my opening. "As simple as . . . I don't know, water freezing at thirty-two degrees Fahrenheit. But what makes science, well, *science* is that you can prove it. And not just beyond a reasonable doubt. There is no doubt at all that water freezes at thirty-two degrees. But a criminal trial—especially a murder trial— is about people, not science. Sure, science plays a role. In fact, if the defense were allowed to go first, I would have been the one telling you about Carolyn McDermott's blood alcohol level. About the drugs in her system at the time of her death. About her pregnancy, which made her particularly prone to passing out. About how each one of these factors was greatly exacerbated by the fact that she was bathing in hot water."

So far, so good. The jury looked engaged, nodding along with my words.

"Mr. Sherman said *who* was the critical question for you to decide. But the real question is *if*—*if* Carolyn McDermott was murdered. Because if she wasn't, then there is no crime."

Nicky and I had discussed whether he would take the stand. I had not wavered in the belief it was indispensable, but he was less sure. Although most people think that defendants are always champing at the bit to tell their story, that isn't usually the case. The smart ones, at least, know that putting your entire future at risk in the hope that you'll be able to withstand cross-examination is a sucker's bet, especially because no amount of practice can prepare you for what it's like in reality.

I had originally told Nicky that it was a decision to be made at the end of the case, when all the other evidence had been presented. But now I realized I could not wait. I needed to tell the jury that Nicky would take the stand and, under oath, swear he had been faithful to his wife and had not killed her.

I took a deep breath, then threw caution to the wind.

"Only one person can tell you what happened on the night Carolyn McDermott died. And he will. Nicholas Zamora is going to take the stand and swear an oath to God, under penalty of the crime of perjury, to tell the truth. After doing that, he will testify to the following: First, that he and Carolyn were in love. Second, that he is absolutely devastated by her death. Third, that he was not having an affair. And most important of all, that he did not kill her. I ask of you, ladies and gentlemen of the jury, one thing, and one thing only, as you sit in judgment of Nicholas Zamora: don't make up your mind about whether this man murdered his new bride until you hear every word of his testimony. And if you keep an open mind, once you hear what Nicholas Zamora has to say, I am confident that you will find him not guilty."

13.

If I had been prosecuting the case, the ME would have been my first witness. That way, the jury would hear about the evidence of a struggle—Carolyn's bruising and Nicky's scratches—while their attention was at its peak. But when we returned from lunch, Sherman called Detective Lynch to the stand. That was the by-the-book approach to trying a case, so I couldn't blame him. The lead detective would serve as a narrator, telling the jury the entire story from beginning to end and establishing why the police had concluded that Carolyn had been murdered—and that Nicky had murdered her.

Detective Lynch performed his master-of-ceremonies role well. He went through the investigation timeline, starting the moment he picked up the call from his CO that a twenty-seven-year-old woman had drowned in her bathtub.

"Did that strike you as odd? The drowning-in-the-bathtub part?"

I objected. "Detective Lynch is not an expert in this area."

Judge Asbill agreed. "Sustained. Stick to what the witness observed and what he did, Mr. Sherman."

Sherman nodded at the rebuke but didn't change tack. Instead, he reframed the question to get the answer he wanted.

"Detective, please tell us what you observed when you entered the bathroom that caused you to conclude that Carolyn McDermott had been murdered."

"Mr. Zamora told us that he first saw his wife in the bathtub that morning and that he had attempted to revive her. However, by eight or nine the following morning, when Mr. Zamora says he came upon his wife in the bathtub, Ms. McDermott's body was rigid and her skin had a definite bluish color, as did her lips. It was clear that she had already been dead for several hours. I was certain that Mr. Zamora would have been able to discern that immediately upon seeing his wife in the tub."

"What conclusions about this matter, if any, did that cause you to reach, Detective Lynch?"

"That Mr. Zamora knew his wife had died the previous night. That he hadn't tried to perform mouth-to-mouth in the morning, as he claimed. That the scene we were looking at in the bathroom had been staged. And most importantly, that he was lying to me."

———

"Detective, let's start at the beginning, shall we?" I said when I began the cross-examination. "When you arrived on the scene, you had already been told that a woman had drowned. Do I have that right?"

"Yes."

"And when you entered the home, you went straight to the bathroom?"

"Yes. That's right, counselor."

"And you saw that Ms. McDermott had drowned in her bathtub. Am I right so far?"

"I saw that she was on the floor, beside the tub. The tub still had water in it. I could tell from looking at her that she was dead. It was my supposition that she'd drowned, in part because that was the way the 911 call came in. As a drowning."

"You testified on direct that it was obvious to you that she had been dead for some time, and therefore that you believed it would have been obvious to Mr. Zamora as well. Do I have that right?"

"Yes. The rigor and the discoloration were clear signs of that."

"To you, Detective. You have how many years on the force?"

"Seventeen."

"And you've seen how many dead bodies in that time?"

"I don't know how many."

"Right. Too many to count. But Mr. Zamora did not have seventeen years of police experience, and he had not seen countless dead bodies, correct?"

"You are correct, counselor, that Mr. Zamora wasn't a police officer. But I don't know if he'd ever seen a dead body before."

Detective Lynch was proving to be a disciplined witness. He answered the question, and only the question, always with a dispassionate tone. I didn't know if it was good coaching or that was his natural affect, but I was nearly certain the jury trusted him.

"At that time, am I correct that you knew nothing about Carolyn McDermott?"

"Other than she was dead, you mean."

There was some nervous laughter by some of the jurors. I decided to use it to push Detective Lynch off-balance. Sometimes you could get cops to mess up on cross because they resented being questioned. In their jobs, *they* ask the questions, and I'd never met a police officer who didn't get off on being in charge.

"There's nothing funny about a woman's death, Detective. You agree with that, don't you?"

Detective Lynch was too smart to rise to the bait I was dangling, "Your question was unclear, and I was commenting on that, counselor. Of course Carolyn McDermott's death was a tragedy."

His reference to me as *counselor* was also a nice touch. It reminded the jury that I was a hired gun. My job was to defend Nicky, without regard to his guilt. By contrast, Detective Lynch's only job was to investigate whether Carolyn had died as a result of a crime having occurred and, if she were the victim of foul play, to arrest the perpetrator.

"Back to my question, then," I said, trying to regain control of the cross. "When you first arrived on the scene, you didn't know anything about Carolyn McDermott's medical condition, right?"

"Not exactly. We asked Mr. Zamora whether his wife had any health issues that might have caused her death. I remember specifically asking if she suffered from a heart condition or a seizure disorder. He said she did not."

This was something Nicky hadn't shared with me. It was understandable that he would forget this detail, considering his mental state when he first spoke to the police. Still, a surprise in a trial can be like quicksand; I needed to move away from it quickly.

"You didn't know she was pregnant at this point, did you?"

"That is correct," he conceded in a tone that made the fact seem irrelevant. I half expected him to add that he also didn't know whether she was lactose intolerant.

I pretended to be surprised by this revelation. I'm quite certain that if Anne had been present in the courtroom, she would have found my acting to be subpar.

"That fact—that Carolyn McDermott was pregnant—was something that you would have expected Mr. Zamora to tell you in response to your question about her medical condition, isn't it?"

"I don't know if I had any expectations of what he would or would not tell me, other than that I assumed that her husband would be truthful with me if he had no involvement in her death, and would lie if he had murdered her."

"Let's break that down, Detective. If Mr. Zamora was telling you the truth and knew his wife was pregnant, you would have expected him to tell you, right?"

"Yes."

"And if he *had* murdered her—as you claim is the case—wouldn't he also tell you that she was pregnant, because it would be an explanation for how she might have passed out in the tub?"

"Now we're speculating, but if you want me to indulge you, I can imagine that he would have lied about her pregnancy because the fact that she was pregnant gave him a motive to murder her."

This was the equivalent of trading chess pieces. I needed to establish that Nicky hadn't known she was pregnant in order to rebut the prosecution's motive theory, but in doing so, I had to give Detective Lynch the opportunity to bring it front and center.

It had seemed like a better bargain before the detective laid it out for the jury.

14.

The prosecution's next witness was Eric Russell, Westchester County's Medical Examiner. George Graham knew a little bit about him from his own days in the Manhattan ME's office, and unfortunately for the defense, all of it was good. *Smart, thorough,* and *honest* were the words George used to describe the man who would tell the jury that Nicky had forced his wife underwater to her death in a violent struggle.

Russell looked like a scientist, with a scraggly beard and hair too long around the ears for the little he had left on top. He wore a standard-issue government suit that screamed midlevel bureaucrat.

During his direct, Sherman took Dr. Russell through the postmortem findings in a workmanlike fashion. The time of death was firmly established between midnight and four o'clock the night before Nicky called the police. Death was caused by drowning, although Dr. Russell actually said that Carolyn "experienced respiratory failure from submersion in liquid," before Sherman asked him if that meant that she drowned. He noted the Tofranil and the wine in her system, as well as the fact that she was five weeks pregnant, but he claimed those things, even in combination, should not have caused Carolyn to pass out in the bathtub.

About two hours into the testimony, Sherman asked, "Dr. Russell, was there anything in your findings that suggested Carolyn McDermott was involved in a struggle?"

"Yes. There was very clear bruising on Ms. McDermott's upper torso. This occurred as a result of considerable force being exerted on her body to push her down under the water. It is also my medical opinion that during this struggle, Ms. McDermott scratched Mr. Zamora, and that was the reason for the skin under her fingernails."

I could not help but make a half turn to gauge the jury's reaction. There were some nods, and even those who didn't show approval demonstrated that they understood the importance of what Dr. Russell had just said.

"Let me focus you on a part of your report, Dr. Russell. It has previously been marked as Exhibit 27. You may look at the actual report, but I have reproduced a portion that I will put up on the screen."

Sherman walked to the overhead projector that was set up on the side of the courtroom. A member of the DA's support staff placed the transparency on the machine and adjusted the lens to bring the image into sharper focus.

"What we can all now see is a photograph of the portion of Ms. McDermott's upper torso," Sherman said. "Dr. Russell, please point to the place or places where the bruising you just testified about is present."

Dr. Russell walked out of the witness box. He picked up the wooden pointer waiting for him beside the screen.

"It's here," he said, tapping the screen with the stick. "And here as well," he added, tapping a second time. "The two discolorations that you see are bruises that could only have been caused by someone applying severe pressure with their hands."

That was the high point that Sherman wanted to end on, but Dr. Russell lifted him even higher, despite the lack of a question to prompt it.

"There is no doubt in my mind that this bruising was caused when the defendant murdered his wife. None whatsoever."

I asked my first question without introducing myself.

"Dr. Russell, is it your testimony that it is inconceivable to you—and I mean that there's no possibility whatsoever—that these bruises were caused by anything other than someone forcibly drowning Ms. McDermott?"

"It is my opinion that these bruises were caused by her husband drowning her. That is correct."

"Is it possible—just possible—that these bruises occurred in some other way that would not be indicative of murder?"

"What other way?"

"That's exactly my point, Doctor. If you're asking me what other options there are, can we all agree that you acknowledge that there might be other explanations?"

"I don't know if that follows. I have no alternative explanation, but perhaps you have something that will cause me to reconsider my conclusion."

The last thing you want to do is get into a discussion with a witness. As a cross-examiner, you can frame the question as you wish and force the witness to answer. In this case, it made better sense to have George put forth the alternative explanation, then tell the jury that Dr. Russell's contrary view should be rejected because he hadn't even considered other possibilities.

"Can you rule out that these bruises were incurred prior to when Ms. McDermott got into that bathtub?"

"I cannot tell precisely when the bruises occurred, but given that she drowned in the bathtub, I made the assumption they were received as part of that drowning."

"So that is your *assumption*. I see. And I take it that you have the same *assumption* regarding how it came to be that Ms. McDermott had skin under her fingernails, even though, as a medical fact, you have no idea whose skin is under her fingernails, correct?"

"Well . . ."

"Yes or no, Doctor? Isn't it a fact that you cannot determine whose skin is under her nails?"

"Yes. We do not currently have the scientific ability to confirm that the skin belongs to one person or another."

"That's right. It could be her own, in fact. And the same is true of the scratches on Mr. Zamora's arm. As a medical fact, you have no idea how those scratches occurred, isn't that also correct?"

"Yes . . . but the logical assumption—"

"If I wanted logic, I would have a logician testify. You are here solely because you are a medical examiner. So please limit your testimony to your *medical* findings."

Sherman objected.

Before Judge Asbill could rule against me, I said, "I'll ask my question a different way. The medical facts do not even allow you to conclude when these things occurred. For all you know, the bruising on Ms. McDermott, the skin under her fingernails, and the scratches on Mr. Zamora all occurred an hour or two *before* she even got into the bathtub on the night she died."

"I have no idea when she actually got into the tub. Therefore, no one could testify that the bruising and scratching must have occurred while she was in the tub or before she got into the tub. What I can tell you, what I *am* certain about, is that the bruising was a result of severe pressure placed on her torso by another person, and that the skin under her fingernails was the result of Ms. McDermott scratching someone, and her husband has scratch marks on his forearms that are consistent with such scratching."

"You testified on direct that you were certain that the bruising was the result of her being drowned. Now you're saying that you are not sure if the bruising even occurred while she was in the tub. Which one is it, Doctor?"

Sherman objected. "He's arguing with the witness, Your Honor."

This time Judge Asbill had his say. "Mr. Broden, it does sound that way to me."

I'd done as well as I could. I had the prosecution's forensic witness saying that he hadn't seriously considered any other alternative to Carolyn being drowned, and he could not rule out that the bruising and scratches, which he claimed on direct had occurred during a death struggle, had not, in fact, occurred well before the time of death. That should be enough for reasonable doubt all by itself.

But only if the jury believed any of it.

15.

After court, I told Nicky to go home. Given the number of witnesses still on the prosecution's list, I didn't think it was possible that we'd get to the defense case the next day.

I went back to the office, ordered dinner, and prepared for the next day's battle. But an hour later, I realized there wasn't much for me to do. I had already prepared my expected cross of Carolyn's sister and the managing partner of Carolyn's law firm. The other three witnesses on the prosecution's list were names I didn't recognize. The police hadn't interviewed these witnesses, or if they had, they hadn't taken notes, so I wouldn't find out who they were or what they had to say until they said it on the stand.

I was home by eight—the first time I'd been back before midnight in weeks.

Anne and I lived in a one-bedroom apartment on the second floor of a town house on the Upper West Side. The place was full of "old-world charm," as the classified ad had put it, which meant that, in addition to ten-foot ceilings, an exposed brick wall, and a nonworking fireplace, the kitchen and bath hadn't been updated in years. On the plus side, it was quiet, and the southern exposure allowed us to keep the lights off during the day, or so Anne told me, as I was rarely home during the day.

Much to my surprise, Anne was not only awake but in her pajamas when I arrived home. Tuesday night was a standard open mic night at

Lava, a club downtown where Anne had developed a friendship with the booker, which guaranteed her a slot.

"Taking the night off?" I asked.

"Yeah. Maybe more than just tonight."

"Did something happen?"

She smiled. "More like the opposite. Nothing's happening. I just—I don't know . . . maybe a break will do me good."

"Why? I thought you loved singing."

"Yeah, the singing I love. The rejection, the being out every night, not so much."

I had been waiting for this type of epiphany from Anne, but now that it was at hand, I felt nothing but loss. I'd only ever wanted her to give up singing because she thought she'd be happier if we had a family, and because she had made it clear that she didn't think she could do both. The last thing I wanted, however, was for her to give up her dream because she didn't think she could make it as a singer.

"Well, please don't do it for me. I want you to be happy, and if that means chasing your dream for forever, I won't say another word about it."

"Thanks for saying that. Let me think about it a little more. I don't have to decide right now about the rest of my life."

She smiled again, which reminded me of just how long it had been since I'd seen it before tonight. Of course, with Carolyn's death, Nicky's arrest, and now the trial, there hadn't been many moments of happiness to celebrate.

"How'd today go?" she asked.

"Good. Better than I expected, actually. The state's ME testified, which I'd worried might be a nail in Nicky's coffin. But I think I did a good job of getting the jury to consider the evidence doesn't preclude the possibility that Carolyn died accidentally."

"You think they're buying the oral-sex-caused-the-bruising angle?"

When I first told Anne how I planned to explain away the bruising and scratch marks, she was unconvinced. "I guess it makes some sense, but . . . I've never been bruised during sex," was her response.

I'd pointed out that there are really only two defenses to a murder charge: it wasn't murder at all, or if it was murder, someone other than the defendant committed it. I'd hitched Nicky's freedom to the first, but I continually second-guessed that call. Nicky's house was in a sketchy neighborhood, at least for Westchester, only a few blocks from the train station. I knew that he never locked his doors. The master bedroom was on the main floor, which made it entirely possible that someone could have entered the house, found Carolyn in the tub, and forced her under while Nicky slept unaware down the hall.

"I haven't laid it out in all of its glory yet. Do you think the random-intruder theory works better?" I asked.

"Oh, no. I'm just saying that the bruising during oral sex was a bit hard for me to swallow, no pun intended."

Neither of us had the heart to laugh.

"Right. Well, the problem I always had with the intruder angle was that there's no motive. It wasn't a robbery because nothing was taken. Besides, the fact that the murderer killed Carolyn and left Nicky asleep would suggest that Carolyn had been targeted. But who would have wanted her dead? I went through her caseload, thinking that maybe she had done some criminal case, pissed off a client or something, but there was nothing like that. And Nicky swore up and down that she had no enemies."

"You definitely made the right decision. I'm not second-guessing you."

"I know, but I'm second-guessing myself. I didn't believe that Nicky was having an affair because he said he wasn't. Maybe that was a mistake. Just like an affair gives him motive, it gives the mistress motive too. Maybe that was the better defense—to have him concede the affair and cast the mistress as the murderer. Someone involved with Nicky would have known that Carolyn took a bath nearly every night. That lines up with why Carolyn was killed and Nicky was left alone. It has the added benefit of taking the sting out of whatever infidelity evidence the prosecution offered. I could have argued that the prosecution had almost all of it right—the bruising was when she was drowned, the affair being the motive, and Carolyn's pregnancy or the insurance—or both—was the reason that a divorce was no solution. Then I could have argued that the only mistake the police made was that they arrested the wrong lover."

"But that's not right," she said. "For one thing, that strategy presumes that Nick was actually having an affair, and he swears he wasn't. Also, he couldn't just say, *My lover killed Carolyn.* He'd have to identify an actual person. And God only knows what his lover would wind up saying . . . For all you know, she has a husband or someone else to alibi her, and then where would you be? Besides, even if such a person did exist, and even if she had no alibi, Nicky blaming her for Carolyn's murder wouldn't help his defense. The women on the jury wouldn't waste a second before convicting a man who was cheating on his pregnant wife a month after the wedding, then blamed his lover to save himself."

That pretty much covered all the reasons why I had gone with the rough-sex explanation for the bruising and scratches. Every potential defense has pitfalls, and you need to pick the one least likely to sink your case.

16.

The following morning, Sherman led off the day by calling Carolyn's sister, Allison, to the stand. As soon as I heard her name, I jumped to my feet.

"Your Honor, may we approach?"

Judge Asbill didn't seem to understand what the fuss was about. For his part, Sherman wore a confused expression too, but I assumed that was for show.

When Sherman and I reached the bench, Judge Asbill leaned over. "So what's the problem with this witness, Mr. Broden?"

"I'd like a proffer on her testimony," I said.

"That's rather broad, don't you think?" Sherman snapped.

"I'll be more specific. I would like a commitment from the Assistant District Attorney that he will not elicit hearsay testimony regarding anything Ms. McDermott said to this witness on any subject."

From Sherman's change of expression, I could tell that was exactly what he was planning.

"Is that what's going on here, Mr. Sherman?" Judge Asbill asked.

"Judge, the victim told her sister the defendant was cheating on her. That evidence is highly relevant to our theory of motive."

"That's hearsay 101," I said.

"It fits the mental-state exception," Sherman said.

"How so?" Judge Asbill asked.

"If Ms. McDermott believed that her husband was unfaithful, that would explain what triggered their fight on the night she died."

To my surprise and horror, Judge Asbill looked like he might be buying this explanation.

"The prosecution is attempting to manufacture relevance," I protested. "The entire argument is bootstrapping. *If* there was a fight, it somehow makes Ms. McDermott's mental state relevant, but there is no evidence that there was such a fight between the defendant and his wife. I also cannot imagine a more biased witness than Ms. McDermott's sister. Is there any question she'd lie to help convict the man the police said murdered her sister?" It wasn't my most coherent argument, and I could tell that I'd lost the judge midway through. "On top of which," I added somewhat desperately, "the testimony would be highly prejudicial, and that prejudice would greatly outweigh any probative value, which would be minimal at best."

"I think the motive for the murder is pretty probative," Sherman said.

"But it's not motive for the murder, Your Honor," I pleaded. "It's . . . nothing, really. It's total conjecture that her mental state started a fight." It then clicked how to make my point. "Here's the problem in a nutshell: Mr. Sherman is advancing a theory where it doesn't matter if Mr. Zamora was actually having an affair, but what matters is that his wife *thought* he was having an affair. But if Mr. Zamora *wasn't* having an affair—as we contend—he lacks motive. And that's true even if his wife *thought* he was being unfaithful. That's why her thoughts on the matter—her mental impressions—are irrelevant."

Sherman started to rebut that point, but Judge Asbill waved him off. With that same hand he scratched his cheek, like Vito Corleone in *The Godfather*.

The next few seconds were interminable. If Judge Asbill went against us and allowed evidence that Carolyn told Allison that Nicky was cheating, there would be no coming back.

Finally, Judge Asbill said, "Nope. I'm going to agree with Mr. Broden on this one. You can't go there, Mr. Sherman."

———

Sherman chose not to call Allison McDermott at all, but I didn't for a second think that meant he was done trying to prove Nicky was having an affair. I knew that he'd get that evidence in front of the jury another way with a different witness.

That process began when he called a woman named Lori Swenson to the stand. Hers was one of three names on the prosecution's witness list that Nicky hadn't recognized.

She testified that she worked at the front desk of the Hilton hotel on Sixth Avenue.

I looked over to Nicky.

He whispered, "No idea."

She testified for less than ten minutes, but during that time, she provided the most devastating testimony of the trial. Matter-of-factly, she said that she recognized Nicky as a man who had checked into the hotel "several times." She further said that he'd always paid in cash and she'd never seen him with any luggage.

Sherman hadn't introduced any documentation to support his claim that Nicky had spent time in the Hilton, which meant he didn't have any. I couldn't imagine how he'd come upon Lori Swenson. Even if Nicky had been engaged in an illicit hotel rendezvous, he could have selected any one of two hundred hotels in Manhattan alone and varied them so that he never returned to the same one twice.

Besides, Nicky had assured me that he had never checked into the hotel. Not even once, and certainly not the several times Swenson was claiming she'd witnessed. Which meant that Swenson was either a liar or simply mistaken. Which one it was didn't matter to me, so long as the jury didn't believe her.

Of course, that was a tall order. It's always difficult to convince the jury that a witness with no ax to grind is lying, and even though people often get things wrong and then lock themselves into a story, jurors are reluctant to believe that too.

"How did it happen that the police came to question you about this matter?" I asked right out of the gate.

She stared at me before responding. "What do you mean?"

"Did you seek them out, or did they come to you?"

"They came to me. They showed me a picture and asked me if I had ever seen the man in it before."

That visit could have been dumb luck, but I doubted it. Something had tipped the cops off to flash Nicky's picture around the Hilton. Perhaps a charge on a credit card statement I'd missed. Maybe he'd frequented restaurants around the hotel.

"How many rooms are in your hotel?"

"Nearly two thousand. We're the largest hotel in New York City."

"So you must receive . . . I can't even hazard a guess. Does ten thousand guests a month sound right?"

"I have no idea either. But it's a lot."

"Right. Did the police show you any other pictures, aside from the picture of Mr. Zamora?"

"Um, they also showed me a picture of his wife. But that was it."

"When the police first approached you, did you know that Mr. Zamora had been arrested for murdering his wife?"

"Not at first. Since then, I've seen the story in the newspapers and on TV."

"The police told you that they were trying to prove that Mr. Zamora killed his wife, didn't they?"

"They didn't say it like that."

"But you knew that's what they were doing, and that you would be helping them if you said you'd seen Mr. Zamora checking into the hotel."

Sherman objected.

Judge Asbill agreed, admonishing me to ask questions, not make speeches.

I decided not to do either. "I have no more questions for this witness."

The jury now understood that our rebuttal to Lori Swenson was that she was looking for her fifteen minutes of fame and willing to perjure herself to achieve it. Far from a solution for our side, as the jury had now heard from a witness who claimed that Nicky had checked into a hotel suspiciously several times. That would be a difficult bell to unring.

Swenson was followed by the second witness whose name Nicky hadn't recognized. Soon enough I learned that she was a representative from Victoria's Secret. Without much preface, Sherman placed a Victoria's Secret receipt on the overhead projector, the employee pointed out the item identification code on the corner of the receipt, and Sherman replaced the image with a photo of a black nightgown.

This was the lingerie that Sherman had claimed in his opening Nicky purchased for his mistress. I couldn't imagine why he'd assume that, however. It looked like ordinary lingerie to me, and Nicky and Carolyn were newlyweds.

The final witness whose name was unfamiliar was Jennifer Fried. She was young—early twenties—and attractive. At first I thought she might have been a friend of Carolyn's outside of work who would claim Carolyn had told her that Nicky was cheating. But I couldn't imagine Sherman trying the same gambit that the judge had ruled off-limits with Carolyn's sister.

"Ms. Fried, what do you do for a living?" Sherman asked.

"I'm a sales associate at Tiffany & Co."

"Do you recognize the defendant, Nicholas Zamora?"

She looked at the defense table. "Yes. He came into my store."

Nicky's credit card statements contained a big-ticket charge from Tiffany. He told me it was a necklace he'd purchased as a gift for Carolyn. At the time, I had no reason to doubt that.

"Did there come a time when law enforcement requested that you search Tiffany's credit card receipts to see if Mr. Zamora had made any purchases?"

"Yes."

"What did that search reveal?"

"He did."

Sherman was back at the overhead projector. "Exhibit 19," he said.

On the screen was a credit card receipt, complete with Nicky's signature. The price of the item purchased, including tax, was $1,512.

"Is this that receipt?"

"Yes."

"Can you tell from the receipt what item was purchased, Ms. Fried?"

"Yes. The item number is in the corner—72014."

"Exhibit 20," Sherman said.

On the screen appeared a sapphire pendant surrounded by diamonds.

———

Another detective tied it all together. In a monotone he testified that neither the lingerie nor the necklace was found when the police searched the house after Carolyn died.

"In this case, the absence of evidence was, to our mind, conclusive evidence," the detective said. "The lingerie and the necklace were not for the defendant's wife but gifts he gave to another woman."

Sherman's final witness wasn't a witness at all, but a photograph. Still, a live person had to explain it, and he chose Martin Quinn's managing partner, Ted Quinn, to do the honors. Quinn established that the firm's formal dinner-dance occurred the night after Nicky purchased the Tiffany's necklace.

"I'd like to publish Exhibit 23, Your Honor," Sherman said.

The screen lit up with a larger-than-life image of Carolyn and Nicky dressed to the nines. Carolyn was wearing a black cocktail dress, her dark hair shiny as polished granite. Nicky looked like James Bond in his tux.

"Was this photograph taken during the party you just testified about?"

"It was," Quinn said.

Sherman pulled the photograph off the overhead projector. The screen was white for only a second, however. He quickly replaced it with an enlargement of the prior picture. It looked a little vulgar, as it cut off Carolyn's head and focused almost exclusively on her cleavage.

My stomach sank. I now knew where this was heading.

Sherman didn't ask any questions. Instead, he stood silently as the jury stared at the necklace that Carolyn had worn to the Martin Quinn formal. Instead of the Tiffany sapphire pendant Nicky had purchased the day before, around Carolyn's neck was a string of pearls.

———

That night, Anne asked about the evidence the prosecution had put on about the affair.

"It was a bad day," I said.

"Bad how?"

"I'm not sure I want to discuss it now," I said.

She nodded as if she understood. "Okay. But I'm sure it's not as bad as you think."

I could have left it there. Maybe I should have, but I didn't.

"I'm certain Nicky was having an affair," I said.

She waited for me to say more. To explain why I'd had this epiphany in court. When I didn't, she said, "I thought you said the evidence was all circumstantial."

"Yeah, well, circumstantial evidence can be true. Often it is."

"What did Nicky say about it?"

"What does it matter what he said? He's lied to me from day one about it. I'm sure he'll lie to me about it until the day I die."

She looked at me sharply, waiting for me to answer her question.

"There was this necklace," I said. "Expensive. From Tiffany's. Nicky had told me that he bought it for Carolyn to wear at the Martin Quinn formal, so I didn't think twice about it when I saw the purchase on his credit card. But in court today, the prosecution proved that Carolyn hadn't worn it at the formal, which was something Nicky failed to mention."

"Maybe . . . I don't know . . . maybe Carolyn didn't think the necklace went with her dress or something."

"That's what Nicky says too. She thought it was too showy for a firm function. But the detectives said that it wasn't even in their house. So where'd it go?"

This stopped her for a second. "I don't know. Maybe she didn't like it and returned it. Or she lost it."

"No. Tiffany's would have had a record of the return. And if she lost it, she would have told Nicky."

"Maybe she thought he'd be upset. Maybe she was waiting for the right time to tell him."

Anne was trying hard to restore my faith in my best friend. "Yeah, maybe," I said.

In point of fact, I believed that this had become an Occam's Razor situation—the simplest explanation is the correct one. Nicky had bought the necklace for his mistress, not for Carolyn.

17.

The next day, I began to present the defense's case.

My ME witness, George Graham, told the jury that it was possible that Carolyn had passed out in the bathtub, the victim of a toxic cocktail of wine, antidepressant medication, her early-stage pregnancy, and the hot water.

"On their own, none of these factors is particularly dangerous," George explained, "but combine them, and that could be enough to have caused Ms. McDermott to lose consciousness."

This was the best George could do. I had engaged two other experts, both of whom were willing to provide a less equivocal conclusion, but in the end, I could not stake my friend's future on testimony from an expert less reliable than George.

After establishing the possibility of accidental drowning, I addressed the evidence that there had been a struggle.

"Dr. Graham, were you present in the courtroom when the County's Medical Examiner, Dr. Russell, testified?"

"Yes, I was."

"Do you recall his testimony regarding certain bruising that was found on Carolyn McDermott's upper torso?"

"I do recall that."

"Did you draw any conclusions regarding that testimony when you heard it?"

"I did."

"What were those conclusions?"

"That he had not considered other possibilities."

That was exactly how the Q and A was scripted. Short questions, shorter answers.

"Dr. Graham, please tell the jury what you concluded about the cause of the bruising present on Ms. McDermott's body."

"The manner of bruising is consistent with explanations other than someone drowning her."

I walked up to the railing of the witness box. I only wished that I were taller, so my crotch would line up with George's mouth, to make the point better visually.

"What is another possible explanation for the bruising, Dr. Graham?"

"At the risk of being indelicate, and recognizing that we are in a court of law, I can certainly see it being the result of Mr. Zamora and his wife engaging in a sexual act where he is standing and she is on her knees in front of him. That would cause the same bruising pattern."

"Oral sex, in other words?"

"Yes."

"Would that also explain how Mr. Zamora's forearm was scratched by Ms. McDermott?"

"It would. While this area is outside my expertise as a forensic pathologist, it is not uncommon that during sexual activity, scratching occurs. Therefore, it would also explain the marks on Mr. Zamora, as well as the skin under Ms. McDermott's fingernails."

———

Sherman's first question on cross undid a lot of my good work on direct. "Dr. Graham, can you rule out that Ms. McDermott was murdered?"

"No. All I can testify to competently is that there are factors involved that could have caused her to pass out. And if that happened, she would have drowned."

"I understand. So put another way, what you're saying is that the evidence is consistent with Mr. Zamora murdering his wife?"

It hurt to watch. Like seeing your kid forget her lines onstage and knowing there's nothing you can do to help.

"I wouldn't say that," George replied. "Instead, I'd say that the forensic evidence is ambiguous. It could be interpreted to be consistent with either a murder or an accidental drowning."

———

Nicky was my only other witness.

Electricity fills the air when the defendant takes the stand. Finally, the jury will hear from the only person who can tell them what actually happened. The irony is that the defendant is often the least reliable witness of all. No other trial participant is as incentivized to lie, so it should hardly come as a surprise that, more often than not, they do.

Nicky explained that the life insurance was purchased in tandem with their closing on the house. "I could never have afforded to stay in the house without Carolyn's income," he explained. "That's why the bank required that I have sufficient life insurance on Carolyn to cover the mortgage. It wasn't for me. It was for Citibank. I didn't even remember that we had taken out the policy until I saw it as part of this case. And I never knew that Carolyn had life insurance at work. We never talked about that kind of thing."

He sounded every bit as confident when I asked my next question, whether he'd ever been unfaithful to Carolyn.

"Absolutely not."

"Ever been to the Hilton hotel in midtown?"

"I can't say that I never walked through the lobby, maybe to use the men's room or something. But I never checked in. That never happened."

He was two for two. I moved on to the forensic evidence, hoping that Nicky would be equally convincing on that subject.

"Your wife had some bruising on her body, and she had skin under her fingernails. You also had some faint scratches on your forearm when the police arrived at the scene. Can you explain how those things occurred?"

"The night before Carolyn died, we had sex. As part of that, she . . . like Dr. Graham said, she was kneeling and I was standing. I had my hands on her chest, and she had hers on my arms. Both of us got caught up in the moment and . . . well, marks were left."

We had practiced this part of Nicky's testimony at length. He delivered his lines exactly as rehearsed, complete with the right amount of emotion.

I could now see the finish line. But before I broke the tape, I still needed him to explain away the lingerie and the necklace.

"Please tell the jury for whom you purchased the nightgown and the necklace."

"For Carolyn, of course."

"You heard a detective testify that the police did not find the nightgown among Carolyn's possessions. Do you know why that would be?"

"Yes. This is a little embarrassing, but she wore it on the night I gave it to her, and it was . . . torn. After that, she threw it out, I guess. I don't know. Maybe she brought it to a dry cleaner to be mended. I doubt it, though, because the nightgown cost less than thirty dollars. It probably wasn't worth the cost of tailoring."

"The prosecution made quite a bit of a necklace that you purchased. Do you recall that?"

"I do."

"And that necklace was more expensive than fifty dollars, wasn't it?"

"Much more. I paid about fifteen hundred dollars for it."

"Why did you purchase that necklace?"

"To give to Carolyn."

"Did you give it to her?"

"Yes. The same night I bought it."

"So that would have been the night before the Martin Quinn formal?"

"That's right. I bought it because I thought she might want to wear it at the formal."

"We saw evidence that she did not, in fact, wear it to the firm formal, though. Is that right?"

"She thought it was a little showy for a work function. So she wore an older necklace she had. Obviously, it didn't matter to me."

"You heard a member of the Westchester police department testify that they did not find the necklace at your home when they executed a search warrant looking for it. Do you recall that testimony?"

"I know that's what they said. But it makes no sense because the necklace was there. Carolyn was a little strange in this respect, but she kept jewelry of any value rolled up in a sock in her top dresser drawer."

"How can you be so sure that the necklace was there?"

"Because that's where I found it."

Nicky reached into his pocket. A moment later, dangling from his fingers was the necklace on which the prosecution had premised a large chunk of its conclusion that Nicky had cheated on Carolyn.

———

Sherman was like a bull in a china shop when he got his turn.

"So you're telling this jury that a team of highly trained detectives just missed this necklace? Is that your story, Mr. Zamora?"

"I don't know about them being highly trained, and I'm not telling any stories," Nicky said calmly, exactly the way I had instructed him to respond to aggressive questioning. "But if you're telling me that the police were looking for this necklace and they didn't find it, then I would agree with you that they missed it. Because it was there."

"How about this as an alternative explanation, Mr. Zamora—you purchased the expensive necklace as a gift for your mistress. After you murdered your wife, she returned it to you."

"That's not true," said Nicky.

"And it's your testimony, under oath, that the reason your wife did not wear the necklace after you gave it to her as a gift expressly to wear at the firm formal was because she thought it was—your words—*too showy*. That's your testimony?"

"That is not only my testimony, it's the truth."

Sherman didn't respond, other than to flash a smile as if to say, *Of course. You would never tell a lie.*

He put the photograph of Carolyn at the formal back on the overhead projector.

"Is it your sworn testimony, Mr. Zamora, that your wife thought that this necklace, which appears to have diamonds in between the pearls, was *less* showy than the sapphire necklace we saw earlier, and that she decided to wear this one, and not the one that you had just purchased for her for more than fifteen hundred dollars?"

"It is my testimony, and it *is* more understated. The pearl necklace is costume jewelry. Those are not real pearls or diamonds."

"Where is that necklace today?"

Never ask a question you don't know the answer to is practically the golden rule of cross-examination. Nicky made Sherman pay for the mistake. In spades.

"She was buried in it," Nicky said.

Sherman actually laughed. "You want this jury to believe that you buried your wife in fake gems and costume jewelry?"

"I don't make very much money, Mr. Sherman, and it was the first present I ever gave Carolyn. She always said that made it special to her. I thought it was a fitting tribute to my love to bury her in it."

18.

That night, Anne asked me if I thought I would win. She phrased it like that, as if the victory would be mine, not Nicky's. That's how we often talked about my cases, as if I were the only interested party.

She hadn't seen any of the trial, but each night I'd filled her in on the developments. I'd just finished sharing with her the theatrics of the necklace reveal. I suspect that it was this turn for the better that had prompted her question, one that she'd been afraid to ask before now.

In my career up to that point, I had won slightly less than 20 percent of my trials. When people asked about my winning percentage, I had always hedged that it was too broad a question to have any meaning. "The better indicator," I'd say to them, "is the percentage of cases I've won that I thought I might win." That inevitably resulted in my questioner asking for that figure. "There I'm around fifty-fifty," I'd answer.

In other words, in cases I expected to win when the jury began deliberations, I was wrong 50 percent of the time.

"I don't know," I told Anne.

———

Few things are as simultaneously boring and fraught with peril as the time spent waiting for the jury to reach a verdict. At any moment the jury could come back; every hour was potentially the last Nicky would experience as a free man.

Even though there was nothing to do all day but wait, we were still required to be in court promptly at nine thirty. The judge sent the jury home at five. That added up to seven and a half hours each day spent sitting and waiting.

That's what we did on the first day. And the second. And the third.

During jury deliberations, the dynamic between lawyer and client often switches. Once my job is done, I often can no longer summon the resolve to tell my client it's going to end well. Usually, defendants pick up this slack, expressing confidence in an acquittal, often praising my brilliance in the process. Of course, when the verdict goes the other way, it's my trial work that's to blame.

With Nicky, however, it wasn't professionalism that kept me from predicting the outcome. I was too close to the matter to know what version of Nicky the jury was considering: devastated spouse or philandering murderer.

The Zamoras had largely kept to themselves during the trial, but it wasn't hard to see that they were dying a little bit each day. If I thought that they'd looked elderly at the arraignment, now they seemed downright ancient.

I had taken every opportunity I could to tell them I was confident of acquittal. But the Zamoras were smart enough to know the truth. It could go either way.

The official announcement came from the judge's clerk at three o'clock on the fourth day. Until then, there had not been a peep out of the jury. No request that they be read back any portion of the evidence, no need for further explanation on the law. Nothing.

Somehow, the press already knew; a reporter for the *New York Post* had told me ten minutes earlier that he'd heard there was a verdict. His scoop didn't include what it would be, however.

"The judge will take the bench at five to read the verdict," Judge Asbill's law clerk told the parties. "He has another matter that he has to attend to first."

I couldn't imagine what would be more pressing than the verdict in a high-profile murder case. Then again, perhaps his prior commitment was a ruse, and the delay was to give the media the time they needed to be front and center for the judge's star turn.

I called Anne from the pay phone in the hallway. "There's going to be a verdict at five. Can you come down here and wait with us?"

As she had with my prior invitation, Anne at first declined. "I don't know if I'll be able to take it if Nicky's convicted," she said.

"Please, come," I said. "I wouldn't ask, but I'm afraid *I* won't be able to take it either. I don't want to be alone if it happens."

Two hours later, right before five o'clock, when Nicky and I entered the courtroom from the private space that was reserved for us during deliberations, Anne was sitting in the gallery's first row, right behind defense counsel's table. I smiled at her and mouthed, *Thank you*. She smiled back and mouthed, *Good luck*, then, *I love you*.

Judge Asbill took the bench at five on the dot. Five minutes after that, the jury was seated, and a minute later, the foreman officially told the judge that the jury had, in fact, reached a verdict. After another few minutes of procedural rigmarole, including the reading of the charge, the jury foreman passed the verdict slip to the court officer, who passed it to the judge for review. Judge Asbill told the defendant to rise and turned to the foreman for the big reveal.

"On the only count of the indictment, murder in the second degree, what is the jury's verdict?"

I stood shoulder to shoulder with Nicky, although in actuality my shoulder was slightly below his armpit. I could feel my legs turning to jelly. Nicky looked straight ahead. If he felt any anxiety, he hid it better than I.

The foreman came to his feet. He was one of the younger members of the jury, and he reminded me a bit of Judd Nelson's character from *The Breakfast Club*.

All he said was, "Not guilty."

———

Nicky's parents threw their arms around their son, and I could see the tears streaming down their cheeks. Anne was crying too when she embraced me. Then we switched partners, and I watched Anne whisper her congratulations into Nicky's ear as the Zamoras once again thanked me. I told them that they were the only family I had in the world other than Anne, and they said that they thought of me as their son too.

Anne, Nicky, and I adjourned to our apartment to celebrate. Nicky had suggested we go out—"Anywhere. My treat, of course"—but I told him it was better for us to keep a low profile.

"Being photographed popping champagne because you did not kill your wife isn't something you want to see on the cover of the tabloids tomorrow."

Which didn't mean that we didn't pop champagne. Anne had actually bought a bottle of Dom Pérignon in anticipation of Nicky's acquittal, something she claimed she never doubted for a second. I did the honors, and when our flutes were filled, Nicky made the toast.

"To Clinton, for his friendship and wise counsel, without which I not only wouldn't be the person I am today, but I would be inmate 983702."

Thinking he had finished, I brought the champagne to my lips.

"Not yet," he said. "I think we also need to drink to Carolyn's memory. I'm so sorry about so many things . . ." He began to choke up, but after an audible clearing of his throat, he was able to say, "I'm just so, so sorry."

Anne put her arm on his shoulder. "It's okay, Nick. It's all over," she said. "Life starts over for you now."

PART TWO

ANNE BRODEN

November 2003–May 2004

19.

Dr. Goldman's was the third opinion I sought. He was considered to be the best oncologist in the country, but despite his impeccable references and Ivy League degrees, he told me the same thing that I'd heard twice before from supposedly lesser physicians.

"I'm fifty-one," I said, as if it were relevant to my diagnosis.

Dr. Goldman didn't respond. Instead, he looked down at his chart like it was a script and he'd momentarily forgotten his lines.

"There is a new clinical trial that I might be able to get you in," he said after a pause. "It's an experimental treatment, so the data is somewhat spotty, but we estimate the five-year survival rate at approximately twenty-five percent. I know, still not great odds, but without the treatment, you're looking at a life expectancy measured in months."

Every fiber of my being wanted to say no. That I would not spend my last months as some type of lab rat. It wasn't out of bravery, however. Or because I was a martyr. My knee-jerk reaction to refuse further treatment was born from absolute selfishness—I wanted my last months to be as normal as possible.

"Let me think about it," I said instead.

"That's understandable," he said. "It's obviously a big decision. Unfortunately, time is not your friend right now. But you have to be committed to the treatment's regimen, as it will be extremely taxing on your body. So take another few days to consider it. Discuss it with your husband. But I'm afraid that come December, you won't be a viable candidate any longer. And I do believe that this trial is the only chance you have to extend your life expectancy."

Odd phrase, that—*extend your life expectancy*. It was applicable to everyone, at all times. Infants should be vaccinated to *extend their life expectancy*. Children should be secured in car seats to *extend their life expectancy*. Adults should get regular checkups to *extend their life expectancy*. But in truth, the term applies to only the terminally ill.

I no longer had a life. I had a *life expectancy*. And no matter what I decided to do next, it was short.

———

I had kept secret from Clint that his wife was a very sick woman. At first it was to make sure that it was actually the case while I waited for a second opinion. After that doctor concurred with the first, I simply wanted to hold on to my old life for a few days longer. Now, with Dr. Goldman making it three for three, the time had come to share the news.

But it would still have to wait until later, when Clint and I were alone, because the next time I saw my husband was in the theater of Ella's high school. Charlotte was sitting between us with an excited look on her face. I daresay that the only person who enjoyed watching Ella sing more than I was Charlotte.

When Ella was in eighth grade, one of the music teachers in her private, all-girls middle school suggested she audition for New York City's high school for the performing arts. I knew about the school from the movie *Fame* and was excited about the prospect of Ella having a more diverse educational experience. Clint was a tougher sell, not understanding why we'd give up the benefits of the best education money could buy to send her to a public school—even one that was famous for producing musicians and actors. But it was Ella who made the final decision, and after that, she never looked back.

That night was the school's annual talent show, which they dubbed Rising Stars. Three hours of the most talented high school kids in New York City doing various musical and dance numbers. Ella told us that nearly every one of the 2,500 kids in the school auditioned. Fewer than two hundred made it, and nearly all of them would appear in group numbers.

Ella had a solo. Toward the end of the first act. There it was in the playbill: *Ella Broden . . . . . . Mira.* I had never heard of the song, but Ella told me it was from *Carnival,* about a girl who comes to the big city from a small town.

She walked out on stage alone, an old prop briefcase in her hand, wearing a peasant dress and boots. The costume was no doubt what Ella, a city girl from head to toe, imagined a small-town rube would wear. She looked so tiny on the empty stage, but the moment she opened her mouth, the space became too small to contain her. Her soprano was strong and crystalline, the way I imagined mine on my very best day.

I couldn't help myself and started to cry even before she had sung her last note. Clint thought they were tears of joy. He leaned closer and said, "Can you believe that she's ours?"

That wasn't what I couldn't believe, however. I could not comprehend that my time with my daughters was fast coming to an end. I would likely never see them any older than they were now, never get to watch them walk down the aisle, never know the joy of holding their children in my arms.

———

After the girls had gone to sleep, or at least Charlotte had—Ella would probably stay up until two o'clock talking to her friends about the show—I decided that I could no longer keep my condition from my husband. It was a conversation I had played out in my head a million times since I first heard the word *cancer* connected to me, yet with the matter finally at hand, I still didn't have the first clue how I would break the news.

We were alone in our bedroom. Ironically, we were watching *House*, the medical drama in which the cantankerous Dr. House invariably comes up with a miracle diagnosis that saves a patient's life.

"I have something I need to tell you," I said.

They say that dogs do not recognize words so much as tone. They're happy when you say, "Let's go to the park," because they can sense that you're happy, and they get scared when you say, "Bad dog," because they hear anger in your voice. I tend to think that the same applies to communications in a marriage.

The words of my preface could just as easily have preceded my telling Clint that we'd won the lottery, but he knew instantly that I was going to share bad news. His expression turned grim as he waited for me to continue.

I decided that it would be least painful, for him and for me, if I just blurted it all out at once. So after a deep breath, I said, "I went to the doctor the other day. I have stage-four breast cancer. That means it's metastasized to other areas, including my liver. The prognosis is not good."

I remembered all too vividly the tsunami of emotions that roiled over me when the first of my doctors had uttered those same words. It felt like I was free-falling through the stages of grief, the speed of which left no time for me to be angry, or to bargain, or even to accept my fate before I hit the ground.

The one thing I'd wanted to know then would be at the forefront of Clint's mind now. I'd been afraid to ask the first doctor. I assumed that was why Clint didn't immediately ask me.

So I told him. "If I do this experimental treatment, the doctor said that the five-year survival rate is around twenty-five percent. And without any treatment, I'll have six months, give or take."

Clint was the most thoughtful man I'd ever met. Not the flowers-for-Valentine's-Day kind of thoughtfulness—there he had never excelled—but in the literal sense that he was always thinking.

"You need to get a second opinion," he said.

"I did. And a third. They're unanimous, I'm afraid."

I could see in his eyes that he wanted to ask how long I'd kept this news to myself. He suppressed the question, knowing the answer was unimportant.

Without uttering a word, he pulled me into an embrace and began to sob on my shoulder. I had wanted to avoid crying, but the moment I felt him convulse, I joined in.

My tears stopped his. He sat up straight and wiped his eyes.

"How do you feel?"

I laughed. "Actually, not bad. In fact, no different than I did before I knew I was dying."

Clint's somber expression didn't budge. Obviously too soon for him to share in gallows humor about my condition.

"When will the chemo start?" he asked.

This was my husband in fact-gathering mode, as he called it when retained by a new client. No conclusions or predictions until all the facts were absorbed. It was not lost on me, of course, that he posed the query not as an *if*, but a *when*, there being no scenario in which he envisioned I would forgo treatment. I suppose I would have thought the same thing if this had been Clint's diagnosis instead of mine.

"I still need to think that through a little bit," I said. "I know it's what I'm supposed to do, but I'm not sure it's the right thing for me. As soon as I start, I'll feel sick. And tired. And even with the chemo, I'm likely to die just as quickly. Best case, I'll feel like hell for a year, and have only a one-in-four chance of living another four years. Worse case, I'll die while still on chemo, and I'll feel terrible that entire time. On the other hand, without treatment, I could have another . . . I don't know, four, five, maybe even six good months left."

Clint was losing hope by the second. His face seemed to cave in on itself, his eyes filling with tears, his jaw locking. I understood that he would equate my decision to deny treatment with surrender. I wanted to disabuse him of that thought, to tell him that forgoing chemotherapy wasn't capitulation, but a way for me to triumph over my illness by living the remainder of my life on my own terms.

He didn't give me the chance.

"So let me understand the choice here. One option is that you forgo treatment, and that'll mean that, at best, you can live for another six months, and maybe half of that you'll be okay before you begin to decline. Option number two is that you undergo treatment, and that gives you something approaching a twenty-five percent chance of living at least five years, although the first year of that will be very hard on you."

Just like he did in court, he'd summarized a complex set of facts so that the conclusion to be drawn from them was self-evident. At least to him.

"In three years, Ella will be in college," he said to drive his point home. "Five years is more than half Charlotte's life."

"I know," I said, touching his cheek. "I've done the math too."

20.

The next morning, I made french toast. That was hardly an uncommon occurrence on the weekend. What the girls found strange, however, was that Clint hadn't left for work, which he did at the same time on Saturdays as he did Monday through Friday. Sunday was his only day of rest, and even then only on occasion.

Almost immediately after Nick's acquittal, Clint's practice had taken off. In short order he went from a solo practitioner with very little to do to the lawyer of choice for the rich and famous. Among those early clients was a bond trader who gave Clint a $2 million nonrefundable retainer, which we used to buy the town house off Fifth Avenue that we still called home. It was five stories with a backyard and boasted seven working fireplaces and a dining room that comfortably seated sixteen, which we used only for formal occasions. We had family meals in the kitchen, where a small table with only enough room for the four of us rested against the window. When Clint had last suggested we consider having a third child—"to go for a boy," as he phrased it—I told him that we wouldn't all fit at the table anymore, and I only half meant it as a joke.

Charlotte usually spoke the most and the loudest at our family meals. Today's subject was the solar eclipse that was coming next week. Her third-grade science teacher had devoted a considerable amount of class time to the event, so that Charlotte now spoke with the assurance of an expert in the matter.

"You can't see the sun because the moon is in front of it, so it gets all dark," she said excitedly. "But you still shouldn't look at it because even though you can't see the sun, it's still there, and it'll make you blind if you stare at it. That's why I don't even want to go outside to see it, but Ms. Gilmore says that if you look at it through a box you can see it, and it won't make you blind."

"Or you can watch it on TV later," Clint offered.

Charlotte ignored the remark. "Are you going to watch it, Ella?"

Growing up as an only child, I'd always pitied those with siblings for having to share their parents' attention. But having my daughters taught me that I had missed out on the joys of that sibling bond. As much as it warmed my heart to know that they would always have each other, the realization that Ella would bear the burden of becoming a surrogate mother for Charlotte pained me even more. At fifteen, she was much too young for that responsibility. But at least Charlotte would have her. There'd be no one for Ella to turn to for maternal advice. Clint would try to be both mother and father, of course, but he'd never succeed. That was a tall order for anyone and beyond hope for a workaholic father, no matter how much he loved his children.

After breakfast, Clint asked the girls to come into the living room for a "family discussion." Charlotte bounded in the room, oblivious to what was about to occur, happy just to be included. Ella, however, was intuitive enough to realize that families didn't call meetings to discuss good things. She immediately reached for my hand, which was not something she—or any fifteen-year-old girl, for that matter—was apt to do.

When we were all in our places, the girls looked to Clint to share the reason we had assembled. But it was my cancer, so I broke it to them.

"I'm afraid I have some bad news, girls. I went to the doctor, and I was told that I have breast cancer. I'm going to get treatment for it, and that means I'm going to lose my hair. But, and this is the part we all have to focus on, if the treatment goes well, I'm going to be fine."

That was the trade-off for me. I would endure chemo in exchange for giving my children hope that the world as they knew it would not end.

If that was the message they got, it certainly didn't show on their faces. They both looked shell-shocked. It took all my strength not to break down, but I was determined to hold it together, at least while I was in their presence.

"I know that this affects our entire family, and everyone has their own feelings and their own concerns, but I want to tell you mine first, okay?"

Charlotte whispered, "Okay, Mommy."

Ella sat stone-faced, as if in a trance.

"For me, it's that everything stays as normal as possible. That means we all continue to do our jobs just like we always have. Your jobs are to go to school and see your friends and have fun. Your father's job is to go to work. My job is the only one that is going to change. And I hope my job doesn't have to change too much. I'm still going to be here to help with homework and cook dinner, but I'm also going to have to go to the doctor and be a patient too. And I'm probably going to be really tired a lot."

After I'd shared my news with Clint last night, and the shock of it had slightly subsided, he said that he wanted to fire all his clients, so we could spend more time together. He suggested we travel—wherever I wanted to go. In other words, do the things that people do who are fortunate enough not to have to worry about money or the impending death of a loved one.

There were numerous logistical impediments to such a plan, of course. The girls had to go to school. I had to be at chemo three times a week and check in with my doctor regularly in between. But the real reason I declined was because of what I'd just told the girls—I wanted everything to stay normal. For them and for me.

Clint said, "I'm going to do my best to do my job, just like Mom said. Can we count on both of you to do your jobs too?"

It was Charlotte who cut through all the babble. "Are you going to die, Mommy?"

I had told Clint this was coming. "Ella will be thinking it all through," I'd said, "using her mental energy to keep her feelings in check. But Charlotte will get right to the nitty-gritty."

When Ella was little, probably three or four, she asked me when I was going to die. I was already near forty when we had this discussion, and told her I would live for about another hundred years, because that seemed more than long enough to assuage her concerns. Ella immediately began to wail. "That's too soon. Sleeping Beauty was asleep for a hundred years, and when she woke up her mother was there!" I didn't fully understand how Disney had pulled that off, but my takeaway was that kids need to be comforted in terms they understood. In that instance, I told her I'd meant that I'd live for another thousand years, and she was happy again.

"The doctors are telling me that there's a good chance that I'm going to be okay," I said.

That was as much as I was willing to lie. Not a *certainty*, or even a *very good chance*. Just *good*. Which, of course, was still untrue.

Charlotte was mollified by my response. She had her usual smile back, and she gave me a hug.

"I'm sorry that you're sick, Mommy," she said.

I knew Ella would not be so easily soothed. At fifteen, she was old enough to understand that her world had just changed and would never be the same again. But she followed her younger sister's lead and put her arms around me, pretending to believe what I'd told Charlotte.

Clint left for work shortly after. He offered to take the day off, but I told him that it was important he set the example of everyone doing their jobs as usual, which in his case was working around the clock.

When I went into Ella's room, I found her on her computer. She startled at my presence, as if viewing a website we would not allow. I knew she was doing her own research about cancer survival rates.

"I thought you might have some questions you didn't want to ask in front of Charlotte," I said.

Ella looked at me as if I hadn't said anything. Her blankness was so complete that I was tempted to ask if she'd heard me, but of course she had.

Finally, she said, "What stage is your cancer?"

I had vowed to treat her like the adult she was becoming. I wouldn't sugarcoat or evade the truth.

"Four," I said, as even-keeled as I could utter the word.

I had always thought that Ella was much more like me than Charlotte. Some of that was because she bore such a striking resemblance to me. If it weren't for the advances in photography and fashion since the 1970s, I would have had a hard time discerning whether my high school pictures were of me or her. Her performance last night had further proven what I had long known: that, in addition to my face, Ella had also inherited my singing voice. But when I looked at her now, I saw nothing but Clint. The way he could bore into my thoughts with his intelligence, almost as if it were truth serum.

"I'll do the whole living-my-life thing like you said, Mom, but only if you promise me something."

"Anything," I said, and the moment I did, I prayed that her request would be something that I could actually grant.

"Promise that you'll tell me when you know that the end is near," she said, sounding so much more grown-up than she had been just a few minutes earlier. "You don't have to tell Charlotte, and I won't either.

But I need to know. Otherwise, I'll go crazy. Every day I'll be worried that you know you're about to die and you're not telling me."

"I promise. I'll tell you as soon as I know." Then I added, "If it comes to that, which hopefully it will not."

It wasn't the only promise I made regarding things I'd need to do when the end was near.

The other I made to myself. But it would have to wait. And I wasn't sure whether I'd be able to see it through.

21.

The first week after chemo, my hair was still in place, and I allowed myself to think that I might be one of the tiny percentage of chemo patients who did not suffer from that side effect. That hope lasted only until the next day, when the first clump came out in my hand in the shower. The following morning, my pillow resembled the remnants of a shedding black Lab.

I contemplated waiting for the girls to come home from school and having them help me shave my head, as if it were some bonding activity, like giving each other facials. But it wasn't that, and no amount of pretending would make it anything other than it was—a sign that I was dying. So I stood alone, looking at my old self for what I knew might be the last time. From now on, the image that stared back at me wouldn't be me, but a shell of who I once was. Maybe, if I was lucky, if I was in that 25 percent that I now considered to be a more exclusive club than those who had walked on the moon, I might once again see myself in the reflection. But if I was in the other group, the 75 percent chemo could not save, this was goodbye to that person. Even though the Anne Broden captured in the reflection now wasn't healthy, at least she didn't look sick, and in a moment, that would not be the case.

The only lefty scissors in the house that I could find were Charlotte's. Smaller than my hand, with a bright-green handle, the ones she used for her art projects. I thought about doing it in stages: cutting my hair first to shoulder-length. Then into a sporty chin-bob, and finally an adorable pixie, like Mia Farrow in *Rosemary's Baby*. But without further thought, I brought the scissors to the roots on the top of my head.

It took less than five minutes. It reminded me a bit of those films they show at the end of the evening news when a building is demolished. How the structure comes down in seconds, even though it took years to build. This felt the same, except I was that structure.

———

I visited Dr. Goldman's for my biweekly testing like clockwork until mid-February, when his weeklong vacation in Aruba through Presidents' Day meant it would be three weeks between appointments. The last time I had seen him, he'd said that my cancer seemed to be receding, but we'd need more time to know for sure.

"It's good that we're skipping a week," he'd said. "I should get a clearer indication of where things stand when I get back."

On my next visit, Dr. Goldman entered the tiny exam room sporting a deep tan, the tip of his nose already peeling. I asked if he'd had a nice vacation. He said he had, then looked down at my chart.

It had become something of a parlor game with me to try to discern what Dr. Goldman was going to say, given the look on his face. I had previously assumed that I either wasn't very good at it or that the man had a world-class poker face.

The instant his eyes met mine again, however, I knew that my assessment had been wrong. This time, I knew exactly what he would say.

"The cancer has spread," he said. Then, without letting the import of the words set in, he destroyed whatever optimism I'd clung to. "We could switch to a different protocol, but I don't see any reason to believe it would be more successful." And then, to seal my fate, he uttered the words everyone else had said to me, but which he had thus far resisted: "I'm sorry, Anne."

"What does that mean?" I asked.

The question was rhetorical. I knew what it meant—that my dream of seeing Ella graduate from high school, or at least attending her Sweet Sixteen, would not come true. I likely wouldn't be around for Charlotte's tenth birthday in August. In fact, the odds were long that I'd survive to the end of the school year.

Dr. Goldman took the question literally. "We'll stop the chemo. You'll feel better in the short term, maybe as soon as a week. And your hair will begin to grow back." He smiled, as if regaining some of my hair were consolation for losing my life, although I suspect it was more out of force of habit than any belief on his part that it was a silver lining. "In the longer term, however, it means that the cancer will spread until it overwhelms your system and ends your life."

When I'd first received news of my condition, I became woozy and unfocused, unsure where I was or what had just happened. I didn't remember a single word my original doctor said after "stage-four breast cancer."

This time, my reaction was the opposite. Rather than the world falling out of focus, everything slowed, and I could see with sharpened clarity. I was going to die. Soon. It was a fact. There was nothing I could do about it.

"How long is the longer term?" I asked.

Up until this moment, Dr. Goldman had refused to provide me with a definitive answer to this most crucial question. Like a politician, he'd offer me statistics and ranges, none of which provided any useful information. But, as Ella had done with me, I'd made Dr. Goldman promise that, when the end was at hand, he'd tell me what I needed to know.

Giving credit where it is due, he kept his word.

"Two to three months, give or take," he said softly but with conviction. "You should be fine for the next month, during which you'll be feeling better than you have in some time. Enjoy this period. When the fatigue begins to set in, that will be the beginning of the end.

Sometime during the few weeks after that, you'll begin to have difficulty eating or drinking. Some patients tell me that they begin to lose interest in anything having to do with the outside world, and some report that they no longer want to see friends, or even family. That's when life expectancy becomes measured in weeks. At some point, you'll be sleeping most of the day, and that's when you only have days left. And, I'm sorry to say, the last few days, you will not be yourself at all. You'll be largely uncommunicative, and some patients appear to be suffering from delusions. That said, you should be able to recognize loved ones right up until the very end."

———

I returned home from the doctor as if I were already dead. How could I tell Clint—and Ella, if I planned to keep my word to her—that I had two, maybe three, months to live? How could I *not* tell Charlotte?

I was cursing my decision to endure chemo in the first place. But like so many times since my diagnosis, I stifled the thought, realizing that wishing I could go back in time and do things differently wasn't a productive use of the little time I had left.

When the girls were babies, I always recorded their firsts. Teeth, words, steps, and birthdays were memorialized in the baby books I kept for them. When later firsts arrived—days of school, camp, ballet recitals, subway rides alone—the events might be captured with a photograph, but the true repository was my memory. There were some lasts too, of course, but they always were either acts of abandonment (piano) or the natural progression upward (lower-school graduations). Never an end to something that anyone wished would continue. And now, my entire life would be consumed with lasts. Worse still, no one would know that these events were lasts, except in hindsight.

Clint arrived home a little after ten. As soon as he entered the bedroom, he smiled broadly, which had become something of a habit of late. It sometimes made me feel as if he were expecting me to be dead and was pleasantly surprised that I was still breathing.

At least tonight I knew that wasn't the only reason for his happiness. It was my attire that had lifted his spirits.

I was wearing lingerie.

Even with my baldness, I still looked good in lingerie. In fact, chemo's one positive result was that I had lost ten pounds.

"Where are the girls?" Clint asked.

"Ella's sleeping at Sydney's, and Charlotte is at Olivia Lubins's birthday party. They're going to see *Finding Nemo*."

"How many times is that for her?"

"Three."

"Three times," Clint said with a sly smile. "I think that's a worthy goal, don't you?"

Over the years, I had heard from others who knew Clint from a work setting that he was one cool customer. The type of man who was methodical in his thinking, no matter how inflamed the passions around him. He liked this image of himself, I think. The commander keeping his head while everyone else loses theirs.

I knew that it was an act. Perhaps that's unfair, as *act* denotes subterfuge. More accurately, it was a matter of will. He could keep his feelings in check when he needed that level of control, but when there was nothing to be gained by it, he was as emotional a man as I'd ever known. He cried at sad movies more often than I did, and almost anything sentimental about our daughters reduced him to putty.

So far, he had relied on his control to be my rock. When I cried or felt desperate, he assured me that he had not given up hope.

After our first time that night, while Clint and I lay naked in the dark, basking in the afterglow, I told him what Dr. Goldman had told me. I knew that meant there would be no second time, much less a third. In fact, I doubted we'd ever make love again.

It was a *last*.

22.

I decided I'd tell Ella, but not Charlotte. At least not right away. When the end was nearer, Charlotte and I would have our discussion. Clint concurred with the decision, but even as we were reaching it, I could imagine a grown-up Charlotte telling Clint that she never forgave me for not telling her sooner.

My original plan was to tell Ella first thing Saturday morning, so that we'd have the entire day to be together to act like a normal mother and daughter. But at breakfast, Ella told me that she had made plans to meet up with some friends in Brooklyn.

"I'd like you back by five," I said.

She pouted. "Really?"

"Yes, really. I'm going to make stuffed shells tonight, and I'd like us all together when it hits the table."

She didn't answer, which meant that she had agreed to my demand. After all, stuffed shells were Ella's favorite. The things mothers do that they think will comfort their children. Pasta filled with cheese would not be adequate reparations for Ella losing her mother.

I had read everything I could about how to share this news with teenagers, but it was all the usual stuff—be direct, don't lie or overpromise, provide enough detail for them to understand, but don't overwhelm them with information, let them lead the discussion, and then give them time to process what you've imparted. None of it gave me much insight as to how to phrase the concept that Mom would be dead in two months and Ella would live the rest of her life without me.

By midafternoon, Charlotte was rereading *Harry Potter and the Order of the Phoenix*, her activity of choice whenever I limited her television watching. It must have been her third time through the Potter books, and I had told her that when she finished this go-round, she needed to start something new rather than go back through the series. My most recent nominee was *The Golden Compass*. Charlotte wouldn't hear of it, however. She had similarly rejected my earlier suggestions of *Anne of Green Gables* and the Laura Ingalls Wilder books. "Want me to read some to you and then you can read some to me?" I asked.

Charlotte's face lit up. It was something I had learned from Ella— no matter how old kids get, they love to be read to by their parents.

I had read the Harry Potter books too, always within the week that they came out. Among many more important things, my worsening prognosis meant I would never know exactly how Harry defeated Voldemort in the end, assuming of course that good triumphed over evil in the wizarding world.

For more than an hour, Charlotte snuggled against me, her body in a ball as if she were a lap cat, while I read. At times I assumed she was daydreaming, or full-on asleep, but whenever I missed a word, she was quick to pop up and ask me to reread the sentence.

As I read, I thought about what price I would be willing to pay for more time. This was a normal part of the process of bargaining that comes with grief, or so I'd heard. The truth is, I would have sold my eternal soul to the devil for more time with my family. But how long? To see my grandchildren and die at a ripe old age? In a heartbeat. Until the day after the girls got married? Yes, of course. Until college graduation? That too. High school? Yes. Eternity in hell for one more year with my loved ones? Even that would have been a fair trade.

Ella came home a few minutes before five.

I had been in the kitchen but came out into the hallway when I heard the front door open. In the time it took me to wash the cheese off my hands, however, Ella had already escaped into her bedroom, and I instead found Charlotte parked in front of the television. Even though we had a perfectly nice sofa, she liked to sit on the rug with her chin propped on her fists, elbows on the ground. *Jimmy Neutron: Boy Genius* was on.

"Was that your sister I just heard?"

Her attention didn't break from the show. In another life I might have said, *Earth calling Charlotte*, but this time I decided to get down on the floor beside her, even though it took a fair amount of energy for me to do it and getting up would be even more difficult. Luckily for me, I reached the floor at exactly the same moment that the show ended, which caused Charlotte to smile at me instead of the screen.

"How's my baby girl?"

"Good. How's my baby mommy?"

She giggled after saying that, as she always did.

"She's good too. What's on after the boy genius?"

"SpongeBob."

That settled that question, at least. Charlotte wouldn't budge from her spot in front of the television for the next thirty minutes.

"Enjoy your time at Bikini Bottom."

"Okay, Mom."

She had just started calling me Mom, yet another sign my little girl was growing up. Then again, Ella had jettisoned *mommy* by the time she was five. I kissed my younger child on the top of her head and breathed in her sweet scent, just as Patchy the Pirate asked that age-old question: *Who lives in a pineapple under the sea?*

The few minutes I'd spent on the rug with Charlotte had been long enough for Ella to power up her iBook and stare at the screen as if it held the secrets of the universe. The hours she spent alone with that device made me long for the days when the television was her best friend, because at least then I knew what she was looking at.

"What are you doing?"

"Homework."

"What did you and your friends do today?"

"Nothing too much. Just hung out."

That was about as much small talk as I was going to be able to accomplish before losing my nerve. I took a deep, cleansing breath.

"I need to talk to you, Ella."

Ella's face went blank. Her complexion lost whatever little color her usually pale skin would allow. Her eyes began to fill.

When Ella was born, the nurse who handed me my daughter for the first time said, "Here you go, Mama. I think you have a very old soul in this precious baby girl."

Maybe she said that to all the new mothers. Maybe she was insane. But in Ella's case, I always thought it was true. Neither Clint nor I believed in reincarnation, but sometimes we'd joke that this was definitely Ella's last time through, and it might be Charlotte's first.

"I'm so sorry, sweetheart, but I have to keep my promise to you. The doctor said that the chemo has stopped working. That means that I have only a few more months. It's hard to tell exactly how long, but he said that I would be fine, maybe even stronger than usual, until about mid-April, and then . . ."

By this point she had burst into tears, her head shaking back and forth as if she could change my fate by objecting to it. I'd desperately wanted to be strong for her, like I was when I first shared my cancer news, but this time there was no chance of that.

23.

Almost as soon as I stopped the chemo, I felt better. I knew it was something of a dead-cat bounce, but that didn't mean I didn't enjoy finally going through the day without feeling as if I might puke at any moment. Within two weeks, my hair started to grow back. At first it was just fuzz, and splotchy at that, but by St. Patrick's Day I had coverage, albeit in a Sinead O'Connor way. I suspected that by the time I finally succumbed, I'd be sporting that adorable Mia Farrow pixie style after all.

If Dr. Goldman was correct that I had two to three months left to live, then April was likely the tipping point. If he had been overly optimistic by a month, which he acknowledged might be the case, I was now entering the death-rattle phase.

When my hair began to reappear, I told Charlotte the bad news, for fear that she'd otherwise interpret it as a sign that I was better. She reacted stoically, a response that made me sadder than if she had lost her composure completely. It meant that my baby was already adjusting to her new reality of life without a mother to comfort her.

There now remained only one person to share the news with.

———

Easter Sunday 2004 was April 11. It was Clint's idea that the family go to mass.

All the talk at church of rising from the dead, of being worthy of redemption, finally pushed me over the edge. The next morning, as soon as Clint had left for work and the girls were on their way to school, I turned my attention to figuring out how I could get a message to Nick Zamora.

His phone number was unlisted, of course. I could have told my husband that as part of putting my affairs in order, I wanted to call Nick and say goodbye, but I feared that would be too suspicious. Other than my moments with the girls, I hadn't engaged in melodramatic farewells with anyone. Clint knew too well that I preferred the "Irish goodbye," even at dinner parties. Besides, I had no reason to believe Clint knew Nick's phone number. Their last contact had been before cell phones were even invented.

I began my investigation to find Nick Zamora by running online searches with his name. But they only directed me to web pages where his books were for sale. I called the general number of his publisher, and they told me to contact his agent. When I asked for his agent's name and phone number, they told me that they were not at liberty to give out that information.

Finally, I went to Shakespeare & Company, the bookstore on Lexington Avenue. About twenty copies of Nick's latest novel—*Losing Things I Never Had*—were displayed atop the bestseller table.

It was a big book. So heavy, in fact, that in my current condition, even lifting it off the table took effort. The cover art was a cloud-filled sky, which reminded me a bit of *The Simpsons*' title sequence. Nick's name was in the largest font, embossed in shiny silver above the title. Beneath it was the obligatory *International #1 Bestseller* and a quote from the *New York Times* that said, "Zamora's name must be included among the voices of his generation."

Like I did whenever Nick came out with a new book, even before cracking the spine, I turned it over to see the author photo. He had used the same photo for his last two books, but an updated picture graced the back of his latest tome. The photograph might have been captioned *The Great Man at 50*. It showed Nick with a full head of hair that could be fairly characterized as salt-and-pepper and cut short in a way that he could pass for a Wall Street lawyer. His outfit also suggested a professional turn. Nick was wearing a dark suit, his tie loosened at the top button, as if he'd just finished a night of celebrating. To cap off the image, he wore black-framed glasses that gave him that *serious author* vibe.

On page 579 were the acknowledgments. That was another thing I did every time Nick published a new book—read the dedication and the acknowledgments first. I had long stopped thinking that my name would be listed in either place; still, I checked anyway to see if there was someone else in his life. But the thanks he gave were always to his agent and publisher and PR team. Not a Zelda among them, at least as far as I could tell.

This time was no different. In the first paragraph he thanked his agent, Scott Stonehill of Javelin Media. I called Javelin's main number as soon as I hit the street but didn't make it past Stonehill's secretary. When she agreed to take a message, I said, "My name is Anne Broden. I'm an old friend of Nick Zamora's. Could you please tell Mr. Stonehill immediately to get the following message to Nick: That I'm in failing health, and there are things that I need to share with him while I'm still able. He should call me on my cell phone as soon as possible. My name again is Anne Broden."

I asked her to read back the message. When she did, it sounded more dire than I had intended. My circumstances required that degree of urgency, though. There was no way to sugarcoat it.

———

Later that night, while Clint was still at work and I was eating dinner with the girls, listening to Charlotte strenuously argue that OutKast's

"Hey Ya!" was a much better song than Usher's "Yeah!," my phone rang. A sixth sense told me it was Nick. I jumped up and rushed to answer it.

"No phones at the dinner table," Charlotte said with a giggle, mimicking what I said to Ella on an almost daily basis.

I ignored her and left my girls to continue their debate. My hand was shaking when I grabbed the phone.

"Hello?"

"Anne?"

I shouldn't have given him the satisfaction that I recognized his voice, but I needed to get this part over with. "Nick," I said. "Thank you for calling."

"Is what you said in your message true? Are you sick?"

"Unfortunately, yes. I have cancer."

"Oh my God. I'm so sorry. I . . . I was hoping that your message was some type of joke someone was playing on me. But at the same time, I wanted it to be you who called, just not for the reasons you said in the message."

His babbling revealed that he hadn't rehearsed what he was going to say. I had the sense that he must have just received my message and immediately called, without giving the matter any further thought. I, on the other hand, had been thinking through this conversation for years. In none of those imaginary iterations did we conduct it over the phone.

"I was hoping you'd come to New York so that we could talk in person."

He didn't hesitate. "Of course. When?"

"The sooner the better. Can you be here in the next day or two?"

He fell silent. I didn't think it was because he was checking his schedule. Instead, I assumed my request to drop everything and fly across the country emphasized how little time I had left.

"Yes. I'll leave tomorrow. Is the day after that soon enough?"

"Thank you, Nick."

He asked if I had a place in mind to meet. I suggested that the bar of whatever hotel he was staying at would suffice, so long as it was quiet. He told me that when he came to New York these days he stayed at the Four Seasons, and the bar area there was usually empty after lunch.

We agreed to meet at three. When the plans were done, he said, "Anne . . ." But nothing followed.

"Until then," I said.

24.

When I was a kid, the night before Halloween was called Mischief Night. In college, I learned that for people from other parts of the country, it went by other names—Devil's Night, Goosey Night, and even Cabbage Night. Regardless of the designation, it was when teenagers went around toilet-papering yards and committing other acts of petty vandalism.

The week prior to Mischief Night, Nick had given Clint the manuscript of his novel to read, but an appellate brief had consumed all Clint's time. Left alone at night, I'd agreed to read it in my husband's stead. The book was called *Precipice* and was about . . . well, about Nick. His stand-in was named Alexander, an aspiring painter whom everyone was convinced would achieve greatness, although Alexander was finding it difficult to live up to that promise. The love interest, Nicole, wouldn't hear of Alexander's self-doubt.

When I called Nick to tell him that I had finished the book, he stopped me cold.

"Not another word. Let me buy you a drink and get your full thoughts. Tomorrow. You pick the place."

I selected a French restaurant near our apartment because it was quiet and had a bar area with tables. I invited Clint to come along, but he told me that he had a client dinner. "Besides," he'd said, "you read the book, I didn't."

Nick was waiting for me at the bar, a glass nearly half-full of brown liquid sitting in front of him. He saw my eyes go to it.

"Scotch, just in case it's that type of a discussion," he said.

"I don't know what that means, but I'll have one too."

He signaled to the bartender to get me the same drink. Turning back, he said, "The suspense is killing me."

"You're the one who made me wait until now to tell you." I paused for a beat, to tease him. "It's great, Nick. Really."

His body slackened, as if I were his commanding officer and had ordered him at ease. A smile came to his face that could easily have launched a thousand ships.

Before Clint, I'd dated a lot of Nicks—pretty boys for whom everything had always come easy. I found them boring and shallow, less interested in me than in the concept of me. It was in part why I had fallen for Clint. He didn't expect to be handed anything, and he didn't regard me like an accessory that would make him look better.

In short, Clint was everything that those boys were not.

The bartender delivered my scotch. I had no sooner lifted it when Nick touched his glass against mine. "To my first reader," he said.

"To the soon-to-be bestselling author," I toasted back.

We talked through the plot, Nick peppering me with questions about what I liked and didn't, asking if certain parts rang true to me. I answered truthfully, which wasn't too hard because I truly loved the book.

"What about the ending?" he asked.

"What about it?"

"Nicole's death, in particular."

"Isn't that always the way it goes in fiction?" I said. "The poor girl stands by her man through thick and thin, and right when he's about to achieve fame and fortune, what's her reward? She dies."

"Seriously, Anne. I'm asking for real. I agonized over the ending."

"Okay," I said and put on a more serious expression. "The ending worked for me. In my humble opinion, the type of relationship Alexander and Nicole shared was too intense to survive. That type of passion either burns out, or everyone gets incinerated."

He laughed. "Jesus. I always thought Clinton was the cynic in your marriage, and you were the wide-eyed romantic."

It was my turn to laugh. "You've known Clint since he was eight, and you think he's a cynic?"

"You don't?"

"No. Not at all. Don't get me wrong, he's not Richard Gere sweeping Debra Winger off her feet in *An Officer and a Gentleman*, but Clint has the strongest moral code of anyone I've ever known. If that doesn't qualify you as a romantic—someone who believes in an ideal—then I don't know what does."

"That's not the dictionary definition, though," he countered. "Does your husband believe love conquers all? That's what I think of when I think of a romantic. Which is why I think it applies to me. And, before what you said two minutes ago, I thought it applied to you too. But Clinton . . . I think he would say that reason conquers all, and that's a very different thing."

"Tomato, *tomahto*. The point is that he believes in something greater than himself, and that, to me, is what makes someone a romantic. I know you like to fancy yourself a romantic, but I'm not sure what you believe in to justify that label. Sadly, I'm not worthy of the name either. I wish it were otherwise, and so in that way, you and I, we *are* kindred spirits. We both *want* to be romantics—me with my music and you with your writing—but, for both of us, it's still about us in the end, not the art, not the creation. Which is why, I'm sorry to say, we're both posers when it comes right down to it."

"I believe in true love, Anne. I'm a little hurt that after reading the book you don't see that."

I'd upset him, which wasn't my intent. "No. That's not what I meant, Nick. In the book, it's obvious that you know what it is to believe in true love. But you've given that position to Nicole, right? And you capture that beautifully. *She* believes in true love, which makes her the true romantic in the story. Not Alexander. He's more committed to the idea of being the kind of person who's capable of falling in love than he is to being in a committed, loving relationship . . . if that makes any sense. In that way, he's . . . well, not too surprising here, right? Alexander's more like you."

Nick looked at me curiously. "Alexander isn't me."

I thought he was putting me on.

"I know you're supposed to say that it's fiction, but c'mon, Nick. Even though you made Alexander a painter and not a writer, it's still not even thinly veiled; it's . . . not veiled at all. At least for anyone who knows you. That's fine, don't get me wrong. It's what makes the character seem so real. Because he *is* real."

"Alexander is you, Anne."

"What?"

"I'm Nicole. That's why the initials line up."

Alexander for Anne. Nicole for Nick. And here I'd thought he was playing on a Russian-czar theme by substituting Alexander for Nicholas.

I tried to rethink the story, running through my head each reference to Alexander's beauty or his talent. Nick intended those descriptions to apply to *me*? He thought *I* was the one destined for greatness? The creator of beauty? Just as quickly, another thought hit me. If he was Nicole, did he love me the way she loved Alexander? Was that why he was so interested in my take on the ending? Was he asking if I thought I would be the death of him? Or was he suggesting that he and I could live happily ever after?

"You're freaking me out, Nick."

"I'm sorry. It wasn't my intention, I promise. I know it's a lot to take in. And don't worry, I'm certain no one will ever make the connection without my telling them that I based Nicole on me and Alexander on you, and I'll take that to the grave with me. I would never have offered to let Clinton read it if I thought it was remotely possible he'd see that it's about you and me. I . . . I just thought *you* needed to know. I love you, Anne. And I have for some time. And, sadly for me, I think I always will."

I told him I was flattered but that we needed to remain friends. I couldn't imagine he expected me to say anything else. In fact, I wondered if he'd fully considered the possibility that I might tell Clint about it as soon as I got home.

"I knew that's what you were going to say," he said. "But can you honestly say you haven't thought about me that way? That if *we'd* been the ones set up that night, we wouldn't be the ones married to each other today?"

That was when I made the first of many missteps. I told him the truth, when I should have lied. I could have easily said, "No. I've never thought of you that way. You're my husband's best friend." But what I actually said was, "I don't know about marriage, Nick, but yes, I have thought about you in that way in the past. But part of being grown-ups, not high schoolers, is having the ability to recognize that just because you think something, you don't have to make it happen."

I don't know why I gave him that gift. He certainly didn't need me to stroke his ego. And it's not as if I'd never lied to a man to dampen his expectations. But there was something I always saw as fragile about Nick; I suppose I didn't want to hurt him. Although I can't rule out the more sinister explanation: I wanted him to know I was lonely in my marriage to Clint and was looking for someone to rescue me.

When we left the restaurant that night, I thought we had reached an understanding. We'd each said something that would stay between us, and our lives would go on as before as if the words had never been spoken.

Of course, that's never the way it works. In high school or after.

25.

It was raining. Not a downpour, but coming down steadily enough that I would have otherwise worn a hat. But to meet Nick after all these years, I opted against it. I wanted him to see me all at once, without enduring a slow reveal of my condition.

As he had predicted, the bar area in the Four Seasons was largely empty. It was also dimly lit, as if perfectly suited for a clandestine encounter. Before turning my attention to locating Nick, I scanned the room to ensure that Clint was not there, even though I knew he'd be holed up in his office. Still, "of all the gin joints . . ." was the last thing I wanted today.

Midway through my reconnaissance, I spotted Nick. He had his back to me, sitting beside the fireplace, the flames illuminating his silhouette. I stopped where I was, about twenty feet away. For a moment, I questioned the entire plan. My body was consumed with the irresistible impulse to turn and run. I might have too, had it not been for the fact that Nick made a quarter turn and caught my eye.

He smiled, as I expected he would upon our first sight. But then I held my breath, awaiting his next reaction. That's when most people who had not seen me recently usually morphed into an expression of pity, or at least concern. But Nick continued to take me in with nothing but joy in his eyes.

He looked much like the photograph on the back of his book, except his hair was longer, once again reflecting the shaggy, carefree air of a man who didn't have an office job. The way I recalled from when we were younger. His attire was also old-school Nicky: faded blue jeans and a black sweater. He wasn't wearing glasses.

I had envisioned our reintroduction as akin to the formal greeting heads of state give each other—stiff handshaking before getting down to business. But I walked right into him, even before he opened his arms to receive me. The wisps of his hair tickled my cheek, and his scent instantly transported me back to my younger years. Before motherhood had changed my body, and before cancer had destroyed it.

He ended our embrace and took a step back. I watched him scan me from head to toe. I knew he was finished when he wiped his eyes.

I rubbed the top of my head, a tic I'd recently developed. It might have looked like smoothing my hair, except I was barely sporting a crew cut.

"I haven't changed a bit, am I right?" I said.

"Just as beautiful as I remembered," he lied.

The sofa was long enough that our legs would not touch if I had taken the spot beside him, but I sat on the opposite chair. It was important to look him in the eye for this discussion.

"I'm drinking a very nice scotch," he said. "Can I get you something?"

For all the limitations placed on me during my illness, alcohol was not one of them, as long as it was in moderation. But, in yet another irony of my life, I had lost my taste for it.

"No. I'm fine. I actually want to get through the speech I prepared for this. Can I do that?"

"I flew across the country to hear it. But after, I hope you'll talk to me in a less rehearsed way. And that you'll also give me the opportunity to say some things too."

I nodded to confirm that his request would be granted. Then I heard the words aloud that for nearly twenty years had been relegated solely to my mind.

"I think you know, but there was a time when I truly thought that I could never be as happy as I was with you, Nick. And the last thing I want to do is to reduce Carolyn's life to a sign from God directed at me, but after she died, the way she died, I knew we could never be together. And I understand why you went to California after, and why you broke away from me, and from Clint too, even after all he did for you."

"Should I explain myself?" he asked. "Or do you want me to wait until you're finished?"

"Let me say a little more. Then I'll let you have your turn. I promise."

He smiled and gave me a curt nod.

"Then the oddest thing happened. You and Clint both had this crazy success, almost overnight. His I understood. He deserved it. But—"

"But I didn't."

"No, you didn't."

"Sometimes—"

I interrupted him. "You don't know this, but after . . . when you were already in LA, but not for very long, I gave up singing. Acting too. I thought I was undeserving of anything good ever happening to me. And I needed to make it up to Clint in any way I could. To me, that meant giving him children and being his wife. I got pregnant with Ella even before your first book came out. That's when the strangest thing of all happened. I became happy. And not just a little bit. I woke up one day and realized that I was happier than I ever thought possible."

He didn't protest. Maybe it was because I'd asked him not to interrupt. Maybe he'd already intuited everything I'd revealed.

"And now I'm going to die. And I thought—*of course. This* is the payback. I didn't deserve to be happy. But the worst part isn't about me. It's that my daughters, and Clint too, are going to suffer worse than me. Charlotte, our younger daughter, she's only nine. That's got to be the worst possible age for a girl to lose her mother. Ella is fifteen, which, now that I think about it, isn't any better. This is going to be the worst thing that ever happened to all the people I love. And . . . I know it's irrational on some level, but I blame you, Nick. I do."

"Is it my turn now?" Nick asked.

146

"Yes," I said, while nodding.

"First off, Anne, it's so good to see you. Of course, I'm devastated that it took this news, but I'm glad you called me." He exhaled deeply. "There are things about me too that you don't know. Like the fact that a few months after I got to Los Angeles . . . I tried to take my own life. Sleeping pills." He shrugged. "Of course, I'm still here, so it didn't work. Maybe because I didn't really want to do it. Just wanted to say that I tried. That I was that grief-stricken. I don't know."

He looked at me as if he wanted my sympathy. I was unwilling to grant it to him.

"Kafka once said, one should never doubt one's own sense of guilt," I said.

"What's that supposed to mean?"

"If you feel guilty, you've done something to feel guilty about."

"I suppose that's true. But is there ever a time when you can be forgiven? It's been a long time since what happened between us. I didn't even get the girl in the end."

He smiled at what he must have thought was a witty comment, but I thought it cavalier, as if he were discussing the plot of one of his novels and not real-life people whose lives had been forever diminished because of the mistakes they'd made.

"Carolyn was murdered, Nick. Time doesn't change that."

"I know," Nick said quietly, almost in a whisper. "I can't even begin to tell you how . . . sorry I am."

"About what, exactly?" I asked, a sharp edge to my voice.

He looked confused by the question, although I couldn't imagine why. "Everything," he said.

"*Everything.* That's almost as useless as saying *nothing.* I really want to know, Nick. Tell me. Specifically. What are you sorry about?"

"That I fell in love with you. That it ended my friendship with Clinton. That we were not together in the end. Carolyn . . ." He stopped for a beat. "Like I said. Everything."

26.

Nick called me the day after his Mischief Night declaration of love. It was Halloween, which was why when he reached me on our home phone, I was trying on a costume, deciding whether I could actually perform at a downtown club dressed like Dorothy from *The Wizard of Oz*.

"I've been beating myself up since we said goodbye, and I wanted to apologize."

"It's fine," I said. "Let's just stick to the plan and forget it ever happened."

"Yeah, I agree . . . And I know I have no business asking you this . . . but it would help me get there if we could talk it out a little bit. There's so much that I wanted to say last night but didn't, and what I did say came out differently than I'd intended."

We met a few hours later. We talked, but not for very long. The bulk of our time together that afternoon was spent in his bed.

For that, I have no excuse. Of course, that's not how it seemed to me at the time. A myriad of justifications propelled me to break my marriage vow. That I was starving for affection. That Clint and I were heading for divorce anyway. That Nick was the aggressor, and had he not pursued me, it would never have happened.

That when there's infidelity in a marriage, both parties are to blame.

The truth, however, is black-and-white: I betrayed a man whom I had promised not to betray. And I did so with his best friend. Even setting forth the reasons I assuaged myself with at the time suggests a lack of contrition that is not true. What I did was wrong. I have no excuse.

As we said our good-nights, I told Nick it was a onetime thing, something we'd both needed to get out of our systems. Now that we had, neither of us would speak of it again.

I'm sure Nick didn't believe me. Few women turned him down. But when he suggested we meet again the following week, I refused. Another invitation came after that, and I told him that I'd meant what I said.

———

Nick and I didn't speak again for several weeks. I imagined he was biding his time, waiting for my resolve to crack. Maybe he was thinking that I would make the next move when I realized I couldn't live without him.

Then, right before Thanksgiving, Clint told me that he'd made plans for the two of us to have dinner with Nick and the latest woman he was dating. Clint had met Carolyn previously and thought I'd like her too.

Our double date was at a red-sauce Italian place a few blocks away from Nick's apartment. Nick and Carolyn were waiting in the vestibule when we arrived. The men shook hands, and then Clint leaned over to kiss Carolyn's cheek. When he did, Nick did the same with me. It was when we were in this embrace that I caught sight of Carolyn's hands on my husband's back.

On her left ring finger was an engagement ring.

"Anne, this is . . . well, I guess I might as well let the cat out of the bag right away," Nick said. "This is my fiancée, Carolyn."

Clint looked at me, and I tried my best to smile.

"When did all this happen?" Clint asked.

"I proposed the other day. And for some reason that only Carolyn knows, she actually said yes. Then, because I didn't want her to change her mind, I suggested we get married right away."

"So you two need to keep December 28 free for us," Carolyn said.

I was happy for Nick, or at least I tried to be. The fact that he'd moved on so quickly confirmed that I'd been right about him all along. He'd never loved me. I was something he had wanted for a moment, perhaps to prove something to himself, and he had forgotten about me as soon as a shiny, new thing came along.

Most of all, I truly believed that his engagement meant our one-night stand was now firmly buried in the past. It seemed like one of those rare situations in which a tornado makes a direct strike, but miraculously no one gets hurt.

Privately, Clint predicted that Nick would never walk down the aisle with Carolyn. "I don't know what possessed him to ask her to marry him," he told me. "The last time we talked about her, Nicky said he was thinking of ending it. But I guess it's just Nicky being Nicky. He's always fancied himself as this Great Gatsby character, and so he's become enamored of the idea of this whirlwind romance that's swept him off his feet. But trust me on this, in a few weeks, he'll realize that marriage is forever and he'll slam the brakes."

But when the last weekend of the year arrived, my husband stood beside Nick as his best man, toasting what Clint said would be one of the great love stories of our time. Along with the other guests, I sipped champagne in agreement.

At some point during the reception, someone convinced Carolyn that it was tradition for her to dance with the best man. When she grabbed Clint's hand and took him onto the dance floor, Nick asked me if he could have the honor.

He held me at a respectful distance, and we began to move to Mr. Mister's "Broken Wings." I ran through my head various things to say and settled on, "I think you and Carolyn are going to be very happy together."

He didn't reply. In fact, other than saying "thank you" when the song ended, Nick and I didn't exchange another word for nearly a month. Then, in late January, he called me at home at a time he knew Clint was in the office. He said it was important that we meet.

It had been almost three months since our one and only time over the line. He was now a married man, and so I had every reason to believe that the urgency in his request was about something other than his desire to get me back into bed. About his novel, perhaps. Or maybe he needed marital advice. I convinced myself it could be many reasons, and that I was flattering myself with the thought that he still wanted me in that way when he now had Carolyn.

Even so, I could have declined his invitation. That's what I should have done. And I did, at least once, maybe twice. But he said it was important, and he needed only a few minutes of my time.

So I agreed to meet him at a bar in midtown. He was already sitting in a booth in the back when I arrived. He must have just gotten there himself, because he didn't have a drink, even water, in front of him.

As soon as I sat down, he handed me a box in the distinctive Tiffany's robin's-egg blue.

"What's this?"

"Open it."

I slid the white satin ribbon off the corners. Inside was as beautiful a necklace as I'd ever seen. A platinum pendant with a large sapphire, surrounded by smaller diamonds.

"I love you," he said. "I thought about getting you an engagement ring, but I thought . . . considering that we're both married, that would be unseemly." He grinned sheepishly. "But I wanted to give you something to show you that I was serious. I tried being without you,

Anne. You know I did. Hell, I married someone else to forget you. I'm sorry, but it didn't work. I love you as much now, probably more, than I ever have. And I know that you love me. That means we should be together. We're not doing anyone any favors by pretending otherwise. That includes Clinton and Carolyn, and it especially includes ourselves."

My first thought was that, despite the absence of alcohol on the table, he must be drunk. But when I looked at him more closely, he stared back at me, sober as a judge. My eyes fell to the pendant, if only to break away from his stare.

Since then, I have taken solace in telling myself that I was not in love with Nick as much as I was in love with the feeling I had when I was with him. It was like a perfect drug high—a feeling you never want to end. I realize now that it's the refrain of all addicts and adulterers.

He must have paid for the hotel room before meeting me at the bar. I suspect he used the Hilton's ATM to get the cash, which undoubtedly was how the police later knew to flash his picture to the desk clerks there. When we parted, unlike the prior time, I didn't say that we'd never again be together. Instead, I told him that I loved him.

The next time I spoke to Nick was the following day.

That was when Clint brought him to our home and told me that Carolyn had accidentally drowned in the bathtub.

27.

Hours after I returned from the Four Seasons, Clint casually asked me what I'd done that day. In response, I stroked my stubbled scalp and lied to my husband for the last time in my life.

"I just went for a really long walk in Central Park. It was something I had wanted to do while I still could. Just walk aimlessly and look at everything one last time."

"Is there anything else on that list?" he asked. "Something I can help with, maybe?"

"No. My bucket is empty." I laughed, realizing I had the metaphor wrong. "I guess I should say, my bucket list has been fulfilled. All I want to do now is love you and the girls as much as I can for as long as I can."

He nodded, as if to say he understood, but I could tell he had something else on his mind. Something he wasn't quite sure how to ask me.

Given the state of guilt and paranoia brought about by my meeting with Nick, I assumed Clint had found out how I'd spent my day. Or maybe he hadn't but was aware of the deeper secret I'd kept from him and wanted it out in the open, once and for all.

Over the years, there had been a handful of times that I'd thought Clint was on the brink of confrontation. Sometimes it came when we were arguing, and at others, in moments of tranquility. Circumstances in which he looked at me in such a way that could only mean he *knew*. More than that, actually. It told me that he had always known.

There were other moments, however, when I was certain that my secret was safe. Those times when he looked at me with the starry eyes that made me feel more loved than I could have ever imagined. Ironically, it was in those instances that I most wanted to tell him. To relieve myself of the burden I'd been carrying, or at least ask him to share the weight with me.

Neither of us had ever said a word about it.

Clint's silence might have been unintentional, a product of his not knowing. I often told myself that my silence was the right thing. That telling Clint would have been selfish. Or perhaps we both kept our peace because we feared that the truth would break us, and so we caged it, as if my secret were a wild animal that could never be tamed and could only hurt our family.

That night, contrary to what I'd told Clint, I realized I did have one last item on my bucket list: to set the record straight.

I gathered the strength to make a final confession.

"There's something else that maybe we should talk about," I said, my voice halting with each word. "Something, I don't know, that I've been thinking about a lot lately."

I'm certain that my tone and demeanor conveyed that what I was planning to impart was of the gravest concern—if only because that was the expression I saw on Clint's face as I spoke.

At least at first. But as I fumbled to form the words to confess my greatest sin, Clint broke into a wide grin.

"I know what you're going to say, but there's really no need."

Of course, he didn't. Or at least if he did, he was trying to trick me into thinking he didn't with some comic relief.

"Is that so?"

"Absolutely. There is only one thing that matters to me now that you could possibly say, so that has to be what's so important. Because if it were something else, you'd know it doesn't matter anymore."

"Yeah? What do you think it is?" I said through a smile, my way of letting him know that I had dropped the weightier subject that had started us down this path.

"With the caveat that reading your mind has never been my strong suit, I would say that you're worried that I won't be able to go on without you."

When he finished saying this, Clint was no longer smiling. In fact, he looked even sadder than I'd felt when I began this conversation.

"And," he continued, filling the awkward pause, "I'm sorry to tell you that the answer is that I won't." He forced another smile. "But on the positive side, I will go on because I don't have any other choice, and because Ella and Charlotte need me to do that. Actually, I think the main reason that I'll go on is that I know it's what you want me to do, and even after you're gone, I won't want to disappoint you."

His eyes were wet, and I was losing the battle to hold back my own tears.

"You're wrong about one thing, Clint."

"Yeah, what's that?"

"You're very good at reading my mind."

———

Within the week, I started to feel the fatigue that Dr. Goldman had warned would be the marker that my life would be measured in weeks. Just like he said, I lost my appetite and slept most of the day. I took solace that I didn't lose interest in my family. The last decision I made was for their protection: I asked Clint to transfer me to hospice.

"Are you sure you wouldn't be more comfortable here at home?"

"I might be, but it's not good for you or the girls to see me like that. To just wake up one day and find that I'm dead."

Everyone in my family disagreed. But as with many other decisions I had made for my family through the years, I knew what was best. So on May 1, I entered hospice. Mother's Day was the following week, and I wondered if I'd still be alive by then.

My room was nice enough, with more flowers than I was accustomed to being around. Seemingly everyone I had ever encountered in life had sent flowers when news spread that I was entering hospice. During the day the sun streamed in, making the place seem like something other than what it was. But at night, after Clint and the girls left, I felt lonelier than I could ever remember.

It's a strange thing to imagine making your case for entry to heaven. I had never really believed in an afterlife, and even if there were one, I couldn't imagine that admission rested on your advocacy skills. Nor did I think of it as a ledger of sins and good deeds that were tallied. I imagined it more like college admissions, with no single factor being dispositive, but instead a weighing of different strengths and weaknesses.

On that scale, did I merit entry to the good place? I had tried my best to be a good person, although that effort had not always been successful. But I felt that, on balance, I had done as well as most, maybe better. Sometimes I was reminded of something Clint said about criminal law—how a lie, no matter how small, could poison the entire defense. Did infidelity do that in a marriage? Do you give up your right to say that you were a good spouse, or even a good person, if you committed that single sin?

———

The last thing I remember was the girls beside me. Someone must have told them that it was the end, because Clint suggested that they each spend some time alone with me.

Charlotte went first. Almost at once, she climbed onto my hospital bed and nestled next to me, the way she did on Sunday mornings. It pained me that I lacked the strength to move my hand atop hers. She cried the entire time we were together. I have no recollection of how long we lay like that, Charlotte sobbing, but at some point, Clint came in to get her, finally lifting her off the bed, as if she too lacked the strength to move.

When it was her turn, Ella cried as well, but she was able to rein in her emotions. She talked to me for a few minutes, but I didn't say anything in response, unable to engage on any level that she could discern.

Finally, she said, "I thought that you'd like it if I sang something, Mom."

I don't know if I smiled or cried at the thought of it, but inside me it felt as if I was doing both. For a moment, Ella was still, and I felt a shooting fear that she'd thought better of the gesture. It turned out, however, that her pause was to consider which song to sing.

She started slowly, almost in a whisper, but soon enough I realized that she had selected "My Heart Will Go On" from *Titanic*. As I listened, I knew beyond any doubt that I was in heaven.

PART THREE

NICHOLAS ZAMORA

July 2020

28.

"Liars are like criminals. Only the bad ones get caught. The good ones ply their trade without consequence. The very good ones, like me, can make millions from it." After a dramatic beat, I added, "Of course, I'm only confessing that I'm a liar."

At that point, I'd laugh to make sure that everyone in the audience knew I was joking. "As a novelist, I have to own the fact that I lie for a living—and that I'm well paid to do so."

It was part of the presentation I made at book-signing events. It never ceased to be an applause line.

If I had been born twenty years later, reaching adulthood in the internet era, when my entire life was available for review at the other end of a Google search, I'm quite certain *Precipice* would never have been published. Even if by some act of God it had been, there's no way that Hollywood would have adapted it, or that my Oscar wouldn't have launched a thousand protests and boycotts, effectively ending my career. Lucky for me, I enjoyed these successes and the many others that followed before my life story was available for public consumption. By the time my Wikipedia page went up, complete with an entire section about my trial for Carolyn's murder, my reputation as a perennial bestseller and Hollywood go-to script doctor was solid enough that I could weather the decades-old whiff of scandal. If anything, my clouded past burnished my image as a literary bad boy.

In the years that followed the publication of *Precipice*, my professional fortunes knew no bounds. Everything I wrote almost immediately shot to the top of the bestseller list, and I was often short-listed for one prestigious prize or another. I didn't win another Oscar, but Hollywood paid me a boatload of money for my work.

My personal life was less successful, which was not to say that I lived like a monk. There were many women through the years, but none of them made me rethink my commitment to bachelorhood, the tragic end of my first marriage having caused me to swear off the institution.

Until I met Samantha Remsen.

Like many of the women I'd dated since finding success, Samantha was in the "business," and younger than I. Young enough that when we met—on a movie based on one of my less successful novels—she'd been cast as the love interest, while I was closing in on eligibility for social security.

Despite our thirty-year age difference, we clicked from day one. It was a connection that I'd felt only once before. Not with Carolyn, but with Anne.

I was long over whirlwind romances, though, so things proceeded slowly. Glacially, by Hollywood standards. We dated for the better part of a year before she agreed to give up her LA apartment and move into my house in Malibu. A year after that, we got married.

I'd written a lot about love in my life, usually mining my feelings for Anne as the basis for my characters' emotions. But being married to Samantha showed me that whatever it was that Anne and I had shared—lust, loneliness, fear of never being happy—it wasn't truly love. With Samantha I experienced for the first time the pure bliss of being with another person and desiring nothing else but more of the same.

Like any modern woman, Samantha had googled me early on, which led her to ask about the death of my first wife. At the time, I gave her my standard response: *It was a tragedy, compounded by my being falsely accused. She really did die in the bathtub. Sometimes these things happen.*

That was the one and only time we discussed it until, one night, shortly after we became engaged, I told Samantha things I had never shared with anyone—about my affair with my best friend's wife, about my love for Anne, about how it had led me foolishly to marry Carolyn, as if she were some spirit that would ward off my impure thoughts.

Of course, I left out the one thing she wanted to know.

"Did you kill her?" Samantha asked, nervousness in her voice suggesting she was afraid to hear the answer.

"No," I said. "But I wasn't there to save her, so yes."

"Everything makes so much more sense now."

"What does?"

"*Precipice, Redemption.* Everything you've written, actually. They're all, at their core, stories about guilt."

"Like they say, you write what you know, I guess."

"You know other things too, Nick. Maybe you should write about them."

From time to time, the same thought had occurred to me. I had always come at it from a different angle, though. Not that I should write about different things, but whether I would have written anything in the first place had it not been for my sins.

———

For the first few years of our marriage, I was happier than I'd ever been. But somewhere around the three-year mark, I began to fear that Samantha was pulling away from me. At first, I attributed her distance to career troubles. She was now on the wrong end of thirty for lead roles and had stubbornly refused to give up that persona when her agent pitched her the young-mom parts that were the normal progression for an actress of her age. As a result, she didn't work for nearly a year.

It was therefore something of a godsend when Samantha was offered the female lead in a new thriller that was being directed by Tyree Jefferson. Although my wife was over the moon about it, I had reservations. Tyree had a well-known reputation for bedding his leading ladies, and I did not want to be the cuckold in a Hollywood scandal. When I mentioned this to Samantha, she said, "If I turned down parts because the director was known to stick it in the talent, my IMDB page would be blank."

So she booked the job, and only afterward told me that she'd be on location in the Hamptons all summer. When I expressed displeasure with the arrangement, she suggested I come to New York with her.

"The studio rented me this house on the beach. You can write looking out on the Atlantic just as easily as you do overlooking the Pacific."

She sounded sincere, but she was well aware of my aversion to being on the East Coast. I'd been back to Manhattan many times since Carolyn's death, as it was necessary to meet with my agents and publisher from time to time, but I felt claustrophobic every minute I spent on the island. Just being in the same time zone as Carolyn's grave, as Clinton, as Anne while she was alive, as the memories of a life I'd left behind long ago, made me deeply uneasy.

Had I felt more secure in my marriage, I'm certain I would have declined the offer. The last six months, however, had not been Samantha's and my best. The age difference, which we had thought of as other people's problem, had finally caught up with us. Samantha was showing every indication that she had become disenchanted with being married to someone she saw more as a mentor than an equal partner. Besides which, she wanted children. She knew going in that I felt too old for fatherhood. I assumed we had reached an understanding on that point, but as her fertility window began to close, the issue clearly remained a live one for her. Last, but certainly not least, I was experiencing the insecurity inevitable when a man in his sixties marries a beautiful woman half his age. It manifested in needy and controlling behavior that, not surprisingly, served only to push Samantha further away.

So against my better judgment, or perhaps because I was more afraid of losing Samantha than I was of confronting the ghosts of my past life, I followed my wife to East Hampton.

29.

The house that the studio had rented for Samantha was the quintessential one-percenter summer home—five bedrooms, as many baths, double-height living room, statement staircase, and a towering deck overlooking the Atlantic Ocean. We quickly fell into a routine. Samantha went to the set in the morning, and I wrote at a bay window with an oceanfront view. Sometimes the shoot would run late, but Samantha assured me that Tyree was behaving like a professional, and I took comfort that my wife seemed happy to see me when she came home each night.

In mid-July, Tyree had a dinner party for the leading actors of the cast, including plus-ones. Although there were few things I could imagine enjoying less than listening to Tyree go on about how Fellini and Scorsese were profound influences on him, I told my wife that I was looking forward to meeting her coworkers after hearing so much about them, not to mention admiring their work for years.

The guest list included our host, who was presently unattached and didn't have a plus-one at dinner; Samantha and me; Jaydon Lennox, the male lead in the movie, and his wife, Paige Anderson-Lennox, an Oscar-nominated actress in her own right; Chloe Lassiter, the film's ingenue, who I was hoping would be the conquest Tyree fixated on instead of my wife, and her boyfriend, a rapper I'd never heard of who went by the stage name T-Rex. I was told to refer to him as either *T* or *Rex*, but not both.

The studio had rented Tyree a house that was less than a ten-minute walk from ours. Whereas ours was a traditional colonial, his was all glass and steel and sharp angles. I recognized its exterior from a movie a few years back about a ruthless hedge-fund billionaire.

Wardrobe must have outfitted Tyree for the evening. He was clad in white linen from head to toe. He was more than handsome enough to pull it off, still looking every inch like the model he had been in one of his previous incarnations. He had made the leap to behind the camera less than five years ago, first trying his hand at fashion photography, then short films, which led to his breakout indie effort that won the top prize at the Toronto Film Festival. Two bigger-budget features had followed, the latter of which was a box-office success, paving the way for a major studio to put up $50 million for his new thriller, the movie that had caused all of us to assemble in the Hamptons.

Tyree greeted me with a firm handshake, and a "Good you could come, mate," just in case I'd forgotten that he was British. Then he pulled Samantha into him and kissed her on the lips, which might have been the way he greeted all women, but I got the sense it was meant as a message to me.

"Sam, looking gorgeous as ever," Tyree said.

No one called my wife *Sam*. She had told me during our initial introduction that she hated the diminutive of her name. Apparently, she had made an exception for Tyree.

The others were on the patio, the rain forcing them to congregate under the protection of the awning. A spectacularly beautiful woman dressed in a revealing toga appeared, holding a tray. On it were a glass of scotch, a cotton-candy-colored mixed drink of some sort, and several white tablets slightly larger than an aspirin.

"Tonight's signature cocktail is a Suck, Bang, and Blow," Tyree announced. "It's a real drink. I did not name it. Google it, if you like. It's got . . . a lot of stuff in it. Tequila, vodka, some peppermint schnapps, the list goes on and on. Nick, Sam told me that that you were a scotch man, so I broke into my private stock and opened up this little Glenfarclas forty-year-old. I think you're going to like it."

The others were holding, or had already finished, the signature cocktail. I wasn't going to turn down a hundred-dollar glass of scotch, even if I thought it the height of pomposity to serve it at a party.

"And, of course, a little X to start the evening off right," Tyree added.

Samantha didn't hesitate to reach for both the pill and the drink.

"That's my girl," Tyree said. "Mine's just kicking in, and this stuff is . . . *Damn.*"

Chloe said, "I only took half. How long before I'm allowed to take another one?"

T-Rex said, "No time like the present," and scooped up two pills. One he popped in his mouth, and the second he inserted into Chloe's.

Jaydon Lennox was a good decade younger than I but still the closest thing I had to a contemporary among the group. Not to be outdone by the younger set, he summoned the server and took a tablet as well.

"Look at you," Paige said to her husband.

"When in Rome," Jaydon replied.

Paige waved away the tray. "One is enough for me for now," she said, making it clear that I was the odd man out in this crowd.

Within an hour, the drug had done its work. While we ate dinner, Chloe intermittently made out with T-Rex, and I had the sense that something was definitely going on under the table between the Lennoxes. I was by now on my third scotch, but I could have consumed the entire bottle and still not achieved the others' level of inebriation.

After dinner, despite the downpour, Chloe and T-Rex went into the pool, sans clothing. I was pleased that the Lennoxes drew the line at nudity and dancing with their hands all over each other. I excused myself to go to the bathroom, and when I returned, Tyree and Samantha were beside the Lennoxes, swaying to the music, their bodies far closer than I—or any husband—would have deemed appropriate.

I put my hand firmly on Tyree's shoulder and pried him off my wife.

"Relax, mate," he said.

"I think you're maybe a little too relaxed, my friend."

"Well, it *is* a party. I don't know what old men like to do, but I intend to have fun while I still can."

"Have all the fun you want, just not with my wife."

"Don't you think that's something for her to decide? I don't hear Sam saying anything."

The smile that had prefaced his prior remarks was now nowhere to be seen. In its place was a stern look, like he was itching for a fight. If I'd been ten years younger, I might have answered him with a right cross; instead I turned to Samantha, expecting her to tell him off.

To my surprise and embarrassment, she didn't say a word. In fact, when we made eye contact, she looked away.

"Samantha?" I said.

"I don't want to get into a thing with you here," she said.

"Then let's get out of here."

Chloe and T-Rex were still splashing around naked in the pool, seemingly oblivious to the drama I was engaged in. The Lennoxes, however, had stopped their dancing and were taking in the scene in all its horror.

"I know you told Sam not to do this picture," Tyree said, his voice now at full argument level. "And I know you said that because of me. But I told her that her husband was a fucking twat. She's doing the picture because she believes in my artistic vision, and because she *knows* you're a fucking twat."

I shouted back: "She didn't agree to be in your film because of your *artistic vision*, you asshole. She did it because the studio's paying her a shitload of money."

It degenerated from there. He called me an old man. I yelled that he was a poser. There were taunts at my manhood, at his reputation.

All the while, Samantha continued to stand by mutely. She finally pulled me aside and said, "You need to leave."

"Not without you," I said.

"I don't mean the party, Nick. I mean you need to go back to LA. Give me some space out here, and we can talk again in a few weeks. I'll stay here tonight, and until you leave for LA."

I stormed out of the house alone. It was only once I was in the car that I realized what was still to come. The other couples would depart shortly, leaving Samantha and Tyree alone. She would tell him that she had sent me back to LA, and then he'd do what he had undoubtedly been thinking about doing with my wife from the moment he'd cast her as his leading lady.

I considered turning the car around and heading back to the party to settle matters with Tyree once and for all, but decided that discretion was the better part of valor. That meant waiting until morning before raising the issue with Samantha. We'd both be calmer and could discuss what had happened at the party like adults. If she wanted me to go back to LA, I would, but not before telling her that I would await her return, either when the shoot ended or whenever whatever was going on with her and Tyree had run its course.

And I'd make sure that Samantha knew that I loved her and wanted us to stay married.

30.

Less than two hours later, Samantha stepped into our bedroom. Her gait was shaky, a testament to the fact she had probably taken another pill after I left and was still high as a kite. Her expression confirmed that she was feeling no pain.

"I left my phone here," she said.

I hadn't realized it until then, but she was right. Samantha's phone was atop the charging pod on her nightstand.

"Can we talk?" I asked.

"There's nothing to say," she answered.

"Please. I . . . just need to say a few things."

"Then talk."

I was lying in bed, with her standing above me, her arms folded across her chest. It was the absolutely wrong dynamic for me to profess my undying love. I wanted her to sit, to listen to me. Unfortunately, there were no chairs in the bedroom, and I knew suggesting she join me in the bed, or even asking her to sit on it, would be a nonstarter.

"Okay," I said, getting out of the bed. "Can we do it outside?"

I was wearing only my boxer shorts, so I grabbed a T-shirt but still felt underdressed, especially with Samantha still in the little black dress and high heels she'd worn to the party. She shrugged and followed me out onto the deck. The rain had stopped, but the air was still moist, giving the impression that this was a short interlude in the storm and the skies would open again shortly. For the moment, though, the air had cooled substantially, and I felt a pleasant sea breeze, the likes of which we hadn't experienced in days.

This was my chance. To convince Samantha not to leave me. To swear that we could still be happy together. To beg, if it came to that.

The first step in that process was to get her to sit down. I motioned for Samantha to sit beside me on the outdoor sofa.

"Everything is soaking wet," she said, holding her ground at a distance as she steadied herself against the deck railing and shivered slightly in the breeze.

She was right about that. I'd felt the wetness the moment I sat.

"Okay. Let me first say that I'm so sorry for losing my temper. I love you, Samantha. And I'll do anything—and I mean *anything*—to keep us together. Just tell me what it is, please, and I'll do it."

Her expression remains etched in my mind, and yet, no matter how many times I conjure it, I can't for the life of me decipher what she was feeling in that moment. Would she reciprocate? I wondered. Or tell me my feelings were unrequited?

Her initial response was to hoist herself up onto the deck's railing, as if to regain the high ground for the discussion to come. But the railing was slick with rain, and her hand slipped as she sought to balance herself. Without a word, she fell backward, over the edge of the deck. A half second later, I heard the thud of her body hitting the ground.

For a moment, I couldn't move, paralyzed by the unreality of the moment. Then I leaped up, ran to the railing, and peered down. The moonless sky rendered everything so dark that I couldn't see the ground, much less my wife.

I shouted her name. No response came back.

Racing downstairs, I held out hope that she was okay. But as soon as I came outside and saw her, I knew by the unnatural turn in her neck that she was dead. Her expression was not one of horror or fear; instead she appeared contemplative, as if still considering what I'd said.

This was the second time in my life I had stared at my wife's dead body. The shock of someone being alive one moment and gone the next felt much like it had thirty-four years ago. But whereas Carolyn's death had freed me from a life I didn't want, Samantha's ended a marriage I had loved more than life itself.

As shock gave way to grief, I began to cry, at first haltingly, then sobbing beyond my control. Samantha was so young, she'd had a full life ahead of her, and now she was gone. I wished more than anything that she'd never come home, that she'd stayed at Tyree's. We could have sorted things out later. Or never. The last thing I'd wanted was for her to die.

As I convulsed, I cradled Samantha's head in my arms. I brought my hand up, and even though I couldn't see the blood in the dark, I could feel its sticky wetness on my palm.

That's when I realized I would be blamed for Samantha's death. No one would believe that Samantha had fallen from the deck. They'd assume that, having gotten away with murder once, I'd thought I could do it again.

That realization flipped a switch in me. My tears subsided and my grief moved aside, replaced by the impulse of self-preservation.

I had to act quickly or else be blamed for killing Samantha.

Our neighbors were all weekenders. One of those inverse relationships of the ultra- wealthy—the more expensive the real estate, the less often it's occupied. The houses on either side were dark inside, and while the exterior lights of the modern home to my right were fully illuminated, I assumed that they were set on a timer to scare off would-be intruders approaching from the beach, and that no one was actually home on a Wednesday night.

My choices had become binary. I could call the police and explain exactly what had happened and likely be arrested for a murder I did not commit, or I could carry Samantha into the ocean, swim out as far as I could, and then hope the currents did the rest.

"I'm sorry, Samantha," I whispered.

The summer before my senior year in high school, I worked as a lifeguard at Jones Beach. To get the job, I had to swim fifty yards in the ocean in under fifty seconds, or something like that. During training, I learned everything from the fireman's carry to pulling live bodies through surf. That had been almost half a century ago and the last time I'd tried either.

With great effort, I hoisted Samantha onto my shoulders. That was the hard part. Carrying her out into the surf was not as difficult as I had feared. The ocean was much colder than I anticipated, but the shock lasted only a second, until Samantha and I were fully submerged. I adjusted her body so I now had her in a towing grip. Looking back to shore, I spotted the lights of our neighbor's house, but when I turned toward the horizon, I saw only darkness.

It didn't take long to get farther out than I'd be comfortable going if I weren't trying to discard a dead body. Maybe a hundred yards. But this was no time for half measures. I needed to go farther. As far as I possibly could.

That turned out to be maybe another fifty yards. By that point my arms ached, and I was tired enough that I worried about my ability to swim back safely. The lights on the shore were small now, like pinholes in the distance, and the waves had started up again, causing me to swallow the brine more than once.

I took the deepest breath I could and dived under, pulling my wife's lifeless body with me. I descended as far as I was able, probably no more than ten feet. Then I pushed down on Samantha's corpse with my feet and launched myself up.

I waited there, treading water, praying that Samantha would not rise to the surface. My visibility was limited, but it seemed as if I had succeeded in my objective.

The deed done, I swam a steady breaststroke toward the lights in the distance. For what seemed like an hour, I didn't seem to be getting any closer to shore, the current continually pulling me back. Finally, my knees hit sand and I could stand. By then I was as exhausted as I could ever remember being, on the verge of passing out. I fell to my hands and knees, panting.

I felt a spatter of drops on my back. The rain had begun again. I looked up at the sky with gratitude. Like the ocean, it would be my accomplice in washing away all evidence of what had happened that evening.

As my adrenaline waned, I was overwhelmed by loss, by my shame. And once again I began to sob.

31.

Shortly after nine the following morning, a knock came at the front door. I waited a full two minutes (watching the numbers on my phone switch over) before heading downstairs to give the appearance that the visitor had awakened me. I added to that half a minute to brush my teeth and throw on a robe. Catching my reflection as I headed downstairs, I thought I'd properly captured the look of a just-awakened man my age who had not spent the prior evening watching his wife fall to her death from the balcony or dragging her body into the ocean.

It surprised me how easily I was able to compartmentalize. But the path ahead was clear, and the stakes too great for me to falter. I had no choice but to play this part—the concerned husband, unsure about his wife's whereabouts. In a few days, even if Samantha's body weren't found, she would be presumed dead, and then I could grieve.

A young female production assistant had been assigned the task of gathering Samantha for the day's shoot. The poor kid had been calling Samantha nonstop for the last two hours, thinking that my wife was too hungover to answer the phone, when in reality, I had turned the ringer off and let the calls go to voice mail.

"Hi, Mr. Zamora," she said cheerfully. "I'm so sorry to wake you. Tyree Jefferson sent me here to see if Ms. Remsen was at home."

"I just woke up," I said, "but isn't she at the shoot?"

"No. That's why he asked me to come here. He thought that maybe she had overslept or something."

My strategy was simple: Show no concern, not at first anyway. Give off the *I'm sure Samantha is on her way* vibe.

"Come in. I'm pretty sure Samantha's not here, though. I'm sorry, what was your name?"

"Katlyn."

"Katlyn, I'm sorry you came all the way out here. She's probably held up in traffic."

Tyree must have given Katlyn instructions not to return to the set without Samantha, because she didn't budge. "The thing is, Samantha was supposed to be on set at seven." She looked at her phone. "It's 9:12. She's never been late before, and Mr. Jefferson's worried about her."

I put on my slightly concerned face. "Uh, okay. Let me call her. My phone's upstairs. Just make yourself comfortable, and I'll be down in a second."

Once I was alone in the bedroom, I prepared myself for the next level of distress. A husband whose wife had not shown up for work, and who wasn't answering her phone.

I walked back downstairs with a confused expression. "Her phone is on the nightstand. She must have forgotten it this morning."

"She never arrived on set," Katlyn said, a note of concern in her voice suggesting I was not treating the situation with the appropriate urgency.

I sighed. My way of telling her that the studio was making something out of nothing.

"Let me check if her car's in the garage," I said with exaggerated exasperation.

After opening the door to the garage, we both saw the red Porsche convertible that Samantha had rented, right beside my black one. "Did the studio send a car for her this morning?" I asked, now acting as if I were confused by this turn of events.

If Samantha had to be on set extremely early, they'd typically send a car. But a seven o'clock call didn't qualify for that treatment, which meant that she should have driven herself out to Montauk this morning.

"No. Her call wasn't until seven. That's the regular time, and she always drives herself."

I rubbed my face like an increasingly worried husband. "It's not like Samantha not to show up for her call," I said. "Do you mind calling Tyree and see if . . . I don't know, maybe she's there by now? Maybe she called an Uber."

Katlyn did as I requested. Even though the phone was pressed against her ear, I could hear it ring.

"Is she there?" Tyree said without a *hello*.

"No. Her phone's still here and her car is in the garage. Her husband says he has no idea where she is."

"Let me talk to him," I said.

As Katlyn handed me her phone, I focused on showing her and Tyree that I was now concerned about my wife's whereabouts, which required that I pretend as if any acrimony from the previous evening was the last thing on my mind.

"Tyree, it's Nick. You sure she didn't show this morning? I mean, that she's not in her trailer or on a walk or something?"

"Yeah. We've looked everywhere for her. If her car's still there, I don't see how she got here."

"Right. I thought Uber maybe. I gotta tell you, I'm worried." Then I laid the groundwork for my defense. "I'm not sure she even came home last night. She hadn't by the time I went to sleep, and she wasn't here this morning."

My lie was met with a few moments of silence. Then Tyree said, "I drove her there at about one thirty, so I know she went home last night."

I considered challenging him on that but decided the less I said now, the better. "If she shows up, call me immediately. You know my number?"

I knew he didn't.

"Give it to Katlyn," he said and disconnected.

I gave Katlyn my phone number and asked for Tyree's. She said she wasn't at liberty to give his number out, so she gave me hers instead. We promised each other we'd call immediately upon any sighting of Samantha.

As soon as Katlyn's car receded from view, I considered what I'd do if Samantha had legitimately disappeared. If I truly had no idea of her whereabouts.

The logical assumption, if Samantha hadn't arrived at work or even taken the car, was that she'd gone somewhere on foot. But where? A walk along the beach? A morning swim in the ocean? Either way, a concerned husband would check that out.

When I exited the back of the house, I saw that the previous evening's rain had washed away all evidence that I'd been on the beach. So after having worried about leaving my footprints in the sand last night, I made new ones today. I even jogged to the shoreline, in case forensic techs could determine my level of urgency by my gait.

I didn't go into the water. That seemed too much, too soon. But, standing at the water's edge, I took some comfort that Samantha's body hadn't floated back to shore on the first tide.

After this bit of reconnaissance, I returned to the house. I sat there, staring out at the ocean view for the next forty-five minutes, trying to convince myself that I'd done nothing wrong, not really. I was not responsible for Samantha's death. It was an accident. And everything I was doing now fell under the category of extreme measures to survive extreme circumstances.

At ten, I called Katlyn. "Samantha still isn't back," I said, "and now I'm really worried. I think . . . I think I should call the police."

32.

The police arrived within an hour of my call. By then, I had showered and put on clothes.

More importantly, I'd rehearsed how this would go. My guiding mantra was that I was completely in the dark. I wouldn't deny that there had been drinking and drugs the night before, or even that Samantha and I had fought at the party, after which I'd stormed off alone. All of that was easily verified. Instead, I would say that these things happened from time to time. *Showbiz people, you know.*

I would be emphatic, however, that Samantha had never come home last night.

Two plainclothes detectives knocked on my door. Detective Yuhas was the younger of the duo, midthirties at most. It wasn't hard to imagine that his thinning blond hair had once been down to his shoulders, and he was probably the kind of kid who'd surfed more than he studied in high school. His partner, Detective Hibbitts, had a more hardened look, sporting a goatee with a hint of gray. He carried himself with a swagger that suggested he was a second- or even third-generation cop.

Befitting his seniority, Detective Hibbitts took the lead. "Mr. Zamora, I understand that your wife didn't show up for work this morning. That she was expected on the set in Montauk at seven a.m., and you don't know where she is, and you haven't heard from her at all today. Is that right?"

"Yes. That's right. The last time I saw her was at this party we went to last night at the home of her director, Tyree Jefferson. There was a lot of drinking and some drug use, and things got a little out of control between Tyree and me. I wanted us to leave, but Samantha said she needed to stay behind to smooth things over. She said she'd be home later. I left the party . . . I don't know . . . my guess is sometime around midnight. I waited for an hour or so for Samantha, but then I went to sleep. Tyree told me he dropped her off at about one thirty, but I didn't hear her come in. And when I woke up, she wasn't here. She forgot to take her phone to the party last night, and it's still here. And her car's in the garage."

Detective Hibbitts asked, "Have you looked in every room of the house?"

I could feel my already-heightened heart rate kick up a notch. I hadn't gone into the guest rooms or guest bathrooms, of which there were four each. It hadn't occurred to me to do so. But the question suggested that a concerned husband would have left no corner of the house unchecked.

"Yeah. I've looked everywhere," I lied.

Both detectives nodded. Apparently, that was the right answer.

"Outside too?" Detective Hibbitts asked.

"Yes. I went out to the beach to see if she might have taken a walk. I also went to the pool because . . . well, I thought that maybe she had gone for a swim or something and . . ." My voice was trembling, as I was off-script now, telling them things that I might later regret.

"Could she have gone into the ocean? Either last night or this morning?"

"I don't think so," I said and left it at that. Less is more in these situations, as Clinton once told me.

"I'm going to go check out the beach," Detective Hibbitts said to his partner. "Why don't you take Mr. Zamora through the timeline?"

Detective Yuhas's invocation of my name snapped my attention back to him. "You told us that last night you left the party alone, then came home and went to sleep. What time was that?"

"Like I said, I left the party a little after midnight."

"Okay, and then you fell asleep? And your wife, to your knowledge, never came home?"

"That's right."

"What was your argument with the director about?" Detective Yuhas asked.

This was the first sign that the police were already considering the possibility of foul play. They'd gone from trying to find Samantha to thinking about why she might be missing.

This would be ground zero of my fight for survival. The first battle in the war to convince the police that I wasn't holding back.

"I think it was mainly about our both being drunk, to tell you the truth. I said something about how I didn't like the way he was acting toward Samantha, and he said something to me like I was too old for her. You know, stupid stuff like that."

"You said that there were drugs at the party?"

"Yeah. I didn't partake, but the others did. Ecstasy, I think."

I put my head in my hands, if only to hide from the scrutiny I was receiving. I had more or less accurately described the altercation. The other party guests would undoubtedly have more colorful iterations of who had said what to whom, but at least the cops wouldn't be able to say that I hadn't been candid from the get-go.

"And after that, you left the party alone?"

He meant without Samantha. And what he really meant was that she had stayed behind with the director that I thought she was sleeping with.

This was the big lie. The one that mattered. To convince the police that Samantha was not angry with me. That Tyree was the villain.

"She said that she needed to make nice with Tyree or she'd get fired. I understood. The movie meant a lot to her. She told me to go home and let her deal with him."

"Okay," Detective Yuhas said, as if he were buying it. "Then when you woke up, tell me what happened at that point."

I was pleased to be back on safer ground. There was no need for me to tell him anything but the God's honest truth about the events of this morning, which I proceeded to do.

"When did you realize that her phone was here?" Detective Yuhas asked.

"I remember her saying something about leaving it at home when we were at the party. I didn't think about it again until the PA came by this morning. She said that she'd been trying to reach Samantha, so I went upstairs and called her myself. That's when I saw that her phone was still on her night table."

"Okay," Detective Yuhas said in a way that made me feel like he accepted my lie at face value. "Can I see your wife's car?"

"Sure. This way."

In the garage, Detective Yuhas put his hand on the front hood. "It hasn't been driven lately," he said, like a Native American tracker in an old western. Then he opened the driver's side door. He took a quick set of pictures with his phone, then turned on its flashlight to peer inside.

"Did you notice anything that was missing?" he asked after turning off his phone's flashlight and closing the car door.

The question didn't make much sense to me. "In the car?"

"No. From the bedroom," he said.

That's when it clicked. He was probing whether Samantha had come home, collected her clothing, and left again. I had apparently done a less-than-persuasive job of convincing him that Samantha wasn't leaving me for Tyree.

My first impulse was to lie. *No, nothing's missing, officer. I checked that too, and everything is exactly as it should be.* But my paranoia worked in my favor this time, and I realized Detective Yuhas had laid a trap. There was no reason for me to check to see if anything was missing because I had told him that I didn't think she'd even come home last night.

"I honestly don't know. I didn't think to check."

Detective Hibbitts reemerged through the living room. "The rain did a good job of washing everything away," he said. "All I saw out there were your footprints, Mr. Zamora."

"The car engine's cold to the touch, and there's no sign she's used it in the last twenty-four hours," Detective Yuhas said, bringing his partner up to speed with how he'd spent the last few minutes. "We were just about to go upstairs to check out the bedroom. In particular, I wanted to see if her suitcase is still here and take a look at her phone."

The detectives walked a step behind me up our grand staircase, and then they followed me down the long hallway. When we entered the bedroom, I immediately went to the closet and opened the door. Among Samantha's hundred pairs of shoes and enough clothes for a small boutique were her two suitcases.

"Is anything missing?" Detective Hibbitts asked.

"No. At least not that I can tell. It looks like it always does."

"Is the clothing she wore last night here?"

"Let me see."

I rummaged through Samantha's closet, pretending to look for the dress she had worn the night before. After I'd touched half of the hanging garments, I announced my find.

"It's not here."

I tried to look terrified now. If her dress wasn't in the closet, that would mean she hadn't come home last night. And if she hadn't come home, that would mean that something was seriously wrong.

Detective Hibbitts was examining Samantha's phone. "Do you know the password?"

"I don't," I said, truthfully.

"Mind if we take it? Someone might be able to open it."

"Of course," I said, momentarily panicked that there might be something in her phone that I wouldn't want them to see. Sexting with Tyree, perhaps.

I decided to put my thumb on the scale a little. "Tyree Jefferson told me he drove Samantha home, but he must be lying," I said, as if shocked by the realization. "Maybe she left his house and walked home. It's only a few houses away along the beach. Maybe someone grabbed her?"

I thought this was clever on my part. I was planting the seed that Tyree Jefferson was a liar, but not going so far as to accuse him of killing Samantha. The detectives were more than capable of connecting those dots on their own.

"There's no reason to leap to any conclusion," Detective Hibbitts said. "Most of the time in a missing-persons situation, it ends up being crossed signals. When the wife finally gets home, she can't understand why all the commotion."

He smiled, as if that might be the case here. From the look in his eyes, though, I knew he didn't believe it.

33.

After the police left, I did what I told them I'd already done—searched every room in the house. My lie turned out to be harmless on that score. Of course none of the rooms contained Samantha. But more importantly, there also wasn't any evidence to reveal that she had ever come home last night.

I'd now have about twenty-four hours of solitude. Time to think through the next steps and mourn Samantha. Come tomorrow morning, when it became clear this wasn't, as Detective Hibbitts had said, a crossed-signals thing, the police would need to go public with the fact that Samantha was missing, and the charade would begin again.

It turned out I was wrong. By about twenty-three hours.

The first call was from a number I didn't recognize. I invariably let those go to voice mail, but today I couldn't follow my usual protocol. A man with a missing wife would answer a call from an unknown number on the chance that it was from Samantha using someone else's phone. Or even a kidnapper making a ransom demand.

"Hello?"

The voice on the other end spoke so quickly that I didn't catch his name, but the TMZ part I heard loud and clear. Someone with the East Hampton police department had apparently leaked the news of Samantha's disappearance. Before I could respond to the caller's introduction, my phone beeped again, alerting me to another call coming in. This one also came from a number outside of my contact list. A moment later, a third unknown caller flashed on my screen.

The media frenzy had begun.

"I'm sorry, I don't have any comment," I said to the TMZ guy and hung up.

I put my phone on the coffee table and asked myself: What would Nick Zamora, worried husband of a missing wife, do now? I concluded he would call the police.

I dialed the number on the card Detective Hibbitts had given me.

"Hibbitts."

"It's Nick Zamora. I'm being inundated with press calls. I don't know what to do. I don't want to answer the phone, but I'm worried that Samantha might try to call me from a different number—one I don't recognize."

Silence from the other end of the line. I thought I might have been disconnected.

"Are you there?"

"Yeah, I'm here. I'm just . . . look, if it's already out, maybe it'll get some tips coming our way. Or prompt your wife to call." I heard some clicking on a keyboard. "Yeah, it's all over the internet," he confirmed.

I was momentarily distracted by a firm knock at my front door. From the window I saw a mob walking up the front lawn, having gained entry through a narrow gap in the shrubbery that surrounded the property. It reminded me a bit of one of those zombie movies, where the undead march en masse.

"Uh, now there are people at my front door," I told him in a bit of a panic.

"Here's what we're going to do," the detective said calmly. "I'm going to send a car there right now. They'll take you back to the station, and then we'll make a public announcement. Sit tight until they get there."

I went upstairs to the bedroom and shut the door behind me. Out the window I could see the press corps growing on the street. I drew the curtains and grabbed my laptop.

It was worse than I had feared. Every website I clicked on had Samantha's disappearance as the lead story under a BREAKING NEWS banner. My phone was now buzzing nonstop—phone calls, texts, tweets—and the doorbell was blaring.

Within minutes, I heard the sirens. They steadily got louder as the police cruisers approached the house. Four uniformed men alighted. Two of them moved back to the front gate, which had automatically closed behind the squad cars. The other two walked up the path to my front door.

Neither cop introduced himself when I opened the door. Instead, one of them said, "The other officers are going to stay here to keep the press behind the gate. There's nothing we can do about them congregating in the street. That's public property."

I nodded that I understood. I'd been told the same thing by the Westchester police thirty-four years earlier.

———

The East Hampton Town Police Department was actually located in the town of Wainscott. It had jurisdiction over everything east of Wainscott, all the way to Montauk. It was not to be confused with the East Hampton Village Police Department, which was located in the village proper and had jurisdiction over only the smaller community. I wasn't clear how responsibility was divided between the two departments, but by virtue of the fact we were in the Town building, I assumed they had taken the lead.

The moment I stepped inside, I was transported back in time. Once again, I was in a police station regarding my wife. The workplace for cops had changed dramatically since Ronald Reagan was president, of course. Computer terminals were on every desk, the phones were modern, and even the coffee station was up to date. It was a Keurig, not a Mr. Coffee in sight.

My police chauffeurs had brought me directly to the detectives' room. I was greeted there by Detective Hibbitts.

"It's for the best that our timeline was moved up," he said. "It'll be a little embarrassing for your wife if she shows up on her own after we go public . . . but if it's something else, we'll be glad we got the jump on it. And I want to tell you that even though we're a small department by city standards, we're not some backwater place. About twenty years ago, there was a big murder investigation here, and we caught the guy and he got life in prison. They made a TV movie about it. *Murder in the Hamptons.*"

I nodded but hadn't caught the film. I winced at the thought that someday, maybe not long from now, this entire sequence of events would be similarly re-created by B-list actors for some Lifetime special.

Through a sliver in the doorway, I saw that the pressroom was filled beyond capacity. Not only were the one hundred or so chairs occupied, but people were also lined up along the back wall.

The Chief of Police was a guy named Richard Dempsey. He was a man in his sixties, tall and thin, with a silver mustache and thinning hair that still managed to cover most of his scalp. He was wearing his formal blues, complete with two rows of medals on the breast of his jacket.

He shook my hand. "I'm sorry about all of this," he said. "But making this type of public statement is the best way of figuring out what we have here. If your wife really is just taking some time for herself, she'll get the message that people who love her are worried, and she'll call in. And if it's something else, we'll know that too because we won't hear from her."

That horrible euphemism again . . . *something else.*

"Okay. Whatever you think is best."

"I'll start off by telling the press what we know, which isn't very much. Just her last known whereabouts. The clothing she was in, that kind of thing. Sometimes family members want to say something too. You know, in case she's watching."

The character I was now playing—concerned husband of missing wife—would have agreed. He would have stepped up to the mic and said how worried he was, how much he loved his wife, and if anyone knew anything that could help bring her back, they should call the police. He would shed tears as well. But I couldn't go that far.

"I . . . don't think I can," I said.

Chief Dempsey squinted, which I took to mean that he would have preferred I was more helpful. But then he said, "Okay, in that case, just stand behind me, and I'll do the talking."

With that, he nodded and headed into the pressroom. I was a step behind, with the detectives bringing up the rear. Chief Dempsey walked to the lectern while I stopped to his right and Detective Yuhas and Hibbitts stood on either flank.

"I want to emphasize that we are literally merely hours into the investigation, and thus far we have drawn no conclusions," Chief Dempsey began. "We are hopeful that Ms. Remsen will be found safe, and soon. She was last seen at approximately one thirty this morning, in the Ocean Avenue vicinity of East Hampton, wearing a black cocktail dress. We have no reason to suspect foul play of any kind. Not at this point. Anyone with any information regarding Samantha Remsen's whereabouts should contact the East Hampton police department. I will now answer your questions."

At that, seemingly every member of the press started shouting at once.

Chief Dempsey shouted over them. "I'm going to call on people whose mouths are shut and hands are raised, just like in kindergarten."

A dozen or so reporters got their turn. The first few questions were all variations on whether the police thought Samantha was dead. To each of those questions, Chief Dempsey said that there was no reason to believe that.

A redheaded reporter of about fifty asked, "Is Mr. Zamora a suspect?" As if I weren't standing feet from her.

Chief Dempsey said, "At this time, there are no suspects because, as I just said, we have no reason to believe that a crime has been committed."

The final question was asked by a guy who looked like he was still in college. "Would the same level of manpower be used if the missing person was not famous?"

Chief Dempsey didn't hesitate: "Yep."

As soon as Chief Dempsey moved for the door, the press started shouting their questions at me.

Detective Hibbitts grabbed my elbow and led me out of the room.

———

When I returned home, the press was still out in full force, but as the police had told me when I left, they were cordoned off the property, relegated to the street.

I entered the house without looking back, poured myself a stiff drink, and focused on the truth.

Samantha was dead. Our marriage hadn't been perfect, but I'd truly loved her. Only the day before, I'd been praying with all my might to a God I'd never believed in for Samantha not to leave me—either for Tyree or just because. And now she was gone forever.

I meandered through the rooms of the rental house without purpose. From time to time, I went out on the deck and peered over, reliving Samantha's fall. I stared at the ocean, imagining her body moving with the current, trying to keep from my mind the image of her providing sustenance for the fish.

I wondered how much longer I could maintain the charade.

For as long as it takes, came the answer in my mind.

———

At ten o'clock that night, Detective Hibbitts's number flashed on my phone screen. He could have been calling for a multitude of reasons—to tell me about a lead or to follow up on something he had previously forgotten to ask me. But I instinctively knew the reason.

"We found your wife's body," he said in a flat voice. Then, as if it were an afterthought, he added, "I'm sorry, Mr. Zamora."

I drove myself to the morgue to make the identification. Lying there in the drawer, covered in a sheet, Samantha barely looked like herself. Bloated and blue, her hair matted. She smelled like the ocean, even through the formaldehyde scent that permeated the room.

Detective Hibbitts told me that her body had been found washed up against a rock jetty, about four miles from our home.

"I don't understand why she would have gone for a swim in the ocean at night," I said.

Detective Hibbitts didn't provide an answer. Instead, he said, "Your first wife, she drowned too, didn't she?"

34.

Samantha's mother lived in a retirement community in central New Jersey, about twenty minutes from where Samantha had grown up. Samantha's sister, Danielle, still lived in their hometown with her husband and three young children.

I agreed that Samantha could be buried near them. In part because the alternative was an LA funeral, and that would have brought out the stars and the paparazzi. The other reason was that it was the least I could do for her family after withholding from them the circumstances of Samantha's death.

After I made this concession, the Remsen family must have decided that I served no further purpose for them, because they broke off all contact. None of her relatives returned any of my phone calls or texts in the ensuing days. Even when we met at the funeral parlor on the day Samantha was to be laid to rest, her mother refused to look at me. Danielle dispatched her husband to tell me that the family would appreciate it if I didn't communicate with them at all during the service and kept at least ten feet away at all times.

Samantha's funeral was a modest affair, especially by Hollywood standards. A few of Samantha's actual friends—the people she saw with some regularity—flew east, but most of the celebrities who tweeted out photographs of themselves standing beside Samantha and professed their undying love were no-shows. Tyree came, as did the other attendees of his dinner party. Each of them showed me the same disdain as Samantha's family.

The only person in attendance whom I counted as a friend was my literary agent, Scott Stonehill. My team in LA, the people who handled the movie and television side of the business, sent regrets, telling me that, for one reason or another, they couldn't fly to New Jersey on such short notice. They all said that they wanted to see me as soon as I returned to LA, and their agencies sent overly elaborate floral arrangements to the funeral home.

It was difficult to obey the Remsens' ten-foot rule at the church, as the minister asked that all immediate family sit in the first row. Danielle and her husband put their children between us, like a human wall, and Samantha's mother sat on the far end of the pew.

When it came time for eulogies, Danielle spoke for the Remsen family. I worried that she'd say something inappropriate—calling me out by name as her sister's murderer, or claiming Samantha never really loved me. But like Carolyn's brother decades earlier, Danielle did not dishonor her sister's memory. She spoke of their childhood, of her sister's devotion to her nieces and nephew, of the future that Samantha would sadly never see.

"She was our star in life, and now, like a star in the sky that sailors use for navigation, we will look up to the heavens for Samantha to guide us from there," Danielle said in conclusion.

When it was my turn to speak about my wife, I did so not because that was what Nick Zamora, who had no idea of the circumstances that had led to his wife's death in the ocean, would do, but because it was what Nick Zamora, who loved his wife, had to do.

"I loved Samantha. More than I thought I could ever love someone. And—I'm sure like all of you—I wondered why someone so beautiful, so young, so talented, would love someone like me." There was some nervous laughter, proof that what I'd said resonated with those who knew Samantha, but the Remsens sat stone-faced, like the opposition party at a State of the Union address. "The answer is . . . I wish I knew, but I don't. What I do know, however . . . what I am absolutely certain about, is that we were happy together. I hope that the years we were together were the happiest of her life, but all I know for certain is that they were the happiest of mine."

I could feel myself choking up and took it as a sign that I'd said enough. As I left the stage, I made no effort to embrace the Remsens. Instead, I placed a hand on Samantha's casket, and then I resumed my seat at the edge of the pew and cried alone.

———

The interment service was brief and handled solely by the minister without any opportunity for the mourners to speak. Scott stood beside me during this portion of the ceremony, and I was careful to maintain my distance from the Remsens.

"Is there anything I can do for you, Nick?" my agent asked after the service had concluded. "I know that . . . well, you don't have the strongest support network."

"That's the nicest way I've ever heard someone say that I'm friendless," I said.

I didn't hear a word of his reply. Something had caught my eye in the distance.

"Nick, are you okay?" Scott asked, low-key alarm in his voice.

"I'm not sure." My sightline was directed toward the edge of the collected mourners as the object of my fascination broke free of the crowd. "If you'll excuse me for a second, I think there's someone here I know."

My first thought was that Clinton looked better than I thought possible. He'd aged in a way that smoothed out the skinny, bookworm look that he maintained in my mind's eye. His hair was now silver, and he'd gained just enough weight to fill out his suit the way the designer had intended. The one thing that remained consistent was that Clinton held himself with the same gravitas he'd had since his childhood.

He was already walking toward me. When we met midway, I extended my hand.

He grasped it and immediately pulled me into him, wrapping his arms around me, his face pressing into my chest. Before he could speak, I was sobbing.

"I'm so sorry, Nicky," he whispered in my ear.

Nicky. When was the last time someone called me that? As soon as I asked myself that question, the answer came: It was Clinton. Thirty-four years ago.

When I was finally able to regain my composure, I released him from our bear hug. "I . . . I don't know what to say. You have no idea how much you being here means to me."

"I'm so glad you said that, Nicky. When Anne died, and then when I . . . I suffered a tragedy a few years ago, with the loss of my younger daughter, one of the things I wished for was that I still had you in my life. So when I heard about your wife's death, I thought, I need to fix this thing between Nicky and me because . . . because there are too few people in your life that you love, and it's never too late to be there for them."

I knew he didn't mean to evoke this reaction, but I felt an inch high. I remembered when his daughter died. It was all over cable news, even in LA. The days she was missing . . . the manhunt . . . and then the discovery that she had been murdered. I watched Clinton break down live at the press conference. For weeks, even months, after it ended, I thought about reaching out to him. But I was too afraid.

For reasons that I can no longer fathom, thirty-four years earlier, I had convinced myself that I could never be happy without Anne. My heart charted its own course, I told myself on countless occasions, and I had no choice but to submit to its demands. I was a romantic, not a scoundrel. Everything would make sense on the other side, and the only way the story could unfold was with Anne and me together.

Of course, in reality, I was deluding myself. As Anne had told me at the beginning, I didn't *have* to act on my feelings, and a better man—no, simply a decent man—would have refrained.

When we were younger, I always knew that Clinton Broden was the better man. That unpleasant feeling you have deep inside but can't deny. The things that transpired during our estrangement did not cause me to reconsider that assessment, even as I tried to live the best life I could. Even as Clinton became rich and famous by representing the worst of humanity. Yet his presence today emphatically settled the question, incontrovertible proof that I had been correct all along.

"I . . . I still don't know what to say."

"Say that we've been out of each other's lives for too long."

"Yes. Of course. I've missed you, Clinton. You have no idea how much."

"I think I know exactly how much," he said with a smile.

PART FOUR

CLINT BRODEN

July–October 2020

35.

Like that old Hemingway line, I think about my estrangement from Nicky as occurring slowly, and then all at once. After his trial for Carolyn's murder, Nicky couldn't get out of New York fast enough. That I understood. I've had too few clients acquitted to constitute a large enough statistical sample size, but to a person, they all exiled themselves.

When Nicky first arrived in LA, we spoke by phone a few times, but I knew that our friendship, which I'd once taken for granted would last forever, was on borrowed time. I could have blamed our estrangement entirely on Nicky, but that wouldn't be fair. Which is not to say that he made much of an effort to maintain our relationship, or that I wasn't convinced he was relieved to have me out of his life—only that I felt that way about him too.

The night after Samantha's funeral, Nicky and I went back to my house in the city. A few glasses of scotch down, Nicky offered an apology. "You've never been anything less than a brother to me, Clinton. And I . . . well, I've loved you like a brother, on that I'd stake my life, but—"

"But sometimes a brother can be a real sonofabitch," I interrupted.

"Exactly," he said with a sad smile. "And for that, I'm truly very sorry."

"Apologize by paying it forward, Nicky. By coming back into my life."

And he did. For the next month, we were in steady contact. We talked on the phone two or three times a week, and sometimes those calls went on for hours, remembering our youth or trying to catch up on the last thirty-odd years. More than once he noted that we were like long-lost lovers, and it occurred to me that was exactly what we were.

———

In late August, I went to LA to speak before law students at UCLA. When I told Nicky about my trip, he didn't hesitate to invite me to stay with him. My initial plan was to fly in on Wednesday, the day of my speech, and then fly out the next day, but Nicky wouldn't hear of it, insisting we spend the weekend together.

My speech at UCLA had been advertised—not by me—as "a discussion with F. Clinton Broden, the most celebrated criminal defense lawyer of our time." My student wrangler, a woman named Nancy Wong who had a short Cleopatra haircut and wore oversize glasses, told me that it was the best-attended student-sponsored event of the year. "We had the governor here last month and way fewer people showed up."

The event was held in a small theater. By my estimate, it had five hundred seats, and they were all occupied. A podium was centered in the middle of the stage, and off to the right were two chairs, one of which I occupied, while Nancy stood center stage to introduce me to the crowd. After my opening remarks, I would return to my seat to participate in an interview and answer student questions.

"We're very excited to have F. Clinton Broden with us," Nancy said to the audience. "A graduate of St. John's University and its law school, Mr. Broden began his legal career in the Federal Defender's office in Manhattan, then went into private practice as a criminal defense lawyer. He gained initial fame when he successfully obtained an acquittal for bestselling author Nicholas Zamora, who was accused of murdering his wife. Since then, Mr. Broden has represented a string of A-list clients in virtually every field imaginable—movie stars, politicians, sports heroes, and titans of finance. Mr. Broden has also proudly represented more notorious figures, such as the reputed terrorist Nicolai Garkov. He is, as we say in the title of this talk, the most celebrated criminal defense attorney of our time. Ladies and gentlemen, the Criminal Law Clinic of the UCLA Law School is very proud to bring to you F. Clinton Broden."

The applause was enthusiastic. When I reached the lectern, I thanked Nancy for her kind words and removed from my breast pocket the paper copy of the stump speech I used for this type of event. I'd delivered it so often by now that I rarely even glanced at the pages.

After telling the students what an honor it was to be there and joking about my grades and UCLA, I told them that the topic of my talk would be the role of the defense attorney in the criminal justice system.

"In popular culture," I began, "there are three types of noble lawyers. First, there is the defender of the innocent. Perry Mason and Atticus Finch immediately spring to mind. The second type is the civil rights warrior. Thurgood Marshall and RBG are the patron saints of this category. And lastly, there is the crime fighter. My daughter, Ella, who heads up the Sex Crimes Unit in the Manhattan DA's office, fits this category, as do many other prosecutors throughout the country.

"Obviously, two of those categories don't apply to me at all. Although I've done some civil rights cases, I haven't dedicated my career to the cause. And I've never been a prosecutor. Which means that the only hope I ever had to be a *noble* lawyer—at least according to popular culture—was to defend the innocent. But I have to admit, I'm not that either. From time to time I represent an innocent client, but the vast majority of my clients are guilty as charged. Yet I represent them, and I do so proudly. The conventional wisdom is that I do so for money—and I'm not going to deny that I am lucratively compensated for my services—but I maintain that my role representing the guilty, and fighting as hard as I can for them to be acquitted, is as noble as any other in the justice system.

"As I'm sure you all know from your Crim Pro class, the Fourth Amendment prohibits illegal searches, and the exclusionary rule bars the admissibility of any evidence obtained in or flowing from such an illegal search, under the theory that we lawyers call 'fruit of the poisonous tree.' From TV, you'd think that this entire area of jurisprudence was designed solely to exclude the murder weapon from trial. But without this rule, there would be nothing to stop the police from entering your home without a warrant, or any justification at all, and conducting an illegal search. If they found . . . really, anything, they could use it against you. Now, the judge might yell at the cops for violating the Constitution, but if the prosecutor can still introduce illegally obtained evidence at trial, that doesn't do the defendant a whole lot of good, or deter cops from doing it the next time to someone else. Pretty soon, you're living in a police state.

"So what does any of this have to do with me being a noble lawyer? you ask. My answer is that there are many important procedural safeguards in our criminal justice system that are indispensable for us to live in a free society. The undisputed king of these civil liberty protections is that a defendant is presumed innocent until proven guilty beyond a reasonable doubt. Anything I can do to make the government meet that test keeps us freer than we would otherwise be. And for our justice system to work, for it to truly keep us free, we defense attorneys must make the government meet its burden of proof when representing our clients, whether innocent or guilty."

I went on for another twenty minutes or so, hitting the clichés that law students seem to like, peppered with war stories. During the Q and A, the students asked the usual questions: *Do you really not feel conflicted when representing someone guilty?* "No, not for a second. Any more than a heart surgeon would think twice about saving the life of a patient he thought was guilty of a crime." *What was your favorite case?* "They're like your children, so I don't pick among them." *Are you ever tempted to break the rules to help a client?* "No, never. That would go against the entire idea that I'm doing noble work. If you cheat, even because it is going to get the result you think is just, you have perverted the system, and a lawyer's duty, first and foremost, is to the justice system. Your obligation to your client—even the innocent client—comes second." And, of course, one guy—and it's always a guy—asked, *Is your firm hiring?* .

At the conclusion of my remarks, the law students gave me another standing ovation. As they clapped, I saw Nicky smiling proudly back at me from the second row, the way Anne always looked when she attended my talks.

———

According to Nicky, the best steakhouse in LA was Chi Spacca on Melrose. I had promised this dinner was on me, compensation for his accompanying me to UCLA. When I opened the menu, I realized that Nicky must have confused *best* with *most expensive.*

"Over two hundred bucks for a steak," I said.

"I would have thought that the most celebrated criminal defense lawyer of our time could cover that for the client who made him famous," Nicky said with a smirk. "It's fifty ounces, so we can split it. Anyway, it's the bottle of wine I'm gonna order that will really set you back. And, yes, you can thank me later."

To quote my favorite line from *Pulp Fiction,* paraphrasing because John Travolta was referring to a vanilla milkshake, I'm not sure if the steak was worth $250, but it was a damn good hunk of meat. The wine was also top-notch.

"Do you believe the stuff you told the kids back there?" Nicky asked when we were midway through dinner.

"Absolutely, I do."

"But don't the guilty deserve to be punished for what they've done?"

The question seemed too weighty for dinner chitchat. Was my oldest friend going to confess to me here and now? About Carolyn? Samantha?

The police had already determined Samantha's death to be a homicide, the result of blunt force trauma to the back of her skull that caused her neck to break. The lack of water in her lungs proved that she had been put in the ocean postmortem. That was more than enough evidence for the press—especially the cable news pundits—to declare Nicky guilty.

We'd had a handful of discussions regarding the elephant in the room—that Nicky would likely be charged with murdering Samantha Remsen. Nicky had consistently told me the same thing he had told the police on day one: after the party, he went home alone, expecting to see his wife shortly thereafter, and she never appeared.

I had the sense that our mutual avoidance of the matter was almost superstitious, akin to not talking to your pitcher during a no-hitter. If either of us even mentioned the possibility that Nicky would be charged with Samantha's murder, or worse, if we planned for its eventuality, we might affect the outcome.

"I believe both things, Nicky," I answered. "The guilty should be punished, but only by the state if they are proven guilty beyond a reasonable doubt. What God—or the universe—wants to do with the guilty is a different question altogether, and one that is, thankfully, above my pay grade."

36.

I've never much liked LA. A few years before, a hotshot LA attorney who had just won a multimillion-dollar civil rights suit against the LAPD reached out to me about combining our practices. "You'd be national, Clint," he said. "The first call of every movie star, as well as every finance guy." I passed, in part because I knew that representing Californians meant I'd have to live there at least part of the year. As it turned out, my would-be partner later got himself indicted for cheating his clients, so it was a good decision in the end.

That said, I didn't find much to complain about concerning Nicky's life in the Golden State. Sunshine every day has a certain appeal, and Nicky lived an extremely comfortable, even luxurious, existence. Case in point was his home, which he referred to as a cottage: five thousand square feet smack on the beach in Malibu.

When I awoke the next morning, it was to the smell of freshly brewed coffee.

"It seems as if I certainly made the right choice in accommodations," I said upon joining him in the kitchen. Not only was there coffee, but popovers had apparently just been removed from the oven, because they were still in the baking pan, steam escaping from their tops.

"One bad review and my entire Airbnb business goes down the tubes," Nicky said.

Food and drink in hand, we adjourned to the patio. The view was magnificent. The Pacific in all its glory.

"You've done all right for yourself, my friend," I said.

He didn't acknowledge the compliment. At least not at first.

After a few moments of quiet, he said, "I'm sixty-seven years old. When I turned, I don't know, maybe fifty, certainly by sixty, I started viewing my life backward. Kind of like a Benjamin Button thing. It usually takes me at least three, closer to four, years to write a book. And I might be slowing down. It was nearly five years between my last two, and I'm two years into my latest and I don't see finishing it next year. Even the year after that might be ambitious. Which means I've probably got two more books in me. Three at the outside. That'll take me to seventy-five-ish. Philip Roth hung it up at eighty. So if I'm lucky, really lucky, I will leave this mortal coil with eleven books to my name." He laughed. "And a *New York Times* obituary that says my best book was my first."

"Many writers would kill just to have a *New York Times* obituary."

He shook his head. "That's not my point. I'm not lamenting that I haven't written a book that will be read in English classes a hundred years from now. It's the opposite, actually. When I met Samantha, it was the first time I found something more important in life than my writing. A way for me to be happy that had nothing to do with professional success. I knew she was the one for me because my writing no longer mattered. Being with her was all I cared about. It's what made me happy. And now, without her, I feel like I'm gone too."

"When Charlotte died . . . ," I began, then stopped. "Do you have any idea how many sentences I begin that way? I hate that."

"I'm sorry. I can't even begin to imagine."

I nodded to acknowledge his ignorance on this point. Losing a spouse was nothing like losing a child. I could speak with authority, having suffered both.

"What I meant to say was that Charlotte's murder caused me to question why I was still alive. I'd never be happy again. I knew that. So what was the point, right?"

"Exactly," he said. "What *is* the point?"

"To keep on living. So that you can continue to love the people who you are fortunate enough to be able to love. And live in such a way as to make yourself worthy of their love too."

"Easy for you to say. You have a daughter. I don't think anyone's life would be diminished if I ended it all tomorrow."

He said it without a hint of self-pity or amusement.

"My life would be less without you in it. It *has* been less since 1986. I'm not saying that tragic things happen for a reason, because they don't. It's just random awfulness. But I am saying that sometimes there's some good that comes out of the most horrible tragedies. The fact that we've reentered each other's lives doesn't make up for Samantha's death. I know you'd gladly never hear from me again if it could bring your wife back. I feel the same way about my daughter. But at the same time, I recognize that it was because of what happened to Charlotte that I made the decision to try harder with the people that I loved, to be more forgiving of them, and that positive consequence of her murder is what led me back to you."

For a few moments we fell silent, staring out at the ocean, sipping our coffee. I was about to add that no one should have dark thoughts while enjoying such beauty, when Nicky said, "Can I tell you something in an attorney-client way?"

I hear that a lot. What follows is almost always an admission of guilt.

"I take the position that every conversation we have is privileged," I said, even though, as a legal matter, it wouldn't hold up in court.

"I'm scared. I swear on my life that I didn't kill Samantha. But if I'm arrested for it . . . at my age, I'm not going to go through another trial. If that makes me a coward, so be it. Hemingway offed himself, and people still read his books."

I wasn't entirely sure what to say, or if Nicky expected me to say anything at all. Perhaps this was just his way of warning me not to get too attached to our newly rekindled friendship because it might be short-lived.

"I know that feeling too," I finally said. "And at the risk of being a broken record, *when Charlotte died*, I felt like checking out right then and there. On some days, when it was its worst, it was only not wanting to leave Ella alone that kept me around. But, now, with some time behind me, I'm glad that I stuck around. And I won't lie to you— I'm not happy to be alive every day. Some days, the grief feels like it's physically crushing me, and I fear I won't be able to take it. But then I do. And the next day, I'm glad that I did because even the bad days allow me to hope that tomorrow will be better. So my advice to you is to take it one day a time, and when one of those days becomes too unbearable, call me."

He didn't say anything after that about either the possibility of suicide or his lack of involvement in Samantha's murder. I doubted it was because my words had persuaded him to keep the faith even if everything turned against him. Instead, I got the sense that he was planning how he would end his life, and looking out to the Pacific seemed to provide the answer.

37.

The silence between us was finally broken by my phone. The picture on the screen was of Ella.

"My daughter," I said to Nicky.

"Tell her that I say hello," he said, then excused himself to refill his coffee.

It was conventional wisdom among those who knew us that Anne's passing would be hardest on Charlotte. She was six years younger than her sister; the thinking went that losing her mother would have a more indelible impact on her than on Ella, who was already a teenager and more or less the person she would have become without experiencing such a tragedy.

Anne told me it wouldn't work out that way.

"You have to promise me not to let Ella become a surrogate mother to Charlotte," Anne said shortly before her death. "She can't worry about her sister like a mother does. As much as Charlotte may need that, you have to promise me that you'll do everything in your power to make sure Ella doesn't take on that responsibility. Even though she seems like an old soul, inside that tough exterior is a little girl. Don't let her trick you into thinking otherwise."

"Hey, Dad," came Ella's cheerful voice through the phone. "How'd it go at UCLA? Did you tell the garbageman story?"

I chuckled. "No. I should have, though. That story always kills."

I've asked others with adult children if their kids check up on them the way Ella does with me. They tell me that their children are attentive and vigilantly looking for signs of dementia, but the relationship is as one-way as it's always been—the parent worrying about the child, and the child taking for granted that the parent will always be there to help. I wish it were that way between Ella and me, but it hasn't been for a long time. Even before Charlotte's murder, Ella looked after me as much as I tried to be the one looking after her. Despite doing my best to honor Anne's wishes, I couldn't change my daughter from being the person she was destined to be.

"Tell me about you," I said. "What's going on there?"

"Same-old, same-old. I've been working night and day to get ready for this trial that's been on Judge Kim's calendar for literally three months. We were supposed to pick a jury a week from Monday, and then yesterday her clerk called and said the judge had an unavoidable conflict, and the next available spot she has is early next year."

"So it gives you some time off, then."

"Ha. Not exactly. Just means I have to attend to a dozen other work fires that I was able to disregard with the *I'm about to start a trial* excuse."

"How's Gabriel?" I asked, because I was much more interested in my daughter's life outside the office, even if she wasn't.

"He's good. He wants to get away for a few days, but we didn't budget for a vacation right now."

"Why don't you two go out to East Hampton?"

"Maybe."

I was fluent enough in Ella-speak to know that meant no. Even as a child, Ella was never a big fan of the conspicuous consumption of the Hamptons, and now that she was a public servant at the DA's office, and dating a cop, she liked it even less.

"How's your friend?" she asked.

Another tic I'd noticed with Ella. She never called Nicky by name. He was always *your friend*. I might have chalked that up to her being too busy to remember the names of my friends, but she always said it with an unmistakable tone of disapproval.

"He's good. I'm sitting on the patio of his house in Malibu overlooking the Pacific as we speak."

"So do you no longer hate LA?"

"Nope. Still do. Just not quite as much."

She laughed. Ella had Anne's laugh, throaty and hard, as if it came from somewhere deep within her. Every time I heard it, I closed my eyes in an effort to recapture Anne's timbre. I was already having difficulty recalling Charlotte's laugh, which was higher pitched and lighter than her sister's.

"What's that?" Ella asked.

She was responding to the ring of Nicky's front doorbell, which was apparently loud enough to be heard not just on the patio, but also three thousand miles away. "Just the front door."

"I think it's nice that you have a new friend."

"Not new. Rather old, actually."

"I wasn't finished. I was about to say that I only wish your new-old friend wasn't someone who murdered his wife."

"C'mon, Ella. You don't know that, and I don't believe it."

"Clinton," Nicky yelled from the front of the house.

I could hear the panic in his voice. I'm not sure whether in a different context I would have reached the same conclusion about what was happening, but I knew immediately.

"I gotta go," I told Ella. "Sorry."

As soon as I set foot inside the house, I saw the cops at the front door. Large men, both in uniform.

Nicky's eyes had a vacant look, the kind you get when you no longer care about what's going on around you. I wondered if he was regretting not ending his life when he had the chance. One of the cops was reading Nicky his rights while his partner clicked handcuffs around Nicky's wrists.

"It's going to be okay," I told Nicky. To the cops I said, "Where are you taking him?"

"There's a website for you to find arrestees," the rights-reading cop responded.

They were already moving to the door. Nicky looked at me, and I was instantly transported back in time. He had that same deer-in-the-headlights expression as he'd had at his house in Mount Vernon thirty-four years ago.

"He asserts his right to counsel," I said.

Neither of the two cops acknowledged my invocation. They had by now broken the plane of Nicky's front door, pulling Nicky between them.

"Nicky, tell them you invoke your right to counsel!" I shouted.

"I invoke my right to counsel," he said in a voice much weaker than mine.

"We heard you the first time, counselor," the handcuff-clinking cop said without turning around.

———

As soon as the black-and-white receded from view, I called Joan Celebron. She was my pick as the best lawyer on the West Coast. She was also currently my cocounsel representing Steven Lancaster, the founder and CEO of Tech X, a social media company that was the current fad among the tween set. Lancaster's insider trading case was entering its second year, with no end in sight in large part because Joan and I were sticking to the tried-and-true strategy of delay for delay's sake, especially with a defendant out on bail.

"Hey, Clint. What did Hop-a-Long do this time?" Joan said, referencing the pejorative nickname she used to refer to Assistant District Attorney Hopkins, who was prosecuting the Lancaster case.

"I'm not calling about that. I need your help on something new. Have you heard of Nick Zamora?"

"Yeah. The guy who killed Samantha Remsen."

Criminal defense lawyers are no different from cops or prosecutors in this regard—we think everyone who's not our client is guilty. And most of our own clients too.

"He's a childhood friend, and he was just arrested for *allegedly* killing Samantha Remsen. I'm going to need local counsel."

38.

Lost Hills didn't seem that bad to me—as prisons go, that is. Which is not to say that it wasn't hell on earth. Generally speaking, prisons are like colleges, in that what makes one better or worse has more to do with the population than the facilities.

Joan was already there when I arrived. She said she'd checked in with security, but they hadn't yet been able to locate Nicky.

"That doesn't sound good," I said.

"The people who work at the jail are always the last to know who's been put in their facility," she explained. "Sometimes it takes two or three days before an arrestee is found in the system. I don't know how it is in the Big Apple, but in the City of Angels, they get three days to arraign, which is just another way of saying that they have three days to find your client after an arrest. Does New York have the death penalty?" she asked.

"No," I answered reflexively. "Actually, we do, but not for murdering your wife. Only for murders involving people in the criminal justice system."

"Well, if the potential penalty is life in prison, the judge still can't provide for bail during the preliminary hearing phase. That means your friend will be in lockup for a while. By law, they don't have to hold the PC hearing for ten days."

When a citizen of California is charged with a crime that took place in New York, the local police are not permitted to fly across the country to transport him to New York. Instead, an extradition process must be followed: the New York authorities request permission from the governor of California to make the arrest. That formality had occurred before LA's finest showed up at Nicky's door. The final step before the East Hampton police could bring Nicky back east to stand trial was for a California judge to find "probable cause"—the very low standard needed to obtain an indictment or an arrest warrant—that he was guilty of murder.

"I'm going to waive extradition," I said.

"Really?"

"There's no way he's not going to be extradited back to New York."

"True, but you know as well as anyone that making the prosecution put on its evidence in a PC hearing isn't about winning. It's about getting free discovery. The Hamptons cops will have to put on enough evidence to establish probable cause for the arrest. So you might learn something you wouldn't have, or get one of the cops to lock himself into a story that hurts the prosecution at trial."

Joan's take on the probable cause hearing was the conventional wisdom. So I nodded as if she had persuaded me. She hadn't, though. In fact, I'd already left a message with Jack Ethan, the Suffolk County District Attorney, asking him to have the ADA in charge of Nicky's case call me so we could schedule the arraignment at the earliest possible time.

Jack returned my call while Joan and I were still waiting for Nicky to be found in Lost Hills.

"Clint," he said, as if we were old friends.

I knew Jack from his days as a federal prosecutor in Manhattan, and also because he was the younger brother of Benjamin Ethan, who was considered to be the dean of the white-collar criminal bar, or at least its white-shoe, Big Law version. I'd had no idea that Jack had left the city until about four years ago, when out of the blue he hit me up for a contribution to his campaign for DA. I made the maximum donation, not because I thought Jack would be a great DA but because I considered $2,500 a fair fee for being able to get the Suffolk County DA on the phone if I needed to. By returning my call now, he was repaying that debt, as well as soliciting a contribution for his reelection.

"Hey, Jack. I didn't expect to get the head honcho on this. I was looking for the line ADA prosecuting the Zamora matter."

"You got him. I'm going to try this one personally."

The DA is a managerial job in most places, especially in larger counties. Even though Suffolk was far smaller than New York County, Ethan's office had more than three hundred prosecutors. The fact that Ethan was taking the lead was akin to a general fighting on the front lines of a battle.

"In that case, we'll be talking to each other a lot in the coming weeks, because I'm going to be representing Mr. Zamora. You should know, he's an old friend. We grew up together in Astoria. I was actually visiting his home when we were interrupted by LA's finest executing a warrant to extradite him back to you. I'm waiting for his arraignment as we speak, but I thought I might jump-start the process by getting you on the phone to talk about his voluntary surrender."

"So no PC hearing out there?" Ethan sounded as surprised as Joan about my legal strategy.

"Still thinking that through, but I'm amenable to waiving extradition for the right incentive," I said. "I assume that if Mr. Zamora had been local, you would have asked him to turn himself in. So I'm requesting the same courtesy now, although because it requires a cross-country flight, it might take us forty-eight hours to get there."

Despite what I'd just said, I was certain that the East Hampton police would not have allowed Nicky to turn himself in on a murder charge. They would have arrested him wherever they found him and brought him back in handcuffs, the same way they were planning on doing from LA.

"We can't do that, Clint. Violent crime. Flight risk. You know the drill. It's got to be by the book, and that means he's got to be under our control for the transfer. That being said, I'm always interested in avoiding any delay in bringing someone back, and I'm certain that our LA cousins would prefer that they not have to do a dog and pony show to meet the PC standard. So what I can offer you is, if you waive extradition, we'll do our damnedest to get before a judge within twenty-four hours of your client's arrival."

He wasn't offering much. The arraignment had to be within seventy-two hours in any case. "What about a bail recommendation?"

"No can do on that either, I'm afraid. It's a murder charge."

"It's a spousal charge, and the guy's pretty famous, which means he's got nowhere to go."

This made it even more of a Hail Mary. No prosecutor was going to risk a murder defendant fleeing the jurisdiction. And *pretty famous* was just another way of saying *very rich*, which was another way of saying *flight risk*.

"I'm sorry, Clint. That's a nonstarter with us. You are, of course, free to make that argument to the judge during the arraignment."

"Jack, I gotta say, you're not offering much inducement for my guy not to make you put your PC proof on out here."

"That's your right under the Constitution," Ethan replied.

"Let me talk with my client. But I do appreciate you getting back to me so quickly on this."

"My pleasure, Clint. Always happy to help out a friend."

———

It wasn't until another four hours had passed that the guard told us that they'd finally located Nicky. Joan and I were led through the facility's corridors until we entered a small, windowless room that smelled dank. Inside were a round metal table and three wooden chairs.

Ten minutes later, Nicky appeared. He was not shackled and wore the same clothing he'd been dressed in that morning. His expression told me that he'd had a difficult last several hours. His eyes were puffy, as if he'd been crying, his mouth in a resting frown.

The first thing he said to me, even before acknowledging Joan's presence was, "Clinton, I just can't."

"I know you feel that way, Nicky. But you have to stay strong. Today is the worst day of the entire process. Everything gets better from here. I promise."

That was something I said to clients on the day of their arrest, but it was not always true. If they made bail, then things got better, of course. That is until conviction, which became the new worst day. Those who didn't make bail had *only* worse days.

"This is Joan Celebron," I told him. "She's the best criminal defense lawyer in LA and my colleague on another case. Because I'm not admitted in California, she's going to make the presentation tomorrow."

Joan said, "Nicky—can I call you Nicky?"

I said, "He goes by Nick if you haven't known him since fourth grade."

"Glad I asked, then," Joan said with a smile.

Nicky didn't reciprocate. There was nothing even remotely pleasant about the experience he was enduring.

"So Nick, first thing is that I'm so very sorry that this has happened to you. Tomorrow, we're going to appear before Judge Santiago. The purpose of that hearing is to determine if you will be sent back to New York to stand trial for the charges filed there."

"That's definitely going to happen," I chimed in. "It's a constitu-tional matter. You were indicted in New York, so you have to stand trial in New York, even though you were arrested in California. That means that the real fight is going to be back in East Hampton. And the judge there—not the judge here—will decide on bail."

"So what's the point of whatever's going to happen tomorrow?" Nicky asked.

"You can do one of two things at tomorrow's hearing," Joan said. "You can waive extradition, which means that they put you on the next plane to New York. Or you can fight it, in which case they schedule what is called a probable cause hearing. The hearing has to begin within ten days. It can last for one day or several. The purpose of the hearing is for a judge here to determine whether there is probable cause for the issuance of the arrest warrant. If there is, you're extradited back to New York. If not, you go free. And I'm sorry to say that during that entire time the PC hearing is going on, you're stuck in jail. There's no possibility for bail."

"There's no doubt that you'll be extradited," I said. "It's the same standard that allows the police to arrest you in the first place. The choice we need to make is whether you agree to go back now voluntarily, or we make them do the PC hearing."

"It sounds like you think I should just go now," he said.

"I do. I've already spoken to the DA in Suffolk County. I know him. He promised me that if we waive extradition, we'll get before a New York judge no more than twenty-four hours after you get there. At that court appearance we'll be able to ask for bail. That means that if you waive extradition, with any luck, you'll be out tomorrow night. The alternative is that Lost Hills is your home probably through the end of the month. Then, when you do come back to New York, as you inevitably will when we lose the PC hearing, you'll be before a judge who might be pissed you fought extradition."

I could feel Joan's disapproving stare. She would have made a different call. A PC hearing would have also earned her $100,000 in fees, and that kind of money can cloud your judgment. Joan knew better than to say anything, however. Every year I sent her clients worth five times that much.

"If you both think that's the right call," Nicky said.

"We do," I replied before Joan could advance a contrary opinion.

39.

The following morning, Nicky entered the courtroom wearing an orange prison jumpsuit with *Lost Hills* stenciled on the back. He took his position at the defense counsel table between Joan and me. I couldn't remember the last time I'd been in court and not said anything, but this would be one of those occasions.

The courtroom was full, of course. Press from every state in the union and enough foreign countries to hold a United Nations meeting. As was the California way, the hearing would be televised, which meant clips would play on the news this evening and forever on the internet.

"All rise," the court officer shouted. "The honorable William Santiago presiding. Come forward and ye shall be heard."

The judge strode in, and after he was comfortably seated, he instructed the rest of us to be seated. "So what's it going to be, Ms. Celebron?"

Joan came back to her feet. "Mr. Zamora waives his right to a probable cause hearing so that he may return to New York as soon as possible, where he will contest these erroneous charges and ultimately be exonerated."

"Is that so?"

"Yes. Mr. Zamora is innocent of these charges, and he wants to be able to clear his name at the earliest possible opportunity."

"Wouldn't that be here, though?"

The judge was playing to the cameras, clearly enjoying himself despite the fact that a man's life was at stake.

"It is Mr. Zamora's desire to be exonerated of these charges in the proper forum as soon as possible," Joan said, for the third time. "There is no reason to delay that process by holding a hearing here. In fact, every day that Mr. Zamora is not permitted to have his day in court to contest these false charges is a day that he has been denied justice by being wrongly accused of murdering the wife that he loved."

Judge Santiago practically rolled his eyes. "Mr. Zamora, is it, in fact, your desire to waive extradition and return to New York to stand trial?"

"Stand up," I whispered to Nicky.

Nicky came to his feet and said, "It is, Your Honor."

"And you have, I'm sure, been advised by your counsel that you have the right to demand that the People put on evidence in an open hearing in this court that there is probable cause for your arrest before you are extradited to New York."

"Yes, I understand that."

"And nonetheless, you freely choose to waive that right, as if probable cause has been established."

The question must have tripped Nicky up a bit because he didn't immediately respond. After a beat, he said, "Yes."

"Finally, you make this waiver freely, and not because anyone has induced you or made any promises to you?"

"Yes," he said, with more conviction.

"If there's nothing from the People on this, I'm ready to send Mr. Zamora back east," Judge Santiago said.

The prosecutor, a woman in her thirties with dark hair, who hadn't said a word thus far, said, "Nothing from the People, Your Honor."

The judge struck the gavel. "Godspeed, Mr. Zamora."

———

I booked myself on the next available flight, an afternoon plane that would land at JFK at 9:06 p.m.

After we took off, I walked through the cabin to see if Nicky was on board. He wasn't, so I settled back into my first-class seat, and on the theory that it was almost five o'clock in New York, I ordered a drink.

More than five hours later, the pilot announced that we'd made up time in the air. We touched down at JFK at 8:55 p.m. It would be another two hours of travel for me to get home and then another three hours to drive out to East Hampton. I contemplated going home for the night and driving out in the morning but decided that it was better to get all the traveling over in one fell swoop. That way, when I woke up tomorrow, I could make the ten-minute trip to the police station to get the particulars about Nicky's arraignment and be on hand in case it was held first thing in the morning.

I called Ella from the taxi line to tell her that I was home and that Nicky had been arrested. She had already heard the news.

"I read that some woman was his lawyer," Ella said.

"Joan Celebron?"

"I think so."

"She's a friend who practices in LA. She pinch-hit for the California appearance, but I'm going to be out front from now on. In fact, I'm going to go to East Hampton tonight. You and Gabriel are still invited to use the house this weekend and for as long as you want, but I wanted to tell you that you'll have company."

"The ADA out in East Hampton must be loving you right now," she said.

Ella had extradited enough defendants to know that waiving the PC hearing is atypical.

"The DA's actually going to try the case himself," I said, deflecting her comment. "Guy named Jack Ethan. You know him?"

"Related to Benjamin Ethan over at Windsor Taft?"

I remembered then that not only did Ella know Benjamin Ethan, she had also tried a big case against him only a year or two ago. "That's right. You went up against him in that murder case."

Ella didn't immediately respond, and I worried that I might have upset her by referencing that case. It was a tough one, and though I was proud of the way it had ended, Ella took some flak for it with the DA at the time. But there was another reason for her silence.

"Dad . . . are you sure you want to do this?"

I could have feigned confusion. *Do what?* But I knew what she meant, in all its many layers. Just as I had when her mother asked me nearly the same question in 1986. And as further evidence that some things never change, I answered my daughter the same way I had responded to Anne all those years ago.

With a simple yes.

But just like it had back then, my answer belied much more complicated emotions. Truth be told, I didn't know if I was sure I *wanted* to do it so much as I felt as if I didn't have any choice.

After Ella and I said our goodbyes, I couldn't help wondering what Anne would have said if she had been on the other end of the line instead of my daughter. Would she have approved of what I was about to do?

40.

The Suffolk County Criminal courthouse was located in Riverhead, a working-class town that served as the county seat. The town's median income was approximately $50,000, which was about as much as the average monthly rent for a summer place in the Hampton villages that were also situated within the court's jurisdiction.

As soon as I arrived, I sought out the court officer. "Can I get some time to speak to my client before his case is called?"

"Sorry," he said, actually sounding apologetic. "Only the judge can grant that request."

That's not the way it worked in Manhattan, but I knew pointing that out wasn't going to get me an audience with my client any sooner. With little choice, I took a seat in the gallery to watch and wait.

The arraignment judge was Louis Romatowski. He looked more like an old angler than a judge, with a ruddy complexion and full white beard. I knew nothing about him, but that didn't matter. This would be his sole involvement in the case, and his one and only decision would be regarding bail. Whether he was an easy mark or the toughest SOB in the system, it wouldn't alter my approach.

Two other cases were called before Nicky's, neither providing any insight into Judge Romatowski's views on bail. They were both minor offenses, and the prosecutor was the first to suggest the defendants be released on their own recognizance. I knew that Nicky wouldn't get such kid-glove treatment.

Nicky entered the courtroom from the side entrance, which was reserved for inmates. He was now wearing the beige canvas prison jumpsuit, complete with the handcuff accessory.

The clerk called out, "Counsel, please state your appearances."

"Assistant District Attorney Sandra Washington," the woman who had handled the first two arraignments said.

"F. Clinton Broden, New York City, for the defendant."

"Welcome, Mr. Broden," Judge Romatowski said absentmindedly as he looked through a sheaf of papers, likely reviewing the indictment. When he looked up again, he caught my eye but didn't say anything. Then he shifted his gaze to the ADA.

"Well, you better start reading, Ms. Washington."

"Apologies, Your Honor," I said quickly. "The defense waives reading of the indictment."

"Yeah, I was wondering if you were going to get around to that. We may not be big-city folks all the way out here in Riverhead, but we still don't have time to read every indictment."

I acknowledged the joke at my expense with a smile.

"If you wouldn't mind, now would also be an ideal time for you to share with me how your client pleads."

"Not guilty," Nicky said.

"Nice to hear from you, Mr. Zamora," Judge Romatowski said. "Ms. Washington, on bail?"

As her boss had told me she would, Washington asked for remand. She referenced all the usual prosecutorial babble—the violent nature of the crime, Nicky's wealth, his lack of ties to the community, the long prison term he was facing, his age. She was also quick to point out that Nicky had been accused of murdering his first wife and therefore might well be a threat to the community if let free.

I had little to offer by way of counterargument, other than to point out that Nicky was acquitted of murdering his first wife and therefore now had the utmost faith in the jury system.

"He is confident that he will be exonerated," I said, "which is why he will definitely appear at trial, just as he did when he was previously falsely accused."

"A lot has changed since the last time, Mr. Broden," Judge Romatowski said. "For one thing, my understanding is that back then, Mr. Zamora lived in the community, he didn't have any money, and his parents posted their home and business for bail. But now he's a rich author, without family to leave behind holding the bag. I figure he could skip now and not much miss whatever he was leaving behind."

Judge Romatowski had done his homework. I suggested the only thing I thought might keep Nicky out of jail pending trial.

"Your Honor, allow me to propose that Mr. Zamora be held under house arrest. It'll be at his own expense, therefore freeing up tax dollars for the community. He'll agree to whatever restrictions the court sees fit to ensure his appearance at trial."

I expected a flat rejection. Instead Judge Romatowski said, "Not in California."

That was enough of an opening. "He could live in Suffolk County," I said. "I have a home here, and I would be more than happy to house Mr. Zamora pending trial."

Judge Romatowski laughed. "This is a first for me. I've had lawyers vouch for their clients, but none ever agreed to live with them. I'm not sure if you're the most zealous advocate I've ever met or the stupidest, Mr. Broden." He laughed again.

Washington saw no humor in the situation. "That proposal is not acceptable to the People, Your Honor. Mr. Broden is a close, personal friend of the defendant. Granting this request . . . well, it would be like having the fox guarding the henhouse."

"Your Honor, I strongly resent—"

"Yes, I know, Mr. Broden. You're not a fox, and your client is no hen. Ms. Washington was just using colorful language. Obviously, this issue can be relitigated before the trial judge, but I'm going to grant bail on the following conditions: first, defendant post five million dollars or bond equivalent; second, he will be held under house arrest, at his own expense, complete with whatever monitoring devices and other security measures the Suffolk County Police Department deems appropriate; and, finally, he must hand over his passport forthwith."

———

The house in East Hampton had been Anne's idea. She had wanted a place with a backyard and a pool for our girls, and she'd envisioned a future when *their* children would be excited to visit Grandma and Pop-pop. It had cost a fortune when we bought it, but it turned out to be the second-best financial decision we ever made, outpaced only by the appreciation of our town house in the city. But more importantly, this had been Anne's happy place. She'd loved the garden in the back and the view of the ocean at sunset.

After she passed, I didn't come out at all. I missed Anne most when I was there.

A few years later, I told the girls that I was going to sell it. They begged me to reconsider.

"I think it would make Mom sad," Charlotte said.

Ella joined the full-court press, going so far as to get a summer job in East Hampton at a local bagel store. In the end, I never sold the house but still didn't visit it often.

But now it would be my home for the foreseeable future. More than that, it would be Nicky's prison.

I was sitting in the living room when the police car transporting Nicky made its way up the driveway. Behind it was a second patrol car, and a third pulled up the rear. In all, six police officers entered my home and attended to affixing the monitoring device to Nicky's ankle, then calibrating it to trigger the alarm if he ventured beyond a tight perimeter outside the house.

When they were finished, Nicky said, "Thank you," as if they were fitting him for a suit rather than denying his freedom. Before they left, the cop in charge told us that there would be police stationed on the beach and at the end of the driveway twenty-four hours a day.

"You'll get used to it," I said when I noticed Nicky tugging at the ankle bracelet. "That's what my clients tell me, anyway."

"Does it zap when you leave the yard, like they do for dog collars?"

"No, but they immediately arrest you. I've had clients who claimed that the bracelet activated when they hadn't left the house, and the police showed up with guns drawn. One guy left his house because his dog had bolted. Luckily for him the judge was an animal lover, or else he would've been thrown back in jail. On the other end of the spectrum, my client Nikolai Garkov lives like a king while under house arrest, which is why he's still there, going on . . . I've lost track, it's been so long."

"Don't get me wrong," said Nicky. "I'm eternally grateful for everything you're doing for me. Not only defending me, but letting me live here too. And I'm also grateful that we got to be together again. But I'm afraid I'll go crazy being confined to your house, as lovely as it is."

I laughed. "Well, then I have good news for you."

He looked at me suspiciously.

"You won't be here for long. I'm going to push for an immediate trial date. Hopefully, they won't have all their ducks in a row fast enough to obtain a conviction."

He took a moment to consider that plan. "And what if they do get their ducks in a row?"

"Then I will have made a grave mistake."

41.

A million years ago, Margaret Catalano and I served together in the Federal Defender's office. We shared a small office for a year before we each advanced to "singles." Back then, I called her Maggie the Cat. After she was married and changed her surname to Gallagher, the nickname no longer made any sense, although she told me that I was free to call her Maggie the Gal if I liked. I stuck with Maggie after that.

I had pegged her as a lifer at the FD's office, and she stayed there for a good decade after my departure. Sometime in the 1990s, her husband became a judge in Patchogue, which is one of those towns on Long Island with a train stop and little else, and she moved out with him and their three boys. I'd expected her to continue as a public defender, but she switched sides, joining the Suffolk County District Attorney's Office, rising through the ranks to become the First Deputy under the prior DA.

When Jack Ethan was elected three years ago as the new DA, Maggie decided to strike out on her own. Not long after, I began getting lunch invitations whenever she came into the city.

One tried-and-true way for a criminal defense lawyer to get clients is through referrals from other criminal defense lawyers. At this stage in my career, I easily turned down twice as many cases as I accepted, but I never turned away a prospective client without giving them a name or two to call. Maggie started inviting me to lunch because she wanted hers to be that name in Suffolk County.

Her practice was housed on Main Street in East Hampton, on the second floor, above a J.Crew. She buzzed me in from the street level. When I passed through the office doors, I was greeted not by Maggie but by a black Labrador.

"Sorry, we don't get too many visitors," Maggie said.

"Maggie the Cat has a dog," I said.

I rubbed the top of the dog's head, and he immediately dropped to the floor, exposing his belly.

"You're getting an invite to a belly rub on the first date. Normally he's not that easy," she said with a laugh.

"What's his name?"

She laughed again. "Funny story there. We got him shortly after Larry's diagnosis. The doctor said that having a dog would be therapeutic for Larry, but I think he meant for both of us. Anyway, we couldn't agree on a name. Larry wanted something judicial sounding, and I wanted something more whimsical. As you might recall, I'm an avid reader of mysteries, so I suggested Hercule, as an homage to Agatha Christie. Larry, ever the jurist, came up with the Solomonic compromise that we name him Holmes and keep to ourselves whether his namesake was Oliver Wendell or Sherlock. But from day one, Larry called him Ollie, and it stuck."

She led me into the workspace. It was for the most part open, with what I presumed to be Maggie's desk situated against a series of windows that looked out on Main Street. On the other end of the floor was an enclosed conference room; a modest bullpen with four cubicles occupied the center.

"Big office for one person," I said.

"I think my entire floor is still smaller than your private office, and I'm not paying a thousand dollars a square foot for mine. But it's not just me here. I have a secretary and a paralegal, although both of them work part time. You know how it is, feast or famine. When I'm gearing up for trial, I keep them all busy around the clock, and when I'm not, I don't want the overhead. Anyway, I'd give you the tour, but you pretty much have it by turning your head three hundred sixty degrees. So come sit down and we can chat a little about this case of yours that I've read about."

Our friendship was one of the longest continuous relationships I'd maintained. Maybe *the* longest. I communicated from time to time with college and law school classmates on social media, but I hadn't seen any of them since college or law school. Although I'd known Nicky longer than anyone else, the long gap in our relationship exceeded the period we had been friends. But I'd stayed in touch with Maggie, albeit on and off, for the better part of forty years.

"Before we get down to business, I need to say that you look good, Clint. Taking good care of yourself too, I hope."

The compliment was somewhat backhanded. The unspoken implication was that I had barely survived Charlotte's death. I'd seen Maggie since then, but for her, and many people I knew, the stock image of me was of that grief-stricken man who cried uncontrollably at the press conference. I wanted to tell her that, despite outward appearances to the contrary, I was still very much that broken man. The only difference was that I'd buried that pain deep within myself.

"Thanks," I said. "I'm trying. And I would say the same thing to you. You look good. But I know that looks can be deceiving. How are you?"

She smiled, understanding all too well what I meant. The stock image in my mind when I thought of Maggie was at her husband's funeral, when she was obviously not at her best. That was at least a year ago, maybe two.

"Thank you. I'm trying too. Still tough without Larry, but everyone tells me that it takes time. I think it's getting better, and then every once in a while . . ."

I nodded. "Yeah, I know."

"I know you do," she said, reclaiming her smile. "Spending time with the kids helps."

"What are they up to, your kids?"

"None of them are lawyers, thank goodness, although my youngest, Ryan, is threatening to go to law school. I think that's largely because his start-up failed, and he doesn't know what else to do with himself. My eldest, Michael, is thirty-five, married, three kids, and they live in Boulder, which is not ideal for grandma time. The middle guy, Patrick, he's in Manhattan doing I have no idea what for a company about which I don't have the first clue. I've had some business with your daughter over the years. You must be very proud of her. She's got a great reputation in the office. DA material, if you ask me."

That had been the recent rumor du jour—Ella running for District Attorney, either against the incumbent or as the party's nominee after Drake McKenney retires. But whenever I mentioned it to Ella, she brushed it off as courthouse gossip.

"My daughter's career plans are dispensed on a need-to-know basis. Unfortunately, she long ago concluded that her father does not need to know, and as a result, I don't."

Maggie laughed at that. I imagined her children were equally tight-lipped about their lives.

"Forgive me, I think I knew this at one point, but now I can't recall: Is Ella married?"

"No. She has a long-term boyfriend, and they live together. He's a lieutenant with the NYPD. Unfortunately for me, Ella's romantic life is another thing that requires a higher security clearance than I possess, so I have no idea if I'm going to be paying for a wedding in the near future."

"Okay, now that we've complained about our kids," Maggie said with a wry smile, "let's get down to business, shall we? You want the lowdown on a Mr. Jackson Ethan?"

She was right, but only partially so. "I know his older brother, Benjamin."

"Actually, they're half siblings. Didn't you ever wonder why Benjamin is over seventy and Jack is . . . I'd say forty or so, tops?"

The truth was, I hadn't. I probably should have, though.

"Old man Ethan, Benjamin and Jack's dad, he took on a chippie when he must have been pushing seventy himself," Maggie explained. "Jack was the progeny of that blissful union."

"What are your impressions of the new DA?"

"He's not so new. Three years now. He's smart, aggressive, and generally fair, although I know more than a few defense lawyers who think he sometimes cares more about his own reputation than the merits of the case."

"What prosecutor doesn't?"

"Touché, but some more than others."

"Any bad blood between you? I only ask because I thought you'd never leave the DA's office."

"No, nothing like that. I was very close to Arthur. When he was defeated for reelection, Jack was gracious and said that I could stay on, but I knew he'd want his own number-two, so it was time for me to go. Besides, the idea of working for someone who was only marginally older than my son wasn't very appealing. The irony is that if Arthur had won, I'd likely be the one trying this case against you."

"Lucky for me that he lost, then," I said. "But I'm surprised that Jack is taking the lead on this."

"I think it's just too big for him to pass up. A front-page murder case. The chance to beat the great F. Clinton Broden. From Jack's point of view, if he gives it to an underling and there's an acquittal, it's the same political fallout as if he tried it himself and lost. You have to understand that the job out here is different from being the District Attorney in Manhattan. Jack doesn't want to be governor or run for congress or be the GC of a hedge fund. His only ambition is to keep getting reelected. And the best way for him to do that is to avoid a major screwup. He touts his office's ninety-four percent winning percentage like he's gunning for the DA hall of fame. You don't win that often without being selective about the cases you indict and the ones you take to trial. Of course, yours is an outlier. Jack had no choice but to indict. Otherwise, he seems soft on famous people, and that's an even surer way to get booted from office. Even though the Hamptons crowd contributes to his campaign, they all vote in Manhattan. So Jack's real constituents are the handymen and pool cleaners who cater to the summer folks. Those people will remember on Election Day if he didn't indict a hotshot LA writer who murdered Samantha Remsen. On the other hand, if he loses at trial, they're likely to blame the high-priced, hotshot Manhattan lawyer who got the guy off and still reward Jack with their vote for fighting the good fight."

"How's he in front of a jury?"

"Good. He's handsome, so that helps, especially with young women, so you may want to steer clear of them on the jury. He's not a dazzler, but he is thorough."

"So your typical prosecutor?"

"More or less."

Her assessment ended part one of my reconnaissance, sizing up my adversary. I would have preferred Maggie say that Ethan was a lightweight, but I wasn't surprised by her description. The first indication that he'd be a formidable opponent was when he told me that he was trying the case himself. A lesser lawyer would have been only too happy to pawn the long hours off on an underling.

"What do you know about the judge, Molly Sloane?" I asked.

"She's too new for anyone to know much about her. I never crossed paths with her before she became a Your Honor, and nobody I know had ever heard of her before she ended up on the slate. I understand that she did trust and estate law, which is big out here, obviously, but an odd springboard to the bench. I can ask around a little if you'd like."

"Maybe. I'll find out more tomorrow."

"She already scheduled the initial conference?"

"At eleven a.m."

"That tells you something, I guess. She's eager to start the case."

"Me too. I'm going to ask for a trial date ASAP."

Maggie didn't say anything at first. She looked to be considering the various reasons why I might want to rush headlong into trial. I could tell by the squint in her eyes that she hadn't come up with one that made any sense.

"Far be it from me to second-guess you, but your guy's out on bail. What's the hurry?"

"House arrest."

"Same difference. I'm going to go out on a limb here and guess that the sheets at your East Hampton vacation home are softer than the ones they use over at the Riverhead Correctional Facility."

"Well, not in the guest room."

She didn't laugh at my quip. Instead, her eyes asked me to explain.

"My guy doesn't have an alibi. He's asleep in the house. He's just left a party after a blowup fight with his wife, and she stayed behind. Time isn't going to change any of that. The defense is going to be that Tyree Jefferson killed Samantha Remsen. It's a door-number-one or door-number-two situation. She was either murdered in Jefferson's house—which makes him the killer—or she was murdered after Jefferson dropped her off at her house—which means my guy murdered her. On top of that, as I'm sure you remember, Nicky's first wife died under suspicious circumstances. Even though he was acquitted of that crime, the last thing I want is for that story to take root over the course of months, poisoning the minds of prospective jurors. I figure that if I can move quickly to trial, I might be able to fill the jury with people who haven't heard about Nicky's past."

"I hear you," she said, which is lawyer for *I disagree.*

"So you in?"

"In what?"

"If we go to trial fast, I'm going to need help. You should tell your staff that their paychecks are going to get a lot fatter, real fast."

"I'm flattered, but, no offense, I'm too old to carry your bags, Clint."

"That's not what I'm asking for. I need a real sounding board, Maggie. The last time I represented Nicky, right before the verdict was read, I had this sinking feeling in my gut that I was too personally involved in the case. I don't want to feel that way this time."

"In other words, you want someone else to blame if your friend is convicted of murder?"

"I want someone to make sure I don't do something stupid that *gets* my friend convicted of murder."

"Like going immediately to trial, you mean."

"I'll hear you out on that. But only if you're in."

"I'm too old to play hard to get, Clint. I'm in. And I never go to trial any sooner than absolutely necessary."

42.

Wearing the jurist's black robes, the Honorable Molly P. Sloane looked like a child in a Halloween costume. She had impossibly large, dark eyes, a mouth that stretched across her entire face, and long curls that reminded me of a flower child's. If I'd shared this initial observation with Ella, she would have told me—first—I was getting old, and—second—that I was a creature of the patriarchy who found a young woman judge so threatening that I resorted to belittling her youthful appearance.

"Since when have teenagers become State Supreme Court justices?" Maggie whispered in my ear, proving I was not alone in my impression.

For this hearing, Nicky sat at the end of the table with Maggie between us. He was dressed in a suit and tie, although I had lost the battle with the guards to remove the monitoring device.

Before Judge Sloane took the bench, Jack Ethan had come over to our table to exchange pleasantries. "Good to see a local at the defense table," he said. "And leave it to you, Clint, you found the very best we have."

Given the stiffness of Maggie's smile at the compliment, I wondered whether she had left the DA's office of her own accord.

"Clint and I have known each other since you were in diapers, Jack," she said, triggering a tight smile in return from the DA.

"We have a lot of housekeeping matters to take care of today," Judge Sloane said. "But before I get to setting a schedule, I wanted to ask both sides if they had any issues that they wished to address. Mr. Ethan?"

"Thank you, Your Honor. We would like the court to reconsider Judge Romatowski's bail ruling. We believe that house arrest subjects the community to danger, as well as creating an undue risk of flight. Given the seriousness of the charge, the defendant's resources, his lack of ties to this—or, frankly, any—community, and the circumstances regarding the death of his first wife, this is a case that calls out for incarceration pending trial. Can any of us truly say that if Mr. Zamora were a roofer in Speonk or a gardener in Ronkonkoma he would be allowed house arrest while pending trial on a murder charge?"

That answered two questions right away, though neither had been in much doubt. The prosecution would take every opportunity to point out that Nicky was a rich outsider, and that he'd killed his first wife.

Judge Sloane listened to Ethan's pitch earnestly, which I took to be bad news for our side. I knew the request to revoke bail was coming and hoped the judge would swat it away as unnecessarily dredging up something that had already been decided.

"Mr. Broden, care to respond?"

"Thank you, Your Honor. Judge Romatowski already considered these issues, and there is no reason for this court to second-guess his determination."

"The reason is that it's my case, not his," Judge Sloane replied curtly.

I belatedly heard Ella's rebuke in my ears. *The last thing you want to do with a young, inexperienced female judge is tell her not to make her own decisions because an older male judge already told her what to do.*

"Of course, Your Honor. I didn't mean to suggest you didn't have every right to reconsider Judge Romatowski's ruling. That is your prerogative as the trial judge. I was merely stating that there was no basis for you to do so because your colleague got it right the first time. As you can see, Mr. Zamora is here today, and he will be at trial too. Mr. Ethan for some reason thinks that the defendant should be punished now, even though, as we all learned in grade school, a defendant is innocent until proven guilty. So the only issue at this point is what will it take to get this innocent man to appear for trial. His being confined to my house with electronic monitoring is more than enough to accomplish that goal."

The judge hesitated, then said, "I'm going to leave the bail conditions as they are for now. Mr. Zamora, understand that bail is a privilege, not a right. I can—and I will—revoke your bail conditions if I hear that there's even the slightest problem with you being under house arrest. Do you understand that?"

Maggie stood to remind Nicky that he had to come to his feet before responding. "Yes. Thank you," he said.

"Anything else you want to raise, Mr. Ethan?"

"No, Your Honor."

"Mr. Broden?"

"Yes, Your Honor. When Mr. Zamora is in court, we request that the ankle monitor be removed. Obviously, he's not going to flee from this courtroom. And it's stigmatizing, which might ultimately prejudice the jury pool."

Judge Sloane needed little time to think about this ruling. "No, that's not going to happen. At trial, when the jury is present, he won't need to wear the monitoring device. But for now, I don't see the harm. Is that all?"

"I'd like to be heard on the issue of scheduling," I said.

"Yes, that was the main item on my agenda for today as well. When are you thinking the defense will be ready for trial? And don't tell me it's more than a year from today, because I'm not going to put up with that kind of delay."

"To the contrary, Your Honor. We're ready to try this case as soon as the court can accommodate."

I'd heard Maggie out thoroughly on the issue. She said the same things I'd told countless clients in the past about the benefits of delaying, especially when the defendant was not incarcerated: the extra time might be Nicky's last days of freedom; plus delays almost always help the defense because witnesses can die, memories dim, evidence becomes lost or contaminated. It also lets juror passions cool. The conventionally "optimal" time to go to trial is when the jury can no longer remember reading about the crime in the newspapers.

I told Maggie that I understood her point. I simply disagreed.

"I hope you're right," she'd said.

Judge Sloane apparently agreed with Maggie's assessment, because she laughed at my request, although she quickly covered her mouth, realizing the image was less than judicial. "Not what I was expecting, Mr. Broden. So props to you for that. I was told that Clint Broden was the master of delay. And here you are, in a murder trial no less, wanting to go right away. Care to share why?"

"The obvious reason, Your Honor. Mr. Zamora is innocent. Every day the stain of guilt clings to him is a day that justice is not served."

"You heard the man, Mr. Ethan," Judge Sloane said. "He wants a trial, and he wants it now. You ready for that?"

Ethan looked over at the defense table before addressing the court, the way the opposing coach smiles across the sidelines when his adversary has run a trick play. "I'm not sure what game the defense is playing here, Your Honor, but we need a little more time to get ready for trial. We're happy to put this on a fast track, but I would think ninety to one hundred twenty days is appropriate."

I didn't give him the chance to say more. "Your Honor, I'm really very surprised that Mr. Ethan is not ready to proceed. He was certainly ready to get an indictment. He was certainly ready to ask this court to incarcerate Mr. Zamora pending trial. Is he actually now representing that he does not today have sufficient evidence to prove Mr. Zamora's guilt beyond a reasonable doubt, and he needs another three to four months to acquire it? Because if that's the case, we move for an immediate dismissal of the indictment. That will give the DA all the time he needs to assemble his case, and then he can reindict Mr. Zamora—or whomever this new evidence that he hopes to collect points to as the murderer—at that time. Perhaps he should not have been so hasty to rush to judgment if he was so uncertain about his case."

Ethan was shouting over the last part of my speech, although I couldn't make out what he was saying. Apparently, the court reporter couldn't discern what either of us had said, because she lifted her hands from the steno machine, her way of signaling that she couldn't transcribe anything.

"Gentlemen, please," Judge Sloane said. "I get it. You're both grandstanding. Playing to the jury pool or the news or . . . whatever. But my job is to keep everything real in my courtroom. I made a promise to myself when I was sworn in as a judge that I wasn't going to pretend that I knew what I didn't know. But I was definitely going to figure it out quickly. So here's me putting that into practice: Mr. Broden, I have no idea why you want to go to trial ASAP. But that's not my job. It's your job. Mr. Ethan, I understand why you don't want to go to trial as fast as Mr. Broden. You assumed that Mr. Broden would seek to delay. And I'm certain that if Mr. Broden had asked for a trial date sometime next year, you would have said you were ready to go tomorrow. One of the things that has always seemed unfair to me about the way our system operates is that the prosecution can take its sweet time to bring an indictment, then demand an early trial date to get the defense before it's ready. I suspect Mr. Broden is hoping to turn the tables on you in that regard. Only time will tell if that was a smart move or a dumb one, but he has that right. So here's what I'm going to do. I would like nothing more than to have a big juicy trial on my docket. So let's put that down for three weeks from today. Who doesn't want to celebrate autumn in a courtroom, am I right?"

Ethan looked like someone had shot his dog. "Your Honor, I told our witnesses that nothing imminent was going to happen. As you may know, the last people to see Ms. Remsen alive were the director and costars of the movie she was shooting. Those folks all live in California and have returned there. For all I know, they're out of the country on some type of shoot right now. I don't know if I can get them back for trial."

"Here's another thing that never made any sense to me," Judge Sloane said. "Why do celebrities get treated like their time is so much more valuable than everyone else's? These are people with access to private jets, right? Tell them to use one and get back here for trial. If you told me that your witness was building somebody's deck and they might lose their job if they didn't finish it by the end of the summer, I might be more sympathetic to a delay because of witness unavailability, but not because somebody wants to walk the red carpet or tour the Côte d'Azur rather than give trial testimony. I would think you would be too, considering that those movie-star friends of yours, Mr. Ethan, are not members of this community. I have to say that I was moved by your impassioned plea a few moments ago on behalf of . . . was that the roofer in Ronkonkoma and the gardener in Speonk, or was it the other way around?"

"Your Honor . . . ," he said.

"I could make the trial even sooner."

"I was about to say that the People will be ready to proceed on the schedule set by the court."

"Excellent. I do so love it when a plan comes together."

43.

It is a ritual I've repeated in every case. Before the trial begins, I say a silent prayer. Not for victory, but for justice to prevail. I say it silently because no client would join in the sentiment. The accused pray only for freedom. I pass no judgment on their self-preservation instinct, but before going into battle on their behalf, I have to remind myself to stay faithful to something greater than victory.

This case was different. I still said a prayer, but it wasn't for justice. I was looking for something else entirely.

Trial officially began with the selection of the jury, *voire dire* as it's referred to by lawyers. In most cases, the jury is selected in a day. In those with considerable pretrial publicity, however, it lasts longer. Once I had a *voire dire* that took longer than the trial.

Like every lawyer, I lean toward certain stereotypes in picking a jury. I favor people with nontraditional jobs—freelance writers, dog walkers, and the like—because they tend to skew more liberal, and therefore are more apt to be skeptical of law enforcement. In the same vein, I reject anyone who served in the military or has a relative who has done so. In a pinch, I can find comfort in the most tangential support—selecting jurors who wear casual shoes, on the theory that they're not uptight and therefore are more likely to be open-minded. I therefore avoid men in brogues and women in stilettos. A bearded man usually makes the cut (no pun intended) unless his facial hair is too well groomed. But the gold standard of a defense juror is anyone who can sympathize with being wrongly accused, which is why you rarely see a young African American rejected by the defense.

For Nicky's case, I realized quickly that my plan to rush to trial to find jurors who had not been tainted with the knowledge of Carolyn McDermott's murder was ill conceived. Anyone with a social media account knew the score.

Toward the end of the selection process, an older white man was up for consideration. By sight alone, he was the prosecutor's dream: big and overweight, but with a cocky look that told you that he had never been convinced about something he didn't already believe. When he added that he considered himself a Fox News junkie, Ethan looked positively giddy. Which was why, when I told Judge Sloane that the defense would also seat Mr. Fox News, I thought Maggie was going to slug me.

"What are you *doing*?" she whispered. "That guy looks like he's ready to convict right now."

"Trust me," I said.

———

"My name is Jack Ethan, and I am the District Attorney for Suffolk County," is the way he began his opening statement, so that everyone knew he hadn't sent an underling to swing the sword at Nicky. "Murder is the most heinous act one person can commit against another. It is among the bedrock principles on which our society stands that murderers must be punished. Ladies and gentlemen of the jury, the evidence will show beyond a reasonable doubt that Nicholas Zamora is a murderer."

After this preface, Ethan indulged in a dramatic pause and then attempted to make eye contact with the jurors, one at a time. Mr. Fox News was smiling at him, but so were the freelance blogger, the man with the shaggy beard, and even the woman in the hijab. The others maintained more neutral expressions, but I was certain that none of them disagreed with punishing murderers.

"The evidence will be incontrovertible that Samantha Remsen was murdered. You will hear from police officers that Ms. Remsen's body was found washed up on the beach not far from the home in East Hampton she was renting with the accused for the summer. The medical examiner who conducted the autopsy will testify that the cause of Ms. Remsen's death was a broken neck, not drowning. She was dead before she ever went in the ocean. Dr. Cammerman knows that for a fact because there was not a drop of water present in Ms. Remsen's lungs. That can only mean that she had stopped breathing before she entered the water. Which, in turn, means that someone put her in the ocean after ensuring she was already dead."

At our last meeting before trial, we had conducted mock openings. Maggie had taken the role of prosecutor and delivered a more passionate presentation than Ethan was mustering, at least so far, hitting the same notes. When she was finished, she told Nicky to show more emotion when listening to Ethan detail the prosecution's evidence.

"Remember, she's your wife, and you loved her," Maggie said. "You need to show the jurors that you're more repulsed at what happened to Samantha than they ever could be."

I turned slightly to gauge Nicky's reaction to see if he was following Maggie's instructions. Sure enough, he looked sickened by Ethan's recitation of the circumstances of his wife's death.

"How do we know that Mr. Zamora is the one who murdered his wife and put her body in the ocean?" Ethan asked. "On this, the evidence will be what is called circumstantial, but that makes it no less reliable. If you are standing in front of a bank and you hear the alarm go off, and a moment later someone wearing a mask runs out holding a bag full of money with bank markings on it, all that evidence is circumstantial because you did not witness the robbery firsthand. But that doesn't mean that you can't conclude beyond a reasonable doubt that the man holding the bag of money had just robbed the bank. In this case, there is no eyewitness to the murder. That's not unusual. Most murders are not committed in the plain sight of an eyewitness. This means that circumstantial evidence plays an important role in the conviction of most murderers."

Maggie scribbled in all caps on the legal pad between us—*OBJECT*. She was right that Ethan's detour into the meaning of circumstantial evidence, as well as the hypothetical bank robbery scenario, had crossed the line into argument, which is prohibited in an opening statement.

I rejected her advice with a shake of my head.

"Allow me to lay out this circumstantial evidence—all of which points to Mr. Zamora, and Mr. Zamora alone, as the murderer," Ethan continued. "First, you will hear that there was considerable tension in the marriage between Mr. Zamora and Ms. Remsen. Mr. Zamora was quite a bit older than his wife was—by some thirty years. He did not support her decision to accept a starring role in a movie being filmed in East Hampton, but Ms. Remsen defied him and accepted the part despite his objection. But most importantly, you will hear that only an hour or so before Ms. Remsen was murdered, she and her husband had a terrible fight. That fight was in front of witnesses, people whose names you've undoubtedly heard of from the movies and the music world. Jaydon Lennox and his wife, Paige Anderson-Lennox. Chloe Lassiter and her boyfriend, the musician known as T-Rex. And their host, the film director Tyree Jefferson. They will each tell you what happened at that party. Specifically, they will testify that Mr. Zamora accused Mr. Jefferson of having an affair with his wife, and after speaking briefly with Ms. Remsen, Mr. Zamora stormed home alone. Ms. Remsen not only abandoned her husband in favor of Mr. Jefferson in front of the others, but Mr. Jefferson will testify that, after the others left the party, he had sex with Ms. Remsen. That, ladies and gentlemen, is the motive in this case. The oldest one there is. Jealousy. Mr. Zamora knew that he was going to lose his wife to a handsome, younger man."

Nicky's description of the party had been slightly different, but not necessarily in a way that meant he'd been lying. "It was your usual Hollywood debauchery," was how he had described it. "Lots of drugs and alcohol. At one point, I went to the bathroom, and when I came back out, he was dancing with Samantha. I thought he was getting a little too handsy, and I told him that he needed to keep his distance, and not in a nice way. Some other words were exchanged, I don't remember what either of us said. Schoolyard-type taunts. Stupid shit. Samantha finally took me aside, and I apologized to her for my outburst. She said she understood, but I had to remember that Tyree was her boss. We agreed that it was best if I just went home. She kissed me goodbye and said she wouldn't be too late."

Maggie and I had reached out to the other participants at the dinner party to see if they would confirm Nicky's version of events. Each, through counsel, declined to speak with us or even to offer a glimpse of their expected testimony. It is one of the many inequities of the criminal justice system: if defense counsel instructs witnesses not to cooperate with the prosecution, it's obstruction of justice, but prosecutors can send that message loud and clear without breaking the law.

This was the first time I was hearing that Jefferson was claiming he'd had sex with Samantha the night of her death. From what Nicky had told me, he hadn't known that. The autopsy hadn't revealed any semen, but that didn't mean that Jefferson and Samantha hadn't had sex.

Witnesses at a trial—and maybe people in everyday life too—either tell the truth or lie due to some perceived benefit. I couldn't come up with a motive for Tyree to lie about bedding Samantha, unless it was to burnish his already solid reputation as a lothario.

"After they had sex, Mr. Jefferson drove Ms. Remsen home that same night," Ethan continued. "The plan was for her to pick up some things that she needed, including her phone, which she'd inadvertently left at home when she went to the party, and then she would drive her car back to Mr. Jefferson's home. She was planning to live with Mr.

Jefferson for the rest of the filming. In other words, she was going to leave her husband. The very evening she was murdered."

Maggie pointed back to the legal pad. Her index finger tapping on the word *OBJECT*.

I remained mute.

"Mr. Jefferson will tell you that taking Ms. Remsen home was the biggest mistake of his life. He dropped her off at approximately one thirty a.m. He watched her enter the home she shared with the defendant. He will further testify that he fully expected her to return to his home with some of her things and her car later that night. But she never did. There is one person, and one person only, who could possibly have seen Ms. Remsen alive after she entered her home: the defendant, Nicholas Zamora."

Ethan didn't say that Nicky had seen Samantha because he couldn't prove that. But he worded it so it sounded like the same thing.

"That's where the prosecution's proof ends," Ethan said. "What happened behind the closed door of their home on the beach is known only by the victim, Samantha Remsen, and the accused, Nicholas Zamora. And of course, Ms. Remsen cannot tell us, as she has been silenced forever."

Ethan paused again, and I recognized the trick. He was planting the seed with the jury that maybe Nicky wouldn't tell them what had happened either. That is the defendant's constitutional right, of course. The Fifth Amendment allowed Nicky not to testify and prohibited any reference to his declination before the jury. But that didn't mean that a smart prosecutor couldn't get the point across loud and clear, as Ethan was doing.

"Mr. Zamora told the police that his wife never returned home that evening," Ethan continued. "But that story—the one he told the police—is in direct contradiction to what Mr. Jefferson will tell you, under oath."

Ethan was goading Nicky and, by extension, me. He had promised the jury that his star witness, Tyree Jefferson, would tell them what had happened. The challenge was for me to promise them that Nicky would do likewise when it was my turn to address the jury.

When Ethan finished his opening, I had to decide whether I would rise to the bait.

44.

"Mr. Broden," Judge Sloane said, "you may present your opening statement at this time."

"Request a short recess, Your Honor."

"Very short, Mr. Broden," she said. "I want to finish your opening today."

After the jury left the courtroom, I repositioned myself so I was standing between Maggie and Nicky. Crouching down so my whisper would not be heard by the press or the prosecutors, all of whom were less than fifteen feet away, I said, "I'm not going to open."

The defense has the option of opening after the prosecution or reserving its opening statement until the prosecution has rested its case. Deferring allows the defense not to commit to any position until it hears the prosecution's evidence. But I've never seen a defense lawyer reserve an opening statement. The conventional wisdom, which is backed by considerable research, is that jurors make up their minds immediately—often before the first witness testifies—and therefore it is incumbent upon the defense to put forth its theory of the case as early as possible.

"Why?" Maggie asked before Nicky could.

"If we open the way we planned—without promising Nicky's testimony—it looks weak next to Ethan's promise that Jefferson is going to tell all," I said. "And we can't promise Nicky's testimony until we know how the judge is going to come out on Carolyn. Our best play is to keep our powder dry and not commit to anything until we see how the prosecution's case comes in."

How the judge was going to come out *on Carolyn* had become our shorthand for the most important issue in the trial—whether, despite Nicky's acquittal in his first trial, Judge Sloane would permit evidence indicating that he had, in fact, killed his first wife. Both sides had filed briefs on the issue claiming that legal precedent supported their position. Judge Sloane had taken the issue under advisement, which meant that we wouldn't know her ruling until she made it, and when that would be was anyone's guess.

"If we're voting, I say you should open," Maggie whispered back. "I've never reserved my opening. And if the reason you're thinking of waiting is because you don't want to open without committing Nicky to taking the stand, then I say two things: First, you can open without making that commitment. But if you think you can't, then let's commit to it right now. You know as well as I do, he's got to testify if we're going to win. But like I said, I don't know if we have to make that call right now. But I do know that not opening is worse than a bad opening."

It was certainly an impassioned plea. I was a little taken aback that Maggie would challenge my advice in front of my client. Then again, Nicky was now *our* client, and I hadn't given her much warning or time to prepare a more politic opinion.

"You know my vote, Nicky," I said. "I'm not going to say that Maggie's wrong. I normally open too. But I think it's a mistake in this case. It's your call in the end. What do you want to do?"

Nicky took a deep breath. Of the three of us, he was the only one unqualified to offer an opinion.

"I'm in your hands, Clinton. Whatever you say."

———

There was a buzz in the courtroom when I informed Judge Sloane that I would reserve my opening statement until after the prosecution rested its case-in-chief. Like my cocounsel, the media had not expected that. By the look on her face, neither had Judge Sloane.

"Call your first witness, Mr. Ethan," Judge Sloane said.

Ethan too was caught unawares. He'd undoubtedly thought he wouldn't have to put on a witness until tomorrow, giving him the evening to prepare that direct testimony. In a shaky voice he said, "The People call Dr. Daniel Cammerman."

There was nothing in the forensic evidence that we were going to contest. Unlike in Nicky's first murder trial, we wouldn't be arguing that death had occurred accidentally. There was obviously no way that Samantha broke her own neck, then put herself in the ocean. Nor could we argue that Samantha died at any time other than the eleven o'clock to four o'clock window provided by the ME. She was at the party in plain sight of multiple witnesses until after midnight, and Jefferson claimed that they were alone for an hour or so until he took her back to her house at around one thirty. If I could create my own evidence, the time of death would have been limited to that window when they were alone—midnight to one thirty. We'd talked to five pathologists in hopes that one would tell us that, but none could. The best we got was three thirty, and that didn't do us much good at all.

Dr. Cammerman looked the part of a death doctor. He had a full gray beard, round steel glasses, and a stern resting expression. His testimony came in smoothly, as Ethan walked him through the findings set out in the autopsy report. Time of death (eleven o'clock to four o'clock). Cause of death (broken neck). Possibility of drowning (no). Signs of struggle (no). DNA on the body (no). Semen present (no).

I didn't make a single objection. When Judge Sloane told me I could begin my cross-examination, I said, "The defense has no questions for this witness."

After court, we adjourned to my home. Although Maggie's office might have been more comfortable to work out of, she didn't have a full kitchen and a chef, which I did. Trial time is precious, and spending it in a restaurant or cooking was wasteful.

"Maybe tomorrow you'll actually say something," Nicky said while we ate.

He matched his words with a smile, but it was a nervous one. I saw him catching Maggie's expression after mine.

"No reason to attack a witness who doesn't hurt us," I said. "When we do it to the witnesses we need to discredit, it'll be all the more effective because we didn't cross Cammerman."

Maggie came to my defense. "Not crossing him was the right move, Nick."

But after Nicky retired for the evening, and Maggie and I were alone, she could no longer hold her tongue. In a quiet voice, so as to not reveal to our client that there was dissension between his lawyers, she asked, "Is something going on here that I don't know?"

"No," I said, content to leave it at that.

"You sure?"

"Yes."

The truth, of course, was that there was much going on that Maggie didn't know. More than I could ever explain to her.

———

Before Nicky's first trial, I had gone to Macy's and bought ten white shirts. I wore the first during the initial pretrial conference, the second at the final pretrial conference, and the third on the first day of trial.

That third shirt caused the problem.

I had mistakenly included among my shirt purchases one with French cuffs, and at the time, I didn't own a pair of cuff links. I might have simply put it back in the bag and reached for the next shirt in the pile. If I had, my life would have played out differently. But I didn't. Instead, I remembered that Anne sometimes wore a French-cuffed shirt.

She kept her jewelry in a large mahogany box. I'm not sure I had ever previously opened it or even seen its interior. The box had earrings on top, rings inserted in grooves, and a false bottom hiding Anne's larger pieces.

If only Anne had kept her cuff links on top with her rings . . . but she hadn't.

I removed the false bottom. There were the cuff links I was searching for—silk knots in a lavender shade—among the chains and pendants and lockets that Anne occasionally wore on special occasions.

I shut the jewelry box and didn't think of it again. That is, until Brandon Sherman put on the overhead projector a photograph of the sapphire pendant that Nicky had allegedly purchased for his mistress.

At first, it was a memory I no longer trusted. Hadn't I seen the exact same pendant in Anne's jewelry box? Could two such necklaces look alike?

That evening, I went back to Anne's jewelry box to confirm that I was mistaken. But when I removed the false bottom, the necklace was gone.

I don't know how she got it to Nicky. I assume he called her from the courthouse pay phone, and she went to his home, leaving it in the mailbox. But when Nicky brandished it in court, I knew beyond all doubt that he was holding the same piece I'd seen in Anne's jewelry box.

I never made the deliberate decision not to discuss it with Anne. In fact, the opposite. I decided that I would wait until after Nicky's trial and then confront her about the betrayal. But after his acquittal, I lost my nerve, fearing that I might push Anne further away, perhaps even into Nicky's embrace. So I kept my discovery to myself.

I'm ashamed now that I made the coward's decision then. I should have had more faith in Anne, and in our marriage—that it could withstand the truth. I might have learned things about my wife that will now forever be mysteries, and perhaps in the end it would have brought us closer together.

Once or twice in the years that followed, I sensed that Anne wanted to come clean. In each of those instances, I said something to suggest that there was no need. Anne must have recognized my code, because she always stopped short.

Without knowing the truth, I had filled in a version of events that allowed me to go on with my life. That Nicky had been the aggressor, and in a moment of weakness, fueled by loneliness that I had ignored and was to blame for, Anne succumbed to temptation. That she immediately felt guilty, and perhaps the necklace had not been a gift to promise a future together, but one to entice her back. That Nicky alone killed Carolyn, because Anne would never have been part of the taking of a life. That the murder was for his own twisted reasons and not caused in any way by his desire to live happily ever after with my wife, rather than his own.

For thirty-four years, I told myself that story, and at times it soothed me, but more often than not it burned. By sparing Anne from confessing the truth, I allowed her affair with Nicky to take on mythic proportions in my mind, to the point that I questioned everything that I thought had been true between Anne and me.

This was, at long last, my opportunity to learn the truth. For some reason, even after he had betrayed me in the most fundamental way a friend can, I still trusted him to provide me the answers I longed for. How did it begin? How long did it last? What were their future plans? Why didn't those plans come to fruition? Was Carolyn murdered because she learned of their affair?

Most important, I wanted Nicky to, once and for all, tell me who had murdered Carolyn: My best friend or my wife?

45.

The next morning, Ethan put the police detective in charge of the investigation on the stand. As during the medical examiner's testimony the previous day, I would have very little to do with Detective Hibbitts. As part of the discovery the prosecution was required to produce, I had already seen his interview notes, so I knew what he'd claim Nicky told him, which was the story Nicky was sticking to.

"Detective Hibbitts, when you first met the defendant, Nicholas Zamora, what did he tell you regarding his wife's whereabouts?" Ethan asked.

"That he had no idea where she was. He told us about the party the night before, and he claimed that she had never come home."

"What, specifically, did he tell you about the party?"

"That there had been a party at the home of Tyree Jefferson. That large amounts of drugs and alcohol had been consumed by others, but not by him. That he had a disagreement with Mr. Jefferson, and that he had left the party alone."

"Was that his characterization? A *disagreement?*"

"Yes."

"Did he ever tell you what the disagreement was about?"

"He was never very specific about that. When he first explained it to us, he blamed it on both of them being drunk, and very generally told us that he was upset with the way Mr. Jefferson was acting toward his wife. After we heard from other witnesses and learned more about what actually was said, Mr. Zamora admitted that the argument had to do with his concerns that Mr. Jefferson might be having an affair with his wife."

"He admitted that to you? That he suspected Mr. Jefferson was having sex with his wife?" Ethan asked, even though that was exactly what Hibbitts had testified.

"Yes. That is what he ultimately said, although it took several meetings with him to get there. By the time he admitted it, we already had ample evidence of the affair through text messages, so there was no point in denying it anymore."

Ethan circled back to the prosecution's table, ostensibly to look at his notes for his next line of inquiry. More likely, his purpose was to allow the last exchange to sink in with the jury.

———

On cross, my goal was to lay the groundwork that the police were so focused on Nicky that they neglected to consider Jefferson as a suspect. Although *rush to judgment* was a cliché, there's a good reason for that—it's often true.

"Detective Hibbitts, when you first spoke with Mr. Zamora, were you already considering him a suspect in his wife's murder?"

"I'm a police detective. So whenever I am called to do anything, there is the possibility that a crime has occurred, or I wouldn't have been called in the first place. But in a missing-persons situation, it often turns out that no crime has been committed. The missing person returns unharmed and explains that the entire thing was just a misunderstanding. When I first met Mr. Zamora, I was open to the idea that would occur in this instance as well."

"When you say you were open to it, can we take from that answer that you were also open to the fact that this might be a situation in which foul play was involved in Ms. Remsen's disappearance?"

"Yes. That is also a possibility in any missing-persons case."

"You reached that conclusion—that a crime might have been committed regarding Ms. Remsen—even though there was no evidence of that?"

"There was some evidence of it. She was missing."

Score one for Detective Hibbitts. He was a good witness.

"Did the police search Tyree Jefferson's car for DNA belonging to Ms. Remsen?"

"We did. But there was nothing there."

"In other words, there is nothing the police found to corroborate Mr. Jefferson's claim that he took Ms. Remsen home that evening?"

"That's right."

Score one for me.

———

The production assistant from the movie came next, Katlyn Belton. She reminded me a little of Charlotte, with her dark hair and dark eyes that combined to provide a certain beauty that you knew would never fade.

"Mr. Jefferson told me that he thought Ms. Remsen had overslept and asked me to get her," she said.

Maggie whispered, "Hearsay," but I let it go, even though she was right. What Jefferson had told her should be admissible through only his testimony.

"What were your perceptions of Mr. Zamora's demeanor at this time?"

"What do you mean?"

"I mean, after you told him that his wife was missing, how did he react? Did he seem concerned to you? Worried about his wife's whereabouts?"

This elicited a "leading" whisper from Maggie. I ignored that too.

"No. Not very much. I thought I might be more worried than he was about the situation. I knew I could get fired if I couldn't find Samantha Remsen and get her to the set."

"So you were more worried about losing your job than Mr. Zamora was about losing his wife?"

This time I objected.

"Withdrawn," Ethan said, his point having been made without the need for an answer to the question.

When it was my turn, I asked, "Had Ms. Remsen ever overslept for work before then?"

"No."

"In fact, this was the first time she'd ever been late by even a minute, right?"

"Yes."

"Other actors were late from time to time, weren't they?"

"Yes."

"But never Samantha Remsen."

"No."

"And you say that Mr. Jefferson told you that he thought she was late on set—for the first time ever—because *he* thought she must have overslept? That's what he said to you?"

"Yes."

"You're not a mind reader, correct?"

She laughed. "No. I'm a PA," she said, causing everyone to laugh with her.

"Isn't it possible that Mr. Jefferson was lying to you when he said he thought Ms. Remsen had overslept?"

"I don't know."

"Right. Just like you don't know if he killed Ms. Remsen."

Ethan objected, causing Katlyn to look up at Judge Sloane with a confused expression. "Am I supposed to answer that?" she asked.

"No," the judge said. "I'm pretty sure it was rhetorical."

———

Late that night, Maggie and I were at her office. Tomorrow would be her big day in court, as she was going to take the lead in cross-examining the party guests. All except Tyree Jefferson, who was my responsibility. I'd told Nicky to get some downtime tonight. Watch television or read. Have a glass of scotch, but just one. Get a good night's sleep.

"You know that Nick . . . well, he doesn't understand what you're doing," Maggie said.

"Him or you?"

Maggie didn't insult me with subterfuge. "I'm not being judgmental. I just don't understand what's going on, that's all."

"What is it that you don't understand, Maggie?"

"When you made a different call than I would have about rushing the trial, or about seating a juror or two, or even about reserving the opening, I was willing to give you the benefit of the doubt. But . . . we prepared a defense that was focused on telling the jury that Jefferson killed Samantha, and we agreed that we would hit it hard at every opportunity. Call me crazy, but I expected you to do that with Hibbitts. Hit him at every point that he was so starstruck by Jefferson that he never gave his story the scrutiny it deserved, and in that way we kept the jury's focus on the fact that Jefferson is a lying sack when he says he drove her home. That he never texted her that night, which proved he wasn't expecting her back. But all you did with Hibbitts was show that her DNA wasn't in his car. I'm not sure that gets us anywhere. You don't normally leave DNA in a car after a five-minute ride."

I didn't take offense at Maggie's second-guessing. To the contrary, I would have been disappointed if she had kept her concerns to herself.

"I made a judgment call. Hibbitts was a better witness than I expected. I was worried that if we pushed too hard that he hadn't given Jefferson enough scrutiny, he'd have an answer for that. It seemed unnecessary to risk it. It'll be more effective if we hit Jefferson with that."

She looked at me with a wary expression. "Tell me the truth. Did he kill his first wife? Because that's the only thing I can think of that might be the reason that you're . . . doing whatever it is you're doing here."

That question had hung over every decision we'd made concerning trial strategy. We'd spent hours researching the grounds on which Judge Sloane should exclude any reference to Carolyn's death at trial, as well as discussing how the judge would rule on that issue. But Maggie had never before asked me to answer it.

I had previously assumed that her self-restraint was calculated. The answer didn't matter to our defense, and possessing such knowledge could only compromise it. If Nicky confessed to the murder, even though double jeopardy prevented him from being charged again if we knew of his guilt for *that* crime, he could still be charged with perjury for lying about it under oath in this trial, and we were ethically prohibited from allowing him to testify that he was innocent. Indeed, Maggie's question went to whether I'd already violated that rule—the criminal offense of suborning perjury—when Nicky testified to his innocence in the first trial.

"He testified that he didn't do it," I said.

"I know what he said. I read the transcript. Every word of it. I wasn't asking what he said. I thought you might tell me the truth."

"He never confessed to me, if that's what you're asking."

"It wasn't," she said.

She wanted my opinion.

"I don't know," I said. "But I believe someone killed her."

"What's that supposed to mean? If not Nick, who?"

"His mistress."

46.

All court days begin with the same pomp. First, the bailiff announces the judge's arrival from chambers with three knocks on the doorframe of the courtroom. Everyone rises, and after the judge takes the bench, she instructs them to be seated. After that, the jury is summoned, and everyone rises again as they enter.

The following morning, however, Judge Sloane deviated from the standard routine. Before telling everyone to be seated, she announced that she had given the jury the morning off because she wanted to hear further argument on the motions *in limine*—the Latin term for our request that she not allow any mention of Carolyn McDermott's death or Nicky's first trial for her murder. We had already thrashed out these issues before trial, but apparently Judge Sloane had some unanswered questions.

Like so many things in the law, the answers to those questions could be found only by going back in time. In this case, to Christmas Eve 1898. On that date, a man named Harry Cornish received a Christmas gift by mail at his home at the Knickerbocker Club. The postmark on the package was December 23, 1898. There was no card in the envelope, but the box indicated the gift was from Tiffany's. Inside was a blue bottle bearing a Bromo-Seltzer label.

A few days later, Cornish offered the Bromo-Seltzer to Katherine Adams, who was suffering from a headache. Upon taking the Bromo-Seltzer, Adams collapsed and died.

The police arrested Roland Molineux for the Adams murder. In the prior year, Molineux and Cornish had a nasty disagreement over, of all things, Cornish's management of the Knickerbocker Club. The evidence further showed that Molineux had purchased something from the Tiffany's stationery department in December 1898 (but not what he had bought), and he had been seen in the vicinity of the New York post office on the afternoon of December 23, 1898. There was also some similarity between Molineux's handwriting and the address written on the package, although the science of handwriting recognition at the time was still too new to establish a definitive match.

During Molineux's trial, the prosecution put on evidence that in the month prior to the Adams murder, Henry C. Barnet had died after receiving a gift by mail at his residence at the Knickerbocker Club. The gift was found to be poison of the same type that had killed Adams.

From these sordid facts emerged a rule of jurisprudence that would determine whether the jury would hear anything about Carolyn McDermott's death. The Molineux Rule, as it had come to be known, posited that the prosecution may not introduce evidence of another crime to show guilt in the case presented to the jury. However, like almost every rule in the law, there were exceptions. Evidence of a prior crime could be used to reveal motive, intent, modus operandi, identity, or a common scheme or plan. In other words, if the prior crime was so distinct and similar to the current crime as to be akin to a signature, it was admissible to show guilt.

Maggie and I had argued in our papers that none of the Molineux factors permitted introduction of evidence concerning Carolyn

McDermott's death into the trial for Samantha Remsen's murder. First and foremost, a jury had found that Carolyn had not been murdered at all. Or at least that there was a reasonable doubt as to whether Nicky had murdered her. But aside from that, the thirty-four years between the deaths, the fact that the circumstances in each case bore no similarity—a drowning in a bathtub versus a broken neck—meant that there was no link between them sufficient to consider them signature crimes that could only have been committed by Nicky.

I was convinced that we were right on the law. I was equally certain that no one who was ignorant of the Molineux Rule would agree. Ask a hundred people whether the fact that Nicky was accused of murdering his first wife was relevant to whether he had murdered his second, and every single one of them would answer in the affirmative.

A more experienced judge would likely not have had so much trouble wrestling with the issue. Judge Sloane, however, had apparently been unable to make up her mind.

"Mr. Ethan, the only link that I see you attempting to establish between the crime that Mr. Zamora presently stands accused of and the crime of which he was acquitted some three decades ago is that they both involved his wife," she said at the outset of the hearing. "Am I missing something there?"

"The murder of both Mr. Zamora's wives meets the Molineux Rule exceptions," Ethan said, which answered Judge Sloane's question; she was not missing anything at all. He had nothing.

"In other words, you believe that the law would *always* permit the introduction of evidence concerning the suspicious death of a first wife if the accused is on trial for murdering another wife."

"I'm not prepared to say *always*, Your Honor. But in this case, yes."

"That's where I'm stuck, Mr. Ethan. This case seems to be more of a no, because it is not clear that Mr. Zamora's first wife was even murdered. That's what troubles me. What I see happening here is that we're going to end up retrying the McDermott murder case in its entirety, thirty-four years after the fact. And the sole purpose of doing that is to say, *See, Mr. Zamora killed his first wife, so you should find him guilty of killing his second wife.* It seems to me that is exactly the kind of connection that the Molineux Rule was designed to prevent."

When the judge is going your way, the best way to help your cause is to keep your mouth shut. But when Judge Sloane asked me if I wanted to be heard, I stood to address the court.

"The Molineux Rule prohibits any reference to Carolyn McDermott's death in 1986 because the prosecution cannot say that both of Mr. Zamora's wives were even murdered."

Judge Sloane stopped me there. "I'm not sure that's the key factor, Mr. Broden. Wouldn't you agree that if a defendant was on trial for murder using . . . a blowtorch, for example, and there was evidence of him blow-torching someone else to death, the prior incident would be admissible in the trial, even if the defendant had never been convicted of the prior offense?"

Despite her inexperience, Judge Sloane was obviously smart, which enabled her to see through the smoke screens Ethan and I were creating. He was saying that the murder of the first wife was always admissible in the trial of the murder of the second without regard to the lack of any commonality of the facts, and I was saying that the acquittal in the first murder makes it *never* admissible in a subsequent murder trial, no matter how similar the circumstances.

Ethan saw a glimmer of hope in the judge's hypothetical and came to his feet. "Your Honor—"

"Please sit down, Mr. Ethan. You too, Mr. Broden," Judge Sloane said.

She didn't say anything else for at least thirty seconds. The silence felt interminable.

Finally, she said, "Herewith is the decision of the court."

Judge Sloane read what turned out to be a seven-page decision. At first it wasn't clear which way she was going to rule, as she set forth the facts in a neutral recitation. But it soon became apparent that she would not admit anything into evidence having to do with Carolyn's murder.

We were now free to put Nicky on the stand. He could testify that he hadn't seen Samantha Remsen after he left the party.

Of course, I doubted very much that was the truth.

47.

Having multiple witnesses to an event can sometimes be more of a curse than a blessing at trial. There are bound to be discrepancies with every iteration, and opposing counsel can focus jurors on those small deviations to call into question the larger points of agreement.

That said, I doubted Ethan would have that problem regarding the dinner party. All five of his witnesses were celebrities. Jurors always believe celebrities.

I wondered whom Ethan would choose to put on first. I knew it wouldn't be Chloe Lassiter, who looked like a child, or her boyfriend, T-Rex, who was well known for his antipolice lyrics and a generally thuggish persona. That left one of the Lennoxes to carry the water. My money was on Jaydon Lennox; I even proposed a five-dollar bet with Maggie to make it interesting.

She laughed. "First, I find the case pretty interesting all by itself, thank you very much. And I take it that you never saw *Guilty Minds?*"

A popular film from maybe two decades before. The movie that made Jaydon Lennox a star.

"No."

"Jaydon Lennox played a guy who lied on the stand to protect his best friend. He gets stabbed in the heart by that same best friend in the end, and his last line is something like, 'I would have lied for you again, if only you'd asked.'"

"So you're saying it'll be Paige who goes first," I said with a smile.

"That's what I'm saying." Maggie smiled back. "And I'll bet you *ten* bucks."

Before we could shake hands to seal the deal, Ethan said, "The People call Paige Anderson-Lennox to the stand."

"You can owe me," Maggie whispered.

Judge Sloane had a rule that the lawyer who handled the questioning was the only one who could object during the other side's examination. That meant I'd be a spectator for Paige Anderson-Lennox, as well as the other witnesses to follow, assuming Ethan called the entire dinner party to the stand. To signal this change of lineup to Judge Sloane, Maggie and I had switched seats, so now I sat beside Nicky in the middle of the defense counsel table.

Paige Anderson-Lennox was wearing oversize, black-framed eyeglasses that did little to hide a face most people would recognize in a crowd. She had once been Hollywood's It Girl and, for a brief period, had commanded the highest salary of any actress. By the time she turned forty, however, leading-lady roles had become scarcer, and she started taking on character parts. To the surprise of many, she turned out to be an excellent actress when given the right material. So much so that the conventional wisdom was that she had been robbed when she didn't win an Oscar last year.

"What was your understanding of the relationship between Tyree Jefferson and Samantha Remsen?" Ethan asked her.

"They were close."

"How close? In other words, did you understand that they were having an affair?"

"Objection," Maggie shouted.

Judge Sloane didn't seem to understand the problem. "Basis, Ms. Gallagher?"

"Unless the witness is going to testify to something she observed firsthand, or something Mr. Zamora told her about this topic, her testimony will be either hearsay or speculative."

Judge Sloan looked down at the witness. "Do you have firsthand knowledge about an affair?"

"Just rumors," Paige said.

"Move to strike," Maggie said loudly.

"Yeah, that was my fault," Judge Sloane said, as if that remedied the problem. "Ladies and gentlemen of the jury, please disregard that last answer. Rumors, of course, are not evidence. They have absolutely no reliability whatsoever."

"Oh, and they were dancing together very closely," Paige added.

Ethan saw the daylight provided by a helpful witness. "Too closely for work colleagues, in your opinion?"

"Closer than I would dance with a man who was not my husband," she said in a butter-wouldn't-melt-in-her-mouth voice.

"Did you observe anything else that indicated to you that Mr. Jefferson and Ms. Remsen might have been engaged in an extramarital affair?"

"What Mr. Zamora said to Tyree at the party."

"What was that?"

"I don't remember exactly, but it was something like he'd better keep away from her."

Jaydon Lennox followed his wife on the stand. With the soothing baritone that was recognizable from the ubiquitous television commercials for a European luxury car brand, he confirmed every word of his wife's testimony, virtually verbatim. Specifically, he supported his wife's recollection about the intimate dancing by Tyree and Samantha. He also added that if Tyree Jefferson had held Paige as close as he did Samantha, Jaydon would have made him regret it.

Chloe Lassiter claimed that she saw Tyree and Samantha dancing from the pool and recounted how she'd said something to T-Rex along the lines that she couldn't believe Tyree acted that way toward Samantha in front of her husband.

T-Rex was sworn in under his given name, which caused some snickering in the gallery. Ethan called him Mr. Singleton. His recollection was the shakiest, which stood to reason because he had never met Samantha before the party, and therefore had never seen her interact with Jefferson. Still, his impressions of the argument between Jefferson and Nicky matched the others' versions.

On cross, Maggie made what points she could. She focused on the drug use and drinking, emphasizing the consensus view that Jefferson was as drunk and high as anyone else there. And they all admitted that they left the party shortly after Nicky and had no idea if Samantha had ever gone home.

48.

Tyree Jefferson was not as publicly recognizable as the attendees of his party, but the buildup to his testimony made this his star turn. Nicky had predicted that Jefferson would be dressed like a character in a British period piece, and on this Jefferson did not disappoint. He was attired in a dark suit with a cream-colored waistcoat, a circular-collared shirt, and a bow tie.

Ethan had already told Judge Sloane that Jefferson would be his last witness. He expected to take the remainder of the day with him, after which the prosecution would rest.

I was back in the first chair. I sensed Nicky tensing up beside me as Tyree Jefferson took the oath.

Sometimes, in my imagination, I thought that Nicky feeling the shame of being a cuckold would bring me some relief. During our estrangement, I sometimes fantasized about sleeping with Nicky's future wife, or at least a girlfriend he liked, then asking him how it felt to be betrayed by both the woman he loved and his best friend.

But now I felt no pleasure in the karma being dished out by Tyree Jefferson. I knew firsthand that there was no more humiliating a feeling. Even though Nicky's betrayer wasn't his best friend, I doubted that provided any solace.

"Please tell the jury about the nature of your relationship with Samantha Remsen," Ethan said after he had gotten the introductory questions out of the way.

"We were lovers."

"For how long?"

"Not very. Three weeks."

"Did you know that Ms. Remsen was married?"

"Of course, but she said—"

"Objection."

My main objective for Jefferson's direct was to keep Ethan from getting Samantha to testify from the grave that she'd told Tyree she was going to leave Nicky. That meant being vigilant whenever it seemed as if Jefferson were about to recount something Samantha had told him.

Judge Sloane sustained my objection and then helped my cause even more by saying, "Mr. Jefferson, you are not to testify about anything that Ms. Remsen said to you."

Jefferson testified that he did not know if Nicky had been aware of the affair, but that he wouldn't have been surprised if he'd sensed something, which I took as a not-too-subtle sexual brag. He recounted the party as his guests had, although Jefferson said his use of drugs and alcohol was less than the others claimed, likely because he didn't want to admit that he was under the influence when he drove Samantha home.

It was what had happened after the party that mattered most, however. When Ethan got to that, the courtroom became still.

"What did you and Ms. Remsen do after the party ended, when you were alone?"

Jefferson displayed a prurient smile. "We had sex."

"When did that end?"

"About an hour after we started," he said, looking proud of himself.

"Your Honor," Ethan said, "we'd like to be heard in chambers."

Nicky whispered to me, "What is this about?"

"He wants permission for Jefferson to testify that Samantha told him she was going to leave you," I whispered back.

Chambers actually meant the small conference room to the rear of the courtroom. The space we crammed into was barely large enough to fit the eight of us (including the judge's law clerk and court reporter). There were only six chairs, so Nicky and Ethan's number-two stood.

"Okay, Mr. Ethan, it's your show," Judge Sloane said. "What is Mr. Jefferson going to say that is so important to require an in-chambers conference?"

"That Samantha Remsen decided to return home that evening solely so she could end her marriage to the defendant," Ethan said with none of the flourish he would use if this were in front of the jury. "Specifically, she told Mr. Jefferson that she wanted to go back to her house to tell Mr. Zamora to return to California and that, until he did, she would be staying with Mr. Jefferson. She also intended to collect some of her belongings, her phone, and some clothing, and to get her car. Mr. Jefferson's statements on this score are directly relevant to the People's theory that Ms. Remsen's disclosure triggered a violent reaction by Mr. Zamora, which led to Ms. Remsen's murder. His testimony is therefore firmly within the parameters of Rule 8.41, the state-of-mind exception to the hearsay rule."

The state-of-mind exception allowed the jury to hear statements made by someone who was not under oath or subject to cross-examination if the statement reflected that person's state of mind. It was an important prosecutorial tool in spousal killings. No judge excluded the testimony of a now-murdered wife telling her sister or a friend days before her murder, "I think my husband is going to kill me," even though that statement is pure hearsay.

It was déjà vu all over again. The prosecutor had tried the same gambit in Nicky's first trial. Back then, it had been Carolyn's sister who was going to testify to her mental state to let the jury know that Nicky was having an affair. Thirty-four years ago, I had convinced the judge that the hearsay exception didn't apply.

Now I had to do it again. Only this time, I had to block Nicky's wife's off-the-stand assertion that she was planning to leave him for another man.

The judge's law clerk handed her an open book. Judge Sloane looked down at the page as the rest of us waited.

"I'm going to read the rule—I should say the exception to the hearsay rule—into the record," Judge Sloane said. "As Mr. Ethan said, it is section 8.41 of the New York code. I quote, *An out-of-court statement by a declarant describing the declarant's state of mind at the time the statement was made, such as intent, plan, motive design, or mental condition and feeling, but not including a statement of memory or belief to prove the fact remembered or believed, is admissible, even though the declarant is available as a witness.*"

It didn't seem to me that Jefferson's account of Samantha Remsen's final words were analogous to those of a terrified spouse fearing for her life. Tyree Jefferson had every reason to lie. If Nicky hadn't killed Samantha, then he had.

I made that point to Judge Sloane. Ethan argued otherwise. And after ten minutes of that back-and-forth, Judge Sloane sent us back to the courtroom to wait.

When she returned to the bench, she announced her ruling: the proffered testimony met the state-of-mind exception. My objection was overruled, and Jefferson's recounting of what Samantha had told him would be admitted.

Ten minutes after that, Tyree Jefferson was back on the stand, explaining that right before Samantha was killed, he took her back to her house so that she could tell her husband she was leaving him.

"Did Ms. Remsen tell you why she wanted to go back home, even though it was by that time after one o'clock in the morning?"

"She wanted to go home and tell Nick that their marriage was over. After she did that, she was going to collect her clothing, her phone, which she'd forgotten to bring to the party, and some other things, including her car, and then drive herself back to my house."

"Did she ever return to your house?"

"No."

"Did that concern you?"

"Not at first. I figured that maybe they were still fighting it out, or the discussion took longer than Sam figured. Or she concluded she was too drunk to drive. But when she didn't show up on set the next morning and wasn't answering my calls . . . and then after I heard her car was still in the garage and her phone was still on the nightstand at her house, well . . . that's when I knew he'd killed her."

———

Judge Sloane allowed a ten-minute recess before my cross-examination. She could have given me ten hours, and it still would have been impossible to undo the damage that Tyree Jefferson had inflicted on the defense.

"You need to throw everything we have at him," Maggie said during the break. "The jury has to believe that he killed Samantha by the time you're done."

I smiled at her. "Is that all?"

Nicky wasn't smiling. He looked shaken by Jefferson's testimony. I did not get the sense that he thought Jefferson was lying, however.

He looked at me in desperation. "I'm counting on you, Clinton."

———

I started the cross by taking Jefferson through the timeline.

"Mr. Jefferson, you claim that Mr. Zamora left your party at approximately eleven thirty p.m., is that right?"

"Yes. Give or take."

"And the rest of the guests left within the next thirty minutes."

"Yes. By midnight, Sam and I were alone."

"And you claim that you then had sex with Ms. Remsen, and that lasted until approximately one a.m."

"Yes. Maybe a little later than that," he added with the same smirk from before.

"And at about one fifteen a.m., you claim that you got in your car and drove Ms. Remsen home. Is that your testimony?"

"Yes, that is what happened."

"And you say that the reason you took her home was because she could not wait until daybreak to tell her husband she wanted a divorce, is that right?"

"That is what she said, yes."

"She absolutely, positively had to tell him that night. She couldn't wait until the next day? Your testimony is that she had to leave your warm bed and, in the middle of the night, while she was drunk and high, go end her marriage."

"She told me that was what she wanted to do and she did not want to wait."

"You claim that you were not drunk or high. Do I have that right?"

"That's right. I drove her. I was able to drive."

"Given your clearheaded state of mind, you must have realized that she should wait until morning to discuss ending her marriage."

He shook his head regretfully. "I wish more than anything else I had thought of that. But I didn't. I just wanted to do what Samantha wanted me to do. That's all I was thinking about."

I thought through what he'd just said. Was it resonating with the jury? Would going back over it reveal how self-serving it was, or only reinforce that Jefferson had made a fatal mistake in acquiescing to Samantha's request, nothing more?

These are the split-second decisions that determine how your client will spend the rest of his life. In this case, I moved on.

"And that ride—from your house on the beach to Ms. Remsen's house on the beach—took no more than five minutes. So, according to your testimony, Ms. Remsen got out of your car at the latest, at about one twenty a.m."

"I can't be certain of the precise time, but as a general matter, that's correct."

"Who else, other than you, can support any of this timeline from the moment your last guest left?"

"No one. It was just Sam and me."

"So all we have to go on about what happened after the last guest left is your word and your word alone."

He glared at me. I glared back.

"Do you not understand the question?" I asked.

"No one else was there except me and Sam," he said. "And now she's dead."

"Mr. Jefferson, isn't it a fact that everything you said happened between you and Ms. Remsen is a lie? That she stayed after the party to talk to you about your sexual harassment."

"No."

"Isn't that what it is when a boss—as the director of the film, you are the boss, are you not?—starts such a relationship with an employee?"

"Not really."

"Of course it is. You ran the show. You called the shots. And you made a sexual advance on your subordinate."

"It was consensual," Jefferson said.

"Objection!" Ethan shouted over his witness's answer.

I continued over both of them. "And when she wanted to end the sexual relationship you initiated, you threatened to *fire* her. That's some real Harvey Weinstein action by you."

"Objection!" Ethan yelled, this time even louder.

But I raised my voice above his. "Ms. Remsen said she'd go public, and that's why you killed her!"

"Objection, Your Honor!" Ethan said at a decibel level that hurt my ears.

By now Judge Sloane was pounding her gavel. "That is enough, Mr. Broden!" she shouted. "When there is an objection lodged, I expect you to stop your questioning and allow me to rule. Now there must have been five questions asked there that Mr. Ethan objected to. I'm going to sustain the objection on every single one of them. That means, ladies and gentlemen of the jury, you are not to infer anything—and I mean *anything*—from Mr. Broden's questions, which I'm ruling were improper."

I shook off the admonishment and took a deep breath before reengaging the director.

"Mr. Jefferson, isn't it a fact that Ms. Remsen never told you that she was leaving her husband? She told you the exact opposite—that she loved him. She also told you that she was going to report your sexual harassment to the studio. You knew that meant that your career was over. So you killed her because nothing—not even a woman's life—was more important to Tyree Jefferson than his career."

Ethan objected. I'm quite sure that Judge Sloane would have ruled the same way she had a moment before, telling the jury to disregard my questions, had Tyree Jefferson not answered so quickly.

"No. Everything you just said, mate, it's all crazy. Sam was in love with me. And that's why *her husband* killed her."

I might have gone back at him, asking the same question again and again, if only so the jury heard my conviction that Jefferson was Samantha's murderer. But each time they also would have heard his denial.

In another split-second decision, I told the judge that I had no further questions.

49.

"You're not going to present any case on my behalf, are you?" Nicky asked that evening when we were alone at my house.

I'd told Maggie that was my intent. She must have shared my strategy with Nicky.

"It's your call, in the end. But that is my strong recommendation."

"I've done whatever you said so far, Clinton. Even when it didn't make any sense to me. I still did it. Even when it was the opposite of what you did the last time. Even when I knew Maggie thought it was wrong. I followed your advice because I thought, *Clinton loves you like a brother, and he's the best criminal defense lawyer of his generation.*"

I wasn't completely certain where he was going with this, but I had a strong suspicion I wasn't going to like it.

"I didn't kill Samantha," he said.

I'd heard him declare his innocence before. With regard to Samantha, of course, but also thirty-four years ago, when he denied guilt in Carolyn's murder and claimed he wasn't having an affair.

I had believed him then, and that turned out to be a mistake. I didn't plan to repeat it.

As if he realized I wasn't buying what he was selling, Nicky said, "Here's the God's honest truth, Clinton. Believe me or don't, I don't give a damn. But at least I know I'm telling you what happened. I don't know if Samantha actually said those things to Tyree, but he was telling the truth when he said he took her back to our place. I was shocked when she came back because she'd told me at the party I should return to LA, and she was going to stay with Tyree until I did." He shook his head. "If she hadn't forgotten her damn phone . . . That's why she came back that night. At least that's what she told me. I thought it was my last chance to save my marriage. I begged Samantha not to leave me. I thought . . . I don't know, that I could still talk her out of it. We went outside to the deck. Samantha didn't want to sit on the furniture because it was soaked from the storm. So she pulled herself onto the railing and . . . she slipped off. She was dead as soon as she hit the ground."

I tried not to show my shock. It had never occurred to me that Samantha's death was an accident.

Perhaps a more objective lawyer would have considered that possibility. Then again, I doubted Maggie had thought of it either.

"And then you put her body in the ocean?"

"That's my only crime. I know it's not nothing. And if they'd let me plead guilty to that, I would. I swear that I would. But I didn't kill Samantha, and I knew no one would ever believe me. I didn't have a choice, Clinton." He looked at me with eyes as big as saucers. "You've got to believe me. I didn't kill Samantha. It was an accident."

When I was slow to confirm that I believed him, Nicky said, "I guess you don't really care one way or the other about whether I killed Samantha. All you care about is making me pay for Carolyn's murder."

It was the first time he had ever said it. The look in his eyes when the words came out suggested that he wished he could take them back.

"I don't care about what you did to Carolyn," I said. "I've only ever cared about what you did to Anne."

Nicky Zamora, the voice of his generation, was mute. Finally exposed for who he was to me—a murdering, lying backstabber who'd had an affair with his best friend's wife.

I could have asked him point-blank whether it was Anne or he who'd killed Carolyn. But I didn't. Instead, I walked away before he could say another word.

————

The next morning, before the court day began, I told Maggie that I needed to discuss something with her. Once we were alone in the room usually reserved for the next witness, I shared my exchange with Nicky.

"Do you believe him?"

"I do. There was something about the way he said it that . . . I don't know, but yes, I do believe him."

"The good news, I guess, is that he's innocent," she said. "I didn't think he was."

"He's not innocent, Maggie. He was my best friend. Not like a brother, because I've known plenty of people who can't stand their brothers. Like a soul mate. Before I met Anne, he was the person I loved the most. I loved him differently than I did her, obviously, but no less completely. And then they both betrayed me."

I'd never said this aloud before, although the thoughts had reverberated in my head a million times, in countless combinations.

For Maggie, the revelation came out of left field. Probably no less a shock than if I had admitted to killing Samantha Remsen myself.

"Clint," she said, "when you say *betrayed*, do you mean like having an affair? Our client and your wife?"

I'd put myself in the most compromising of positions. No matter how much I believed that *I* was the aggrieved party in this situation, Maggie was looking at it from an ethics perspective, and there I was 100 percent in the wrong.

"It was a long time ago," I said.

"I'm not sure there's a statute of limitations on the ethical rules," she said. "You shouldn't have taken the case."

"What's done is done. If nothing else, I've given him a surefire appellate argument if he loses."

"I'm not sure that's going to be much comfort to him in jail."

"Do you want to take over from here?"

It was the only thing I could think of that might ameliorate the situation. But I knew it was an empty gesture.

"We don't have any other witness aside from Nick, and we can't put him on the stand to say that she accidentally died, then he dumped her body in the ocean and lied to the entire world about it. And if I close, that sends a terrible message to the jury." Maggie sighed. "Unless you want to make an already completely fucked-up situation a thousand times worse, you've got to see this through."

"You mean I have to get him acquitted."

She shrugged. "I honestly don't see how you avoid being disbarred *unless* he's acquitted." She smiled, at a private joke, it seemed. "It does seem almost poetic, though."

"How so?"

"Well, you said you two were soul mates." Another shrug. "Now your fates are joined forever."

———

After Judge Sloane took the bench but before the jury returned, I told her that the defense had no witnesses to call.

"Not even your client?" she asked.

"No. Mr. Zamora is going to assert his constitutional right not to testify," I said.

This waiver is deemed so important that it is the one time in a criminal case that the judge actually addresses the defendant to make sure that he understands the ramifications of the decision. Judge Sloane went through the script, eliciting from Nicky his understanding that he had the right to testify, that he was freely choosing not to testify, and that no one had made him any promises or assurances or offered any inducements regarding that decision.

"Okay, then," Judge Sloane said when that part was finished. "What say I call in the jury and we do closing arguments?"

A few minutes later, Ethan was at the lectern, going through the reasons that the jury should convict. It was more or less a rehash of his opening, but this time he was able to point out that the witnesses had said exactly what he'd promised they would.

"Mr. Jefferson is the key," he told them. "He has no reason to lie to you. He freely admitted a sexual relationship with Ms. Remsen, whereas someone acting in a calculated fashion might have denied it. So you should believe him when he said that Ms. Remsen was returning home on the night of her murder to end her marriage to the defendant. And we know to a certainty that no more than a few hours later—and likely much sooner—Samantha Remsen's neck was broken and she was discarded in the ocean like a piece of garbage."

For my part, I gave a reasonable-doubt closing, arguing that the prosecution had failed to meet its burden. "If you think there's any reasonable possibility that Mr. Jefferson is lying—for example, that maybe something did happen between Tyree Jefferson and Ms. Remsen that caused a fight, and that in anger he killed her—or even that Ms. Remsen suffered a terrible accident while she was with Mr. Jefferson, and he lied to cover that up—then you must acquit, because, by definition, that means that you have reasonable doubt that Mr. Zamora is guilty of murder."

The prosecution gets the first and last word in closing arguments. As a result, the jury heard my recitation of what-ifs after Ethan claimed that only Nicky had the motive, means, and opportunity to murder Samantha Remsen. Then they heard him say it again after me.

The last point Ethan made was to rebut my theory of reasonable doubt.

"Reasonable doubt is not *any* doubt, ladies and gentlemen," he said. "Mr. Broden could tell you that aliens came down from Mars and murdered Samantha Remsen, and just because the prosecution couldn't prove that didn't happen, it's not grounds to acquit."

———

A quick verdict is almost always a guilty finding. So, when that first day came and went without a jury note indicating their unanimity, I knew we had at least one holdout among the jurors. The following day also ended without a verdict. When we still had no decision by late Thursday, Maggie predicted that the jury would hang.

Friday is often make-or-break in jury deliberations. Jurors know that if they fail to reach a verdict before the weekend, they have to return on Monday, and that often convinces the holdouts to switch sides.

Even though we had been, more or less, shoulder to shoulder for a week with absolutely nothing else to do, Nicky and I hadn't said anything of consequence to each other. Our last substantive interaction had been when I'd confronted him about Anne. Nothing I could say now would matter in the least to Nicky. The only truth that mattered now was the verdict.

At noon, word came that the jury had reached a verdict.

"Good luck," I said to Nicky as we waited for Judge Sloane to take the bench.

Nicky didn't reply, but if looks could kill, I'd be a dead man.

Judge Sloane summoned the jurors to the courtroom. After everyone was seated, the process that would end with a pronouncement of guilt or acquittal began.

Nicky sat ramrod straight beside me, his eyes focused straight ahead, taking in the theatrics occurring before the judge's bench. The bailiff had just completed his four-foot trek from the jury box to the judge to deliver the jury's verdict slip.

"Will the defendant please rise?" Judge Sloane said.

Maggie, Nicky, and I did as directed. I looked over to Ethan. The prosecution team remained seated.

The foreperson was the oldest woman on the panel. I hadn't wanted to select her, but Maggie had thought she'd side with us in the end. We'd know in a minute which of us had been right.

Out of the corner of my eye, I saw that Maggie had taken Nicky's hand in hers. For my part, I couldn't summon the will to engage in any physical contact with my client.

In a clear, strong voice, the jury foreperson announced the verdict. Oddly enough, it did not register with me. In fact, the full import of what had just occurred hit me only when I saw Nicky embracing Maggie.

Before hearing it announced, I had imagined the aftermath of both outcomes numerous times. *Guilty or not guilty?* My mix of emotions now that Nicky had been acquitted was not any different from how I had imagined I'd feel. Even so, I doubted I would have felt any more satisfaction had he been convicted.

Judge Sloane broke the courtroom roar with a strike of her gavel. "Back to order, everyone."

Once quiet was restored, she turned to the jury and said, "Ladies and gentlemen, I thank you for your service. As soon as you leave this courtroom, you are free to act as you please regarding this trial. Talk to the media or not. Stay in touch with your fellow jurors, or never speak to them again. All of that is entirely your prerogative the moment I excuse you. But before I do that, I'm going to let you all in on a little secret. If I remember the jury selection correctly, this was the first time being a juror for each of you. Well, it was my first time being a judge in a trial too. And, if I do say so myself, I think we rocked it."

The jurors made a hasty exit out of the courtroom, like students after the bell. Almost all of them were smiling, although few met Nicky's eyes. That told me they had voted to acquit because the prosecution had not met its burden rather than out of any belief in Nicky's innocence.

After the last of the jurors had left, we remained standing to allow Judge Sloane to exit. As she made her way toward the door, she wore a broad smile on her face.

If Nicky had been convicted, every ruling Judge Sloane had made against the defense—especially her decision to allow Jefferson to testify about Samantha's state of mind—would have been scrutinized on appeal, subject to rejection by appellate judges. But there can be no appeal of an acquittal, so now the judge's conduct was beyond anyone's reproach.

That was not true of me, however. My performance was still a matter to be reckoned with.

50.

A blockade of press awaited us at the mouth of the courthouse. A podium was set up, complete with microphones. A narrow passageway had been created by court officers to allow us to bypass, but doing so would have made it seem as if we were running away, and that was not what winners did.

The first thought I gave the words I would deliver was when I walked toward the lectern. "On Mr. Zamora's behalf, we thank the jury for their service, and Judge Sloane for hers. We are, of course, thrilled beyond belief that the jury reached the correct verdict and acquitted Mr. Zamora of this crime. He is still in mourning over the death of his wife, and now he can at least grieve without the ugly specter that he was, in any way, responsible for her death."

The press started shouting questions the moment I stopped speaking. *Did Tyree Jefferson kill Samantha Remsen? Is the verdict truly an exoneration? Why didn't Nick Zamora take the stand? Would the verdict have been different if the judge had allowed evidence regarding the death of his first wife?*

I stepped away from the podium without responding. Nicky and Maggie followed me while the reporters continued shouting.

———

We returned to my home, the three of us. When we arrived, Maggie's support staff—Kevin and Jessica—was already there. Maggie must have alerted them to the verdict and invited them to the celebration, which was their victory too.

I was surprised, however, by the presence of Ella and her boyfriend. After what must have been a hundred invitations, my daughter had finally taken me up on my offer to spend some time in East Hampton.

I made the introductions. Ella and Gabriel shook Nicky's hand, as they would that of any other stranger. I looked for some suggestion Anne had told Ella of her affair but didn't see any. I couldn't imagine that she had, but once a secret invades a marriage, anything seems possible.

"You look just like your mother," Nicky said.

It was a compliment Ella had heard many times. She smiled and thanked him.

I recalled vividly the celebration after Carolyn's trial. Anne, Nicky, and I in our apartment. The bottle of champagne that Anne had purchased. My mental images were replaced with the real-time pop of the champagne cork; this time, Maggie had done the honors. She filled the flutes, and everyone took one. I nodded that she should deliver the toast.

"Clint and I want to thank Kevin and Jessica for their assistance on the trial, and I want to thank them for helping me every day," she said. "We also want to thank Nick for the trust he put in us. This is to Nick Zamora. Justice has been done."

I quickly scanned the room, watching Nick and Maggie and Maggie's staff sip the champagne. Gabriel too downed his glassful. Ella, however, left her flute untouched, and when the party resumed, I saw her put it on the table and walk away.

———

At five, Kevin and Jessica went home. They thanked me for the experience, and I said that I looked forward to working with them again someday.

Maggie's departure came not long after. "Ollie misses me," she said. "Tomorrow I'm going to spend the entire day in the park with him to make up for how much I've been away lately."

I walked her to her car. Before she got in, I said, "I couldn't have done it without you, Maggie."

She smiled. "I don't think that's right, but it is nice of you to say it."

"It was the result I wanted," I told her. "I want you to believe that."

"I know you do, Clint. But how can I when I'm not even sure you do?"

She was right. I still wasn't sure what I'd wanted. My desires had been all over the map for so many years when it came to Nicky.

"But it doesn't matter," she said. "All that matters is that he's been acquitted. And you did that. And what I do believe, really and truly, is that you were working toward that, and only that, from day one."

It was kind of her to say, and I wanted to believe she felt that way. I also hoped that it was true.

"So what's next?" she asked.

For the entirety of my professional career, or at least since Nicky's acquittal in 1986, each verdict meant only that I moved on to the next case. Although it would have been easy to rely on my rote response and tell Maggie that more clients awaited me in New York, the words stuck in my throat. Her question reminded me of Nicky's musings about his life becoming Benjamin Button–like, counting back from the end to see how many novels he still had left to write.

"Not entirely sure, to be honest with you."

"Well, whatever tomorrow brings, I hope it brings more time for us to spend together. The best part of this case for me was getting to share an office with you again."

She leaned in to kiss me goodbye. I couldn't remember the last time I'd kissed a woman on the lips, but fortunately for me I had not forgotten how. It was not a lascivious exchange, but it was enough for Maggie to convey that we could be more than we'd been, if that were my desire.

———

Not long after dinner, Ella and Gabriel excused themselves and adjourned to the guest bedroom, leaving Nicky and me alone. In the hours since the verdict, others had formed a buffer between my friend and me, preventing us from conducting any type of postmortem. But the time had come to say the things that needed to be said.

"Let's sit outside," I said.

He knew what this was about, apparently. "Sure, just let me get a bottle to lubricate this discussion."

"With two glasses," I added.

The air was cool enough to forget that it was still summer, and the sunset was the way it always seemed in your mind. I couldn't help but smile at how Anne would have enjoyed this view, the ocean as blue as it gets in the east, the sun a fireball touching it, the rolling waves providing the soundtrack.

"Are you still my lawyer, Clinton?"

"Do you still need a lawyer?"

"I have a legal question about double jeopardy. Does it cover the fact that I put Samantha's body in the ocean?"

It was a good question. One that required legal research if I were to provide a professional opinion.

"There's a provision in the double jeopardy protection that includes lesser offenses. I suspect obstruction of justice is one. But, honestly? I don't see how you'd be prosecuted for it."

"I was thinking about admitting it. Telling Samantha's family what actually happened."

"If I were your lawyer, I'd advise against that."

"What if you were only my friend?"

"Even more strongly, in that case. They won't believe you. On top of which, I don't think it's a more comforting version of events that their loved one fell to her death in a drug-addled, drunken stupor. Telling them serves only one purpose: it transfers the blame from you to her."

"You're probably right," he said. "So that's the end of it, then."

"Not completely. I have a question for you."

He nodded to tell me he was ready. I'm sure he expected me to ask about Anne.

"Did you kill Carolyn?"

He blinked at the implied accusation, but to his credit, he didn't dodge it. In a quiet voice, while looking into my eyes, he said, "I did."

"Did Anne know?"

"Not before, if that's what you're asking. We never talked about it after. I took that to mean she knew."

That made sense. During the trial, Anne would have known Nicky was lying about being faithful to his wife. So she probably realized he was lying about other things as well. Maybe Nicky had known Carolyn was pregnant. Maybe he'd shared that information with Anne.

I could have followed up on those parts. If I had, I was reasonably sure that Nicky would have told me the truth. There was no point in him lying to me about small things, now that his bigger lie had been exposed.

But I went in a different direction. There was something more important that I wanted to know.

"How do you go on after killing someone who loved you?"

He thought for a long moment, as if he had never pondered the issue, though I couldn't imagine *not* thinking about it every second of every day.

"You carry on as best you can. At some point, you kid yourself into thinking it's over, but it never really is. So then, you try to make use of it somehow. To help you be a better person. For me, in my work, I suppose. Because what else could I do?"

It was a fair answer. Fairer than I had expected.

"At least tell me you regret doing it."

He nodded emphatically. "Every day. It wasn't premeditated. Carolyn and I had this terrible fight that evening, and . . . well, I just snapped. I know that's what people say all the time, but it happened so fast and I felt like it wasn't even me doing it. Sometimes it still feels that way. Like someone else killed Carolyn. Like a murderer somehow got in my head and made me force her under the water. I guess it's easier to tell myself that's what happened than to admit that I am capable of such horror."

I finally had my answer. Deep down, I'd always known it had to be Nicky. Anne was not capable of such horror, as Nicky had put it.

"Anything else you want to know?" he asked.

"No. I think I know everything now."

"At least that makes one of us."

I raised my eyebrows at that. "Then ask."

"When did you learn about Anne and me?"

I told him it was the necklace.

"So since before the verdict in the first case, then?"

"Yeah."

"You were just sitting around, waiting all these years to find some way to get back at me, and when you heard Samantha was missing, you figured that this was your chance? I gotta say, that's some long-term revenge there, Clinton."

"No. That's not right at all. I didn't take the case to ensure you'd be convicted. If nothing else, I would think you'd have enough respect for my legal abilities to know how easy it would be to throw a case. And the one thing you wouldn't do, if that was your intent, would be to hire someone like Maggie to second-seat. Rest assured, if I'd wanted you in jail for the rest of your life, that's where you'd be sitting tonight."

"Then I really don't understand," he said.

"I did it for Anne, Nicky. Not for you."

He looked at me as if my words had been spoken in a language he didn't understand, his expression practically begging me to provide the translation. But after a few seconds, he must have realized that I had no intention of enlightening him.

"Did you know that I saw her shortly before she died?" he asked.

That cut me. At this point, I'd thought nothing Nicky could say would even sting, but the fact that he and Anne had a history beyond 1986 opened a Pandora's box.

He must have sensed my distress, because he quickly attempted to defuse it. "Just once. About a month before she died. I think she reached out to me for *you*, to be honest. She wanted to close things out on her own terms. To make it clear to me that she had made the right decision in picking you over me. It was unnecessary, of course. I always knew Anne chose the better man. And Anne did too. It's been sixteen years, but I remember her words nearly verbatim. She said that one day she woke up and realized that she was happier with you than she ever thought possible."

The fact that I have not yet untangled this knot after decades of trying provides little hope that it will ever be loosened. But the God's honest truth is that I defended Nicky to the best of my ability the first time because I truly believed that he was innocent of Carolyn's murder. When I realized that was not the case, it was too late for me to do anything about it, at least within the ethical rules that govern attorney behavior.

Which isn't to say that after I learned the truth about him and Anne, I didn't fantasize extensively about exacting my revenge. But I'm not a violent man, and certainly not a lawbreaker or believer in vigilantism.

When I heard about the suspicious death of Nicky's second wife, however, it was as if the opportunity for retribution had been handed to me on a silver platter. All I had to do was reconnect. From there, I could imagine how it would all unfold. I'd represent him at trial, and he would be convicted. Then, when it was all over, I'd visit him in prison. The scene was so clear in my head: me on one side of the bulletproof partition, him on the other, wearing the prison jumpsuit. Phones in both our hands. He might think we were meeting to discuss his appeal. But then I'd tell him that I knew about his affair with Anne, that he had murdered Carolyn, and this was payback.

Then I'd walk away, not even allowing him to reply. In the movie version, the final shot would be of my dangling phone and Nicky screaming into the other end, unheard.

But I went the other way. I did everything in my power to secure Nicky's freedom, even when I believed he was guilty as charged. Even when I knew I might be assisting him for the second time in getting away with murder.

I did it because, in order to forgive Anne for her transgression all those years ago, I also needed to forgive Nicky. For some reason, I'd been convinced that if I protected him now, it would prove to my long-dead wife—and, more importantly, to myself—that I forgave her too.

It was for Anne. It had always been about Anne.

51.

Early the next morning, Nicky left for the airport on his way back to Los Angeles. I offered to drive him to JFK, but he said that he had imposed on me enough, and the least he could do was spare me the three-hour round trip. As a result, our final goodbye was in my driveway, the Uber driver bearing witness to the exchange.

"Will we speak again?" he asked.

"I don't think so."

"I get it. But if you change your mind, always know that I welcome you being in my life. I can't undo what happened, but it was a long time ago, and it never meant that I didn't love you. Just like I don't for a second think it meant that Anne didn't love you."

It was not Nicky's place to tell me that my wife loved me. In fact, he might have been the last person from whom I wanted an opinion on the subject.

"Good luck with everything," I said. "And when you write about this, and I know you will, be kind about me."

He laughed. "You're always the hero, Clinton. Isn't that the greatest irony? Even in my telling of our lives, you're the protagonist, and I end up the villain of the piece."

"Anne once told me no one should ever doubt their own guilt."

"I know. Believe me, I do."

———

I returned to the house to the smell of frying onions. Ella was in the kitchen making breakfast.

"Candy eggs," she said, referencing the one egg dish I cooked well, the caramelization of the onions giving the eggs something of a sweet taste that Ella and Charlotte had loved when they were kids. I hadn't made the dish since Charlotte's death, and I was grateful to Ella for cooking them today, a reminder of those breakfasts we'd all eaten together at the small table in our kitchen, where Anne had insisted we share our meals.

As she stirred the eggs into the pan, Ella told me that she had been following the trial closely in the press. "I have to be honest with you, Dad. At times I wondered what the hell you were doing."

"You and Nicky both. Truth be told, Maggie too. But that's the great thing about winning, isn't it? All the decisions you make—even the wrong ones—are validated as testaments to your genius."

"What mistakes did you make?"

In truth, not many. Certainly, none that mattered. My decision to waive extradition had been out of concern that Nicky would take his life if he were confined to Lost Hills for the duration of a PC hearing. My other calls—rushing to trial, reserving my opening statement, not putting on a defense—were now validated by the verdict. Even my decision to put Mr. Fox News on the jury had worked the way I thought it would, at least according to the interview he subsequently gave on, of course, Fox News. He confirmed that there was serious dissension among the jurors during deliberations, something I'd been angling for. An inharmonious jury is a defense jury. I couldn't imagine the woman in the hijab and Mr. Fox News working well together, and apparently they had not.

"Taking the case," I answered.

She laughed, not understanding that I meant it literally. She looked at me, inviting me to comment further, to provide some context to my regret over winning an acquittal for my best friend. But I only smiled, as if I'd made a lame joke.

I'm certain Ella knew me well enough to tell that I was being serious. She also clearly intuited that I couldn't explain without divulging certain things I didn't want her to know.

Ella's life experience and professional training made her better than most at understanding human foibles. But no matter how understanding or forgiving their offspring, parents always keep certain things from their children. First on that list is any deficiency in moral composition embedded in the family's DNA.

"You think you'll stay friends with him?" she asked.

"Yeah," I said.

Five minutes earlier, I'd told Nicky the opposite. I still wondered to whom I'd lied.

Ella's expression changed. She got that look in her eyes, the one Anne described as the Clint-stare.

"I'm not going to ask you to break privilege, even though double jeopardy attaches," she said, "but I am going to ask if you know what happened."

"I do."

"Both to Samantha Remsen and to his first wife?"

"Yes. I know everything."

She accepted my response and read my expression for further information. I suspect it was too opaque for her to get a clear take. Ella knew me well enough to understand that I do not lament victory on behalf of a guilty client. And while I'm always overjoyed when I win on behalf of an innocent one, I hadn't represented enough of them for her to recognize the emotion.

Gabriel's presence made itself known as he clumped his way down the stairs. He's a big man, filled out the way a police officer should be, even though he's a detective, not a uniform cop. That morning he wore the type of pajama top that buttons up the front. It was not the sleeping attire I imagined him in, and I wondered if it was my daughter's influence. Probably an outfit she'd bought for him to wear during this visit so he'd have something decent to wear in front of his girlfriend's father.

"Something smells delicious," he said.

"Very soon you'll get to try my version of my father's world-famous candy eggs."

"My favorite," Gabriel said.

I suddenly felt unexpected joy that my daughter had continued this family tradition, followed by the familiar pang of Charlotte's absence. And then I felt something else: I wished Anne could be here. Even after all these years, I was happiest when I saw the world through her eyes.

Without my prompting, Ella set the table in the kitchen, eschewing the much larger one in the dining room. This was one of countless ways she reminded me of Anne without realizing it. When the dish was plated, the eggs looked as I remembered them, and the sweet aroma reminded me of the happiest days of my life.

My thoughts were broken by Ella tapping her spoon against her coffee mug. I smiled at her attempt to get my attention. Then I realized that she was about to make an announcement. My mind whirred as I wondered whether she'd reveal that she and Gabriel had decided to marry or she'd decided to run for District Attorney.

But as her mouth began to move, it occurred to me that I was wrong on both counts. There was only one thing that made a young woman's eyes light up like that.

"We're pregnant," she said. "If everything goes according to plan, sometime in late February you'll be the grandfather of a baby granddaughter."

Another girl joining our family . . . How many times had someone told me during my grief in the aftermath of Charlotte's murder that life would begin again when Ella had a child? I knew that they meant well, just as I knew it wasn't true that new life replaced a lost one.

I stood to hug my daughter. As I did, I realized I was crying.

Gabriel answered the question that I had not thought important enough to ask. "We're going to get married as soon as possible. Ella said she didn't care, but my parents will want us to do it in the usual order. First marriage, then baby."

"A small wedding. Just family," Ella added. "We thought we'd have it in the backyard here, before the weather turns, and before I'm showing too much. Maybe the end of next month."

"I'm so happy for both of you," I managed through my tears. "Yes, absolutely. That all sounds perfect. Whatever you want. Whatever I can do to help."

"All we want is for you to give me away," Ella said.

"And to let us use your home," Gabriel added with a chuckle.

"And that," Ella agreed. "But we've got everything else covered. Including paying for everything."

I wasn't going to fight with my daughter over the bill. Not then, anyway. Later, I'd insist on paying for the wedding, although I knew I'd be no more successful than the time I offered to buy her an apartment after she graduated from law school. My elder daughter is her own person, as she has reminded me time and time again, in both word and deed.

"There's one more thing," Ella said. "I wanted to get your view about naming the baby after Mom and Charlotte. Not sure in which order, though."

"That would make them both very happy," I said.

"I was asking about you, Dad. Will you be okay holding a little Annie Charlotte or a little Charlotte Anne? Or will it make you sad every time you say her name?"

The things we think we keep from our children. Had I been asked a moment before whether Ella knew the extent to which I continued to grieve Anne's death and Charlotte's murder, I would have said that I'd effectively shielded her from the full extent of my suffering. Obviously, my efforts to carry on stoically had not prevented her from seeing the truth.

"Of course not," I said. "I can't imagine anything that would make me happier."

ACKNOWLEDGMENTS

One of my favorite parts of the writing process is emailing with readers, so please send me your thoughts about *The Best Friend* at adam@adammitzner. com. I'll write back, I promise (although sometimes it takes a few weeks). Also, if you liked the book, please spread the word by writing a review, posting on social media, sending a tweet, or doing it the old-fashioned way by telling friends and family.

The Best Friend is my eighth novel and, at least according to my wife, my best one, which makes me happy that I might be getting better with practice. But as with all my books, I am indebted to a great many people for helping me along the way, and this is my opportunity to thank them. So, in no particular order:

Thank you to the great people at Thomas & Mercer, most particularly my amazing editor, Liz Pearsons. Liz has been a champion of my work for a long time, and I am grateful for all she has done for my career. This book was edited by Ed Stackler, who provided me with the first feedback I ever received from a professional about my writing, and I'm grateful that he's still making my books better. Thank-yous also go out to all the others at Thomas & Mercer who do so much, including, but not limited to, Sarah Shaw; Laura Barrett and Kellie Osborne, who proofread and fact-checked the manuscript (you would be amazed at the mistakes they caught); the folks who designed the cover; and those who get the word out to reviewers and readers.

Scott Miller has been my literary agent since before I had a book, and I am grateful for his work and the longevity of our relationship, and a thank-you also goes out to his colleague Logan Harper. It is my hope that my writing gets adapted for the screen or television, and therefore a shout-out to Jon Cassir at CAA, who works to make that happen, as well as Emily Siegel and the very nice people of Spectrevision/Company X, who are doing their best to bring the Brodens to television.

I continue to juggle writing with my responsibilities as the head of the litigation practice at Pavia & Harcourt in New York City. My gratitude goes out to all my law firm colleagues, with a special thanks to George Garcia and Jennifer Fried.

I am lucky to have friends and family who either read the book in draft and offer suggestions or read it when it's done and don't tell me what I should have done differently. Many of them also contribute their names (or the names of their children) to the book: my sister, Jessica Shacter; her husband, Kevin Shacter; Jodi (Shmodie) Siskind; Matt Brooks; Debra Brooks; Ellice Schwab; Margaret Martin; Ted Quinn; Lisa Sheffield; Eric Sheffield; Lily Weitzner; Debbie Peikes; Marilyn Steinthal; Bruce Steinthal; Bonnie Rubin; Jane Goldman; and Gregg Goldman.

And yes, dear readers, as the dedication reveals, there is a real-life Clint Broden. He has graciously allowed me to borrow his name for my books, but I fictionalize everything else about the character (and he would be the first to tell you that he is taller and a more involved father than his namesake). I can say with confidence that if I ever needed the services of a criminal defense lawyer, I'd hire him, not only because he's been my friend for nearly forty years but because there's no one who does it better.

Beneath the twists and turns, my books are about family, the one you're born into and the one you create for yourself. That, in turn, makes me treasure my family that much more. My children are all part of my writing, even though only Benjamin reads my books. Hearing his, as he calls them, *constructive complaints*, is one of the high points of the process for me. In *The Best Friend*, he made me change the name of the rapper, and although he wasn't happy with the name I finally selected (T-Rex), my original name was much worse, I assure you. Rebecca, Michael, and Emily: thank you for your love and support, and I know someday you'll read my books.

To my wife, Susan: No thanks can ever be enough. Everything I write, and everything I am, is shaped through the lens of my love for you and our family.

My final thank-you is to each one of you for reading *The Best Friend*. It is truly a dream come true to share my writing with you. I look forward to our meeting again next year when *The Perfect Marriage* comes out.

ABOUT THE AUTHOR

Photo © 2016 Matthew Simpkins Photography

Adam Mitzner is a practicing attorney in a Manhattan law firm and the author of several acclaimed novels, including *Never Goodbye* and the Amazon Charts bestseller *Dead Certain*, as well as *A Matter of Will*, *A Conflict of Interest*, *A Case of Redemption*, *Losing Faith*, and *The Girl from Home*. *Suspense Magazine* named *A Conflict of Interest* one of the best books of 2012, and in 2014, the American Bar Association nominated *A Case of Redemption* for a Silver Gavel Award. Mitzner and his family live in New York City. Visit him at www.adammitzner.com.